THE SCREAM

RAYMOND M HALL

Copyright © Raymond M Hall 2023 All rights reserved.

Raymond M Hall has asserted his right under the Copyright, Designs and Patents Act, 1988, to be identified as the author of this work.

No part of this book may be reproduced in any form or by any electronic or mechanical means, including information storage and retrieval systems, without written permission from the author, except for the use of brief quotations in a book review.

This is a work of fiction. Names, characters, events, and incidents are the products of the author's imagination. Any resemblance to actual persons, living or dead, or actual events is purely coincidental.

By the same author:

THE HAUNTING

THE WATER MAIDEN

CASSEY

SHORT STORIES AND STRANGE ENDINGS

The Harry Bridges Detective Series:

THOU SHALT NOT SUFFER A WITCH TO LIVE
BACK TO THE END

The Roger Sidebottom Comedy Series:

THE IMPORTANCE OF BEING ROGER
ROGER'S RISE TO INCREDIBLE FAILURE
CARRY ON ROGER

The Digby Rolf Mystery Series:

THE HANGED MAN
IN THE SHADOW OF THE REAPER
MURDER AT HIGH TOR MANOR

Maggie's heart pounded in her chest as she stood panting and disoriented on the pavement outside her house. The abrupt cessation of the ear-piercing scream had left her shaken and bewildered. She took a moment to collect herself, her cool and level-headed demeanour now a distant memory.

As she regained her composure, she looked around, trying to make sense of what had just happened. The neighbourhood appeared normal, with people going about their daily routines, oblivious to the terror that had gripped her just moments ago.

"What was that?" Maggie muttered to herself, her voice trembling slightly. She couldn't shake the feeling that the scream was somehow connected to her, that it had been more than just a random occurrence...

Chapter 1

The house looked its age, and Maggie wondered if she could do anything with it. As an architect, she considered herself qualified to answer her own question, but looking along the row of identical terraced houses felt some doubt. Petrie Street in East London had survived the wartime Blitz, attracting the attention of town planners, eager to destroy any building older than fifty years. Terraced houses were built in the early 1920s to accommodate the returning valiant troops from the Great War. World War 1 had not really been that great, taking the lives of some thirty-seven million people on all sides. However, the government loved to give everything a memorable name.

The house Maggie stared at from across the narrow street sat in the middle of the terrace and had the Number 15 in brass numbers attached to the front door. By the looks of the brass, now dull, someone would have polished it hundreds of times from an era when houses were maintained in pristine condition. Even the front step would have been scrubbed at least once a week. Those times had disappeared and given way to couples who both worked all hours in order to keep a roof over their heads.

'It's been in the same family since the day it was built,' explained the young man from the estate agency. Due to the lack of any front garden, the For Sale sign occupied half of one of the downstairs windows.

Pushing the door open for Maggie, the agent stood to one side, ushering her into the narrow hallway. Maggie felt as if the walls were closing in on her. The terrace houses had been constructed down to a price. Cheap accommodation for factory workers and their families.

Maggie had been used to far better. The last house had been in Hampstead, which she shared with her ex-husband, Peter. After selling their home and paying off Peter's substantial debts, this was all she could afford. But at least it would all be hers with no miscreant husband to drain resources.

The memory of their last encounter still haunted her. She had witnessed another side of her husband of ten years, never hitherto suspected. Maggie reluctantly agreed the proceeds of the sale of their beautiful home should first pay off his debts. Either that or she would have to come to terms with the reality of visiting Peter in hospital, if he even survived the brutal treatment dished out by private moneylenders involved. His gambling habit had finally caught up with him. Maggie barely had enough to buy Number 15, whereas Peter was left with nothing.

Peter stood toe to toe with her outside the lawyer's office, his only possessions the clothes he wore.

'You might at least have given me enough to buy a flat or something!' he ranted.

Maggie kept her cool.

'Your debts have left us both poor, Peter. What's left is mine and mine alone.'

Peter's face, already veined from excessive drinking, turned an even darker shade of red as he turned to walk away.

'You're a fucking bitch. I never should have married you.'

'Amen to that,' said Maggie.

She hadn't seen the slap coming. It knocked her off her feet and she sat for a moment on the pavement, feeling the sting of her face together with grazed knees.

Peter stormed off without looking back as passers-by stopped to help Maggie to her feet.

Sitting at an outside table, she sipped a cold glass of Semillon Blanc, reflecting on life. The pub a welcome retreat from the scene of her recent assault.

Maggie decided not to report the incident, it would merely prolong the unwelcome relationship with her ex-husband. Instead, she reflected on their first meeting.

A live band pumped out the latest hits from a raised stage. Maggie sat at the rear of the hall. Beside her, Peter nervously held her hand. It was their first date, Valentine's Day, February the 14th, and they were both just sixteen years old. Peter tentatively sought her lips for a first nervous kiss, and she turned her head to face him. It had been a childish kiss, but felt nice, she decided. When he approached again, Maggie responded with more enthusiasm and kissing, oblivious to everyone else.

That had been the start of their relationship, and thereafter they were seldom seen apart. Adolescent love can be a crushing experience. It was as if they had singularly discovered the joys of falling in love, and nothing else in the world mattered.

Out of all their friends, they were the only couple to make it all the way through the rest of school, both going up to university together. Maggie studied architecture and Peter economics.

Barely scraping through, Peter clung to his certificate as Maggie endured the praises heaped upon her by the Dean of faculty. She had graduated with an honours degree at the top of her course.

Peter and his cohorts, the group at the bottom of their course, looked on as Maggie bathed in the sea of compliments.

'Smart fucking bitch,' said Michael.

'Steady on, she's my girlfriend,' replied Peter, but with no anger in his voice, 'she is making a meal of it though, I have to agree.'

The four friends liked to think of themselves as The Four Musketeers, but secretly, Maggie thought The Four Desperates might have been more appropriate.

She had fallen for Peter at a tender age and he with her.

The kissing and cuddling went on for months before they progressed to fondling. Maggie, certainly not innocent before that first Valentine's Day kiss, sensed Peter was, so didn't think to make the first move beyond kissing.

Peter had been shocked one evening when Maggie's hand

descended to the front of his jeans. They were in the back of a friend's car, kissing and cuddling as usual, when he felt her hand touching him. The touch became an urgent squeezing, and in spite of the pain, he was reluctant to call a halt to her actions.

That had been the beginning of the second stage of their courtship. Peter began to experiment, touching first Maggie's breasts before casually dropping a hand into her lap.

The second stage lasted a few more months until one afternoon, while Maggie's parents were at church, they sealed their love in her bedroom.

Thereafter, they made love at every opportunity. There seemed to be no end to their desire for each other, and at one stage, Maggie decided they had either been very careful or very lucky that she didn't fall pregnant. The sober thought that maybe she was incapable of having children crossed her mind on more than one occasion.

Throughout university, they had been constant lovers. Maggie never looked at another man in that way, and she assumed Peter had been just as faithful.

Then came the party to celebrate their graduation. Maggie never wanted to remember that night!

Chapter 2

Maggie squeezed past the estate agent into the narrow hallway.

'It's a very cosy little house,' said Julian.

'Yes, it certainly is cosy,' replied Maggie with a downturned mouth.

Julian, from the agency, carried on, ignoring her scepticism.

'The previous owners lived here for many years, so it's ripe for renovation. You will be able to put your own stamp on the place,' said Julian.

Maggie thought he must have reeled out that statement hundreds of times to excuse the dowdy and unexciting décor of this type of low budget house.

Ignoring him, she made her way through to the rear of the property. An add-on featured a small kitchen and, beyond that, a tiny bathroom. Maggie's face showed her distaste. The wallpaper, beginning its journey from the walls to the floor, reminiscent of the 1940s.

Trying to remain positive, Maggie thought of what she could do with the place with modern fittings and white painted walls.

'Let's go upstairs, shall we?' said Maggie.

Julian couldn't resist the answer that jumped out of his mouth.

'I thought you'd never ask.'

Maggie's stare of disapproval left him in no doubt he had crossed a line. His crass remark would in all probability cost him a sale.

Brushing past him, she climbed the narrow stairs to a minuscule landing off which led to two bedrooms. The house had originally been constructed as the classic two up and two down. No bathroom, only an outside privy. The back room served as both living room and kitchen, with the front parlour reserved for high days and holidays. A room used to entertain honoured guests and, on occasion, the room where a loved one would lie in state in a coffin on a trestle to be viewed by family members.

The bedrooms were equal in size and Maggie imagined the front one would have been for the husband and wife, with any offspring crammed into the back bedroom. In days gone by, the idea of a separate bedroom for boys and girls would have been seen as overindulgent. All would have shared a double bed, clinging to each other to ward off the cold. No such thing as central heating then.

Maggie's heart sank as the miserable wallpaper echoed the times when brown had been the predominant colour. No wonder people had been less than happy. Apart from the Second World War, the décor would have been as depressing as Herr Hitler's bombs.

Deep in thought at the top of the stairs, Maggie glanced down to catch Julian, rather less than surreptitiously, looking up her skirt. He looked away bashfully, obviously embarrassed at being caught out, while Maggie smiled inwardly congratulating herself that she could still catch the attention of a younger man.

Far from offending her, Julian's little faux par brightened her day, and she descended the stairs smiling, much to the estate agent's relief. Perhaps he would still make a sale.

'I'll think about it,' she said, walking past him and out onto the pavement.

Julian followed her out, locking the door behind him.

The harsh sound of a door slamming echoed onto the road.

'Did you hear that?' Maggie asked, looking back at the house.

'What?' answered Julian, his eyes now glued to Maggie's blouse.

Maggie shook her head in a deprecating manner.

'Young man, either get yourself a girlfriend or I can refer you to someone for therapy!'

Inwardly, Maggie laughed, struggling not to smile openly. It had been a long time since she had been made aware of her own sexuality, and she liked the feeling. Especially as Julian had to be at least ten years her junior.

The noise of the slamming door overlooked, she rejoiced in her new found freedom, free of Peter at last.

Upstairs, the slammed door of the back bedroom creaked open, guided by an unseen hand. It opened to its fullest extent before slamming back into the doorframe violently. The beginning of a scream changed dramatically into a whimper as the door opened and slammed time and time again.

The couple next door held hands and prayed. Descendants of Haitian born parents, Daphne and Ruben had been raised with a mixture of religions. Inhabitants were schooled in Catholicism, but most still followed the old ways of Voodoo. They were no strangers to the spirit world, and next door now appeared to be occupied by an angry one.

They had lived in their house happily for two years and their neighbours, an old couple, made little or no noise. When the couple moved away to live in a retirement home, the house remained unoccupied and blissfully silent until the couple's family arranged to put it on the market. Whoever had inspected the house must have let the spirit in, and by the noise coming from next door, it wasn't a happy one!

Although less than impressed by the idea of living in such a depressing house in an equally depressing street, Maggie decided it had to be the one. The television news the evening before had decided her. The so-called experts were predicting house prices would soar as investors sought real, tangible assets, in the face of the falling share market. It seemed to be a worldwide phenomenon, and she simply couldn't afford to dither.

The following morning, Maggie walked into the estate agents.

Julian, sitting behind a desk, jumped to attention as she walked in the door.

Maggie sighed.

'Good morning, Julian. I've come to make an offer on Number

15 Petrie Street.'

Julian's eyes dropped to the floor in embarrassment.

'I'm sorry, someone else put in an offer late yesterday afternoon, sight unseen,' he said, his right hand twitching nervously.

'Bugger!' exclaimed Maggie.

'I'm sorry,' said Julian.

'Not as sorry as me,' replied Maggie, 'tell me their offer and the terms of the contract?'

'I can't tell you how much they offered, only that it is slightly less than the asking price and they need to raise some finance.'

'Then, make the owners a counter offer. I'll pay the full price with a cash unconditional contract, and they can settle as soon as they like.'

Maggie's decision had been driven by the fact she had been pipped at the post rather than any heart wrenching loss. Number 15 was hardly her dream house, and even with her skills as an architect, it would never be much more than a terraced house in a poorer part of the city.

'Well, don't just stand there, Julian, do it!' she exclaimed.

Julian looked perplexed and shuffled the papers on his desk nervously.

'I'll have to get Mr Yates,' he blurted.

'Good idea, maybe he can perform the task that you seem to be incapable of.'

She knew she sounded cruel, but time was of the essence and Maggie had always been a winner. Except with Peter.

Mr Yates walked ahead of Julian as he approached. Maggie noted the shiny Armani suit and assumed him to be the owner of the agency.

'You want to up the offer and terms on Number 15 Petrie Street?'

'Yes, as I told Julian,' said Maggie.

Mr Yates smiled with more of an undertaker's smile than an estate agent, or perhaps they attended the same training school.

He held out a superbly manicured hand.

'Desmond Yates, Julian is my son.'

That short statement answered a number of questions in Maggie's mind, principally that Julian exuded a false confidence and the fact that his father appeared to be even sleazier than the son.

'Well?' said Maggie, 'are you going to submit my offer or not?'

Desmond Yates almost fawned as he nodded his head.

'Naturally, my dear. We are duty bound to submit all offers until a sale is finalised.'

Referring to her as my dear didn't impress Maggie, but she bit her tongue. Now was not the time to put the chirpy Mr Yates in his place.

'Very well, kindly submit my offer and make sure they know that I am in a position to settle immediately.'

Desmond shook Maggie's hand for rather longer than two Mississippi's, and when he finally withdrew his hand, she felt the desperate need to wash.

Securing his promise to call her the moment the owners accepted her offer, she left the agency, glad to be away from the creepy father and son act.

Back at her rented flat, Maggie poured herself a scotch and sat down to take stock. Had she made the right decision, or had the madness of the moment taken her over?

The trilling of her cell phone broke the spell and, looking at the screen, her heart fell. Peter again. Would he, or rather could he, ever leave her alone?

'Yes, Peter, what is it now?'

'I'm really sorry about the slap and the abuse,' he said timidly.

'Well, it's not exactly a new thing with us, is it? Don't concern yourself, I haven't reported it. If I didn't that first time, I'm hardly likely to now, am I?'

'I wish you could forget that time, Maggie,' Peter begged.

'So do I,' whispered Maggie, as she ended the call.

Peter stared at his cell phone as the screen went blank.

'Fucking bitch!'

Chapter 3

Her phone summoned once again and Maggie picked up on the verge of telling Peter to grow up and piss off. But it was creepy Desmond on the other end.

'I'm pleased to say they have accepted your offer. The owners have instructed me to cancel the other one and take the place off the market. It's all yours.'

Maggie heard herself say thank you, although inside she still wondered if she had made the right decision.

Desmond's next line brought her heavily back to reality.

'It's normal for us to take a successful buyer for dinner. Where would you like to go?'

Lost for words, Maggie said the first thing that came into her head.

'Gusto's is nice.'

'Then Gusto's it shall be. Pick you up tomorrow evening at 7.30,' said Desmond, ending the call before she could change her mind.

Staring blankly at the phone, Maggie wondered why she always seemed to attract the wrong type of man? Surely she should have learnt from Peter.

As she put the phone down and picked up her drink, the hazy memories of that fateful night so many years ago crept into her mind. Downing the scotch, she grabbed the bottle and sat down, refilling her glass almost to the brim.

The following day, Maggie detoured from work and walked along Petrie Street. Had she made the right decision? Only time would tell, she supposed. Pausing outside her new home to be, she was surprised by the sudden appearance of the next-door neighbour.

Startled, Maggie put out her hand.

'Hello, I'm Maggie. I think I am to be your next-door neighbour.'

Daphne flinched but, despite her inner misgivings, shook Maggie's outstretched hand.

'Pleased to meet you. Were you the person inspecting the property the other evening?'

'Yes,' laughed Maggie.

Daphne, recalling the slamming doors from Number 15, began to tremble inside, her ancient Voodoo fears coming to the surface.

'Must run, catch up later?' she said, turning to walk away.

'Looking forward to it,' replied Maggie, thinking that at least one neighbour looked promising. Daphne looked to be younger than herself, but that might be nice. She craved fresh company, away from her old life.

Left alone in the street, Maggie stood outside her new home, wishing she had the keys. It would be nice to begin the task of planning the refurbishment.

On a whim, she bent and pushed in the brass lid of the letterbox. Inside, the hallway offered no joy, its dullness reminding Maggie of her first impressions of the house. She realised that with all doors closed, it lacked natural light, nothing to welcome a visitor. That would be the first thing to be fixed, even if it meant installing hidden lights with natural daylight luminance fittings.

She must have been bending down for some time, peering into the gloom, when something caught her eye at the far end of the hallway. It might have been a shadow, but shadows don't generally move. However, this one certainly did.

'Hi, can I help you?'

Maggie straightened up in surprise. The voice had come from nowhere. She turned and to be met with a wide grin.

'I'm sorry, you startled me. I'm Maggie,' she said. 'I'm buying this house.'

The wide grin straightened into a tight-lipped stare. Then, as the sides of the generous mouth tilted downwards, Ruben spoke.

'Oh, sorry, I didn't realize,' he said.

'I hope we can be friends. I already met Daphne, your wife?'

Ruben's eyes had locked onto the cross around Maggie's neck. It wasn't any old cross. Suspended from a silver chain around her neck, the matt black cross hung upside down.

'Yes, I mean, certainly, yes,' he stammered before rushing off along the street as if he might be afraid of missing a bus.

Maggie stared after him, wondering what she had said to make him rush off, her fingers gently fondling the Petrine Cross, a habit when anything out of the ordinary happened.

To Ruben, the inverted cross could only mean one thing. Their new neighbour must be a child of Satan, a devil worshipper.

Glancing at the clock, Maggie surveyed herself in the full-length mirror. She wore jeans and a blouse which covered her from the neck down. Long sleeves meant she was completely covered. Nothing to stir Desmond's interest. She hoped.

At precisely 7.30 p.m. the intercom sounded and she picked up the phone.

'Good evening, Desmond here, all ready?'

'I'll meet you downstairs,' said Maggie, putting down the phone, not wanting him in her apartment.

Desmond greeted her dressed in a smart suit, gold cufflinks complementing his gold Omega watch.

'If I may say, you look wonderful,' he said, opening the door of his Mercedes.

Maggie's forced smile did nothing to discourage him, and she knew it would be a difficult evening.

Desmond continued his fawning behaviour at the restaurant, making sure that Maggie knew he frequented regularly, and that they treated him as a valuable patron.

As she expected, the evening dragged on. Desmond made small talk whilst Maggie nodded in agreement at his inconsequential observations, hoping she nodded in the correct places. She had to force herself to listen, her mind wanting to wander. Desmond proved to be as boring as his demeanour suggested.

Chairs scraped against timber flooring as they rose to leave.

Maggie, a little too quickly, exhibiting her eagerness to finish the torturous evening.

Desmond appeared to be driving deliberately slowly towards Maggie's apartment, as if he didn't want the evening to end. Which he didn't.

Finally, they arrived at her home. Expecting Desmond to walk around the car to open her door, Maggie made the mistake of staying put. Desmond took this to be a good sign and, leaning over, gently placed a hand on her leg.

'Coffee would be nice, don't you think?'

Maggie froze, all the danger signs were there and her mind leapt back to that other time. Terror invaded her senses and she lost the power of speech. In the dim light, Desmond failed to notice the look on her face, his thoughts narrowing in on his urgent needs.

Desmond leaned in even further, and while tightening the grip on her upper leg, kissed her gently on the cheek. Maggie found herself unable to react, her brain numb. A black haze began to envelop her consciousness, and Desmond took this for acquiescence.

Quickly alighting from the car, he ran around to the passenger side, opening the door and taking Maggie's hand. She behaved like a robot as the downstairs entry door opened under her hand. Making her way to the apartment door with Desmond following directly behind, she opened it.

As the door closed behind them, Desmond grabbed her around the waist.

'Let's not waste time on coffee,' he said while roughly pulling open her blouse, scattering the buttons in his eagerness.

Maggie's trancelike state held as he pulled at her bra, fingers squeezing her breasts. His passion had kicked in fully as he began to pull down her jeans.

Maggie came to her senses, screaming directly into his face, barely an inch from her own. Shocked by her outburst, he drew back his hand and slapped her.

The slap did the trick, silencing her. However, Desmond now

confronted a new side of Maggie. Her cold look surprised him, leaving him motionless and vulnerable. She viciously brought her knee up into his groin, rendering him helpless with pain. As he crumpled to the floor, she once again used her knee, resulting in a wave of blood from a damaged nose.

Shouting, she opened the apartment door.

'Out, and don't come back!'

Desmond limped out into the hallway, painfully aware the evening had turned into a total disaster.

Maggie slammed the door, slowly sinking to the floor in tears.

'Not this time,' she tearfully whispered, 'not this time.'

Chapter 4

East London 1923

Daisy clapped her hands for joy, running from room to room, yelling at the top of her voice.

'Is this really all for us?'

Her mother chuckled.

'Yes, all for us.'

Gladys Pickering had never lived in a house before. Her life comprised one hardship after another, tenement living her only alternative. Now, Number 15 Petrie Street would be their home. Builders were still finishing, but it didn't stop the tenants from moving in. London County Council had embarked on a huge new project to relieve the housing crisis. Families endured appalling conditions for years in the Victorian and early Edwardian periods, but after the First World War, things began to change. Politicians realised that to win the votes of ordinary folk, they must provide a better standard of living.

The Pickering family were typical slum tenants. Gladys had been born and raised in a tenement, meeting her future husband in the same block.

Like so many others at that time, they took comfort in each other and the inevitable happened. At just fifteen years of age, Gladys found herself pregnant, and the father-to-be, Ken, saw no alternative but to marry her. Refusal would have resulted, at best, in a savage beating and, at worst, death from the same beating delivered by Gladys' father and her brothers. As an accepted situation, they made the best of it.

A room became available in the same block and they moved in. Just one room, no bedroom, living room or kitchen. A privy at the end of each floor, shared by all the tenants. The rooms were in bad repair, damp running down interior walls a common sight. However, they were used to those living conditions.

Ken and Gladys welcomed their first child, Keith, swiftly

followed by a second son, Ben, and then a daughter, Daisy. All in three years. It seemed that Gladys was always pregnant. During Daisy's birth, things did not go well. A local midwife delivered all three children in the tiny flat and having only basic skills could not cope with emergencies.

Daisy's birth had been difficult from the start. In the wrong position, the midwife laboured to turn the baby while still in the womb. Extremely painful for Gladys. Finally, the baby had been pulled from her body in a rush of amniotic fluid and blood. Gladys was unable to have any more children after Daisy's traumatic birth and lucky not to have bled to death. The sad fate of many mothers in that era. However, her husband, Ken, viewed it as a blessing. He would be able to enjoy Gladys without the fear of more mouths to feed. In that time, it was not uncommon for women in the same state of poverty to have ten or more children.

However, the arrival of the council man holding a set of shiny new keys changed the lives of Ken and Gladys.

The two boys and Daisy ran from room to room in sheer delight whilst Gladys inspected the small kitchen cum dining room together with a separate front parlour. Upstairs were two bedrooms. One for her and Ken and one to be shared by the children.

A brick privy stood at the end of a small enclosed rear garden. Washing facilities comprised a tin bath in front of the kitchen fire.

But Gladys viewed it as a hundred times better than a single room in a squalid tenement.

Ken, however, wasn't so sure. He enjoyed the anonymity of tenement living. People lived so close together that, paradoxically, they blended into a whole. No one any better off than the next. One-upmanship didn't exist.

Now he could imagine others bettering themselves, and he supposed Gladys would expect more from him.

When the war began in 1914, Ken had been unemployed. In

fact, he had never been employed, surviving by acts of petty theft and the odd rewarded favour to one of the local gangs. A well-built lad, he occasionally collected debts for a local money lender and never averse to dishing out a beating in cases of no money forthcoming.

Gladys knew nothing of this. The creed of the tenement prevented any tittle tattle.

Ken signed up to join the army before they forced him to enlist. The phrase, It will be over by Christmas, didn't fool him. He thought it would be a long, bloody, protracted conflict and sought a way to avoid it, if possible.

On the firing range, he managed to shoot a sergeant in the hand. In disgust, the commander relegated him to store duties, saying that with him in the front line, the Germans needn't worry, Ken would shoot his own men for them.

Ken was in fact an excellent shot, the sergeant's hand an example. It hadn't been a wild shot but calculated to injure, not kill.

Subsequently, Ken moved from supply store to supply store, ending the war with a sergeant's stripes and never leaving England.

He supplied the black market with goods during the entire course of the war, but never capable with money, squandered the lot by war's end in 1918.

After being demobbed from the army, he returned to his old ways, ducking and diving.

Now, he had to endure the constant scrutiny of neighbours and the constant nagging of Gladys. Ken wasn't as happy as the rest of the family, and his persistent dour expression began to concern Gladys.

Physical life with his wife also left a great deal to be desired. After the complications of Daisy's birth, Gladys found intercourse painful and shied away from Ken's attention. She tried in vain to explain to him, but her words fell on deaf ears. To Ken, the only joy from his marriage had been taken away by his daughter, Daisy, and his resentment began to fester.

He began drinking heavily, spending every night at the local pub, The Welcome Sailor, where he spent his ill-gotten gains freely. Gladys dreaded his homecoming, feigning sleep as he collapsed onto the bed, fully clothed and reeking of stale beer and cigarettes.

Thankfully, he had never been violent towards Gladys. Domestic violence from drunken husbands occurred almost daily in the poorer suburbs. It was seldom reported and even then rarely acted upon by the authorities.

Instead, he began to torment Daisy, who did not know why her father seemingly didn't like her. This continued until she entered her early teens, when one late night things turned really ugly.

Daisy liked to read and although books were scarce, when she could find one, she read it night and day until finished.

It had been a chilly day, and to keep warm, Daisy stayed up late while her mother and brothers climbed the stairs to bed. Snuggled up in her father's chair in front of the coal fired kitchen range, open book spread on her lap, she started as the front door slammed.

Ken lurched into the room very much the worse for wear. As usual, he had spent the evening at the local pub, only leaving when the landlord called time and barred the doors after the last customer left. Inevitably Ken.

He studied his daughter through bleary eyes, sitting in his chair.

'It's not enough that you robbed me of my marriage, now you've even stolen my fucking chair!' he exclaimed.

Daisy trembled as she saw her father's anger building. When sober, he ignored her unless finding a reason to chastise, but now in his drunken state, she felt trapped.

'Sorry, dad, I'll go upstairs,' she said in a whisper.

She stood up to make a hasty retreat, clutching the precious book under one arm.

'Not so fast, you little bitch,' slurred Ken, 'you owe me.'

Daisy had no idea what he meant but began to shake

uncontrollably.

Ken lunged at her, gripping her long nightgown as she tried to pass. The gown had been a hand-me-down adorning many previous owners before Daisy and worn almost paper thin. As Ken grabbed it, the gown tore, revealing Daisy's thin white body underneath.

Something snapped inside Ken's brain and he wrapped both arms around her, roughly pulling her to him. Trying to kiss Daisy as she twisted her face away, he pulled the remainder of the gown off, leaving her naked and exposed. All reason left Ken as his drunken desire took over.

Daisy managed to scream, and at first, it shocked Ken into some semblance of reality. However, all the years of sleeping beside his unresponsive wife, together with the sight of a naked girl who, in his eyes, responsible for all his woes, encouraged his anger and he slapped her, stopping her in mid-scream.

'You might as well be of some use, girl,' he shouted.

Fumbling for his belt, he began to undress. Daisy sank to her knees, shattered that her father could even think of such a thing.

She looked up into his face, eyes pleading for him to stop, but Ken had passed beyond reason. Daisy watched as his clothes fell away, revealing his excited state. The unfamiliar sight of a naked adult male horrified her.

She screamed again as he pushed her backwards until she lay on the floor, helpless and vulnerable.

Ken's face lit up with desire as he stumbled towards her, spittle dripping from his chin.

Daisy clamped her eyes shut as she felt him kneel between her legs.

Then he was on top of her. Daisy felt dizzy and began to slide into a faint. Suddenly, everything stopped abruptly.

She felt his weight leave her and dared to open her eyes. Bright red blood cascaded down as her father's face lifted from her. She looked past him to see her mother straining to move him.

At last, Gladys managed to roll him away. Daisy looked at her father's supine body, his face now covered in blood from a gash to the head. She lay still as Gladys picked up the heavy poker and plunged the end into the fire.

Daisy got to her feet and gingerly poked her father's body with a foot.

'He's dead,' said Gladys.

The first chilling scream had dragged Gladys out of her sleep. She lay in bed, wondering where it had come from. Screams were not uncommon in the neighbourhood, and she waited for another. Maybe there would only be the one. Someone suffering at the hands of a violent husband, no doubt.

The second scream, even louder, sounded more desperate. It appeared to be close at hand, too. Gladys leapt out of bed and ran downstairs in time to witness her husband about to defile his own daughter. So drunk, he didn't notice her walk to the range and pick up the heavy poker. Without hesitation, Gladys raised the poker high above her head before bringing it crashing down upon the back of Ken's head. The blow sounded like the dull crack of an egg, and she knew she had killed him. Blood streaming from the wound in Ken's shattered skull left no doubt in her mind.

Gladys struggled to lift him off Daisy, calling on her inner strength to roll the body sideways. Thinking coolly and coldly, she put the bloodied end of the poker into the fire. The hot coals would take care of any evidence.

Daisy's scream had not disturbed the boys, Keith and Ben. Both sound sleepers, they were roused from their slumber by Gladys vigorous shaking them as she summoned them downstairs.

Sleepily, they stumbled downstairs into the kitchen. Both boys' eyes widened as they stood over the body of their father. The bleeding had stopped and the red pool surrounding his head, already beginning to congeal.

They stood, speechless, as Gladys spoke in a quiet, commanding voice.

'I killed your father. He was drunk and trying it on with your sister.'

The boys stood together searching for words but finding none.

'You can either call the police and condemn me to hang for murder or help me,' said Gladys.

The boys both looked at Daisy, still naked and holding her hands to cover herself.

'We don't want you to hang.' The boys echoed.

Chapter 5

Maggie stood at the front door of Number 15 Petrie Street with the old set of well-worn keys in her hand. It was hers, her own home at last. Nobody to consult on how to decorate or furnish. From now on, she would be the one to make all the decisions.

Opening the front door, she stepped inside the dim hallway and, for a moment, shivered. It must be because the place had been vacant for a while, she thought.

That twerp, Julian, told her that the house had been in the same family for years. When she obtained the deeds, she would check. It would give her a project.

Desmond Yates made a point of absenting himself from the remainder of the transaction. His son, Julian, took over the reins from his father. Since the fateful night of the dinner with Maggie, Desmond wanted to avoid her.

As Julian handed Maggie the keys, his hand lingered unnecessarily over hers.

'Congratulations, Maggie, if I may call you by your Christian name. I'm sure you will make this place as beautiful as yourself.'

Maggie sighed.

'Like father like son, I see.'

'Oh no, I intend to be much more successful,' said Julian, winking as he walked away.

Maggie made a mental note to cross that particular agency off her list.

'Grubby little shit!' she exclaimed, hoping he heard.

All thoughts of the agent disappeared as her mind flooded with ideas of how to pull this dreary little house into the twenty-first century. She decided that colour, lighting, and furnishings would make all the difference.

As she climbed the stairs, Maggie failed to notice a faint shadow flit across the hallway, followed by another seconds later.

The next few weeks flew by. Tradesmen came and went as the old house began to emerge in its new livery. White paint on walls and ceilings brought light into the house. The odd picture would add colour to walls plus indoor plants.

Maggie sat on the comfortable new sofa she had purchased, surveying the results of her plans. The house now unrecognisable from when she first stepped over the threshold as the new owner.

Walking through to the kitchen, she looked lovingly at the new hotplates and under bench oven set into a modern stone topped bench with cupboards under.

At first, it appeared to be a scream coming from outside. Faint but certainly female, she thought, cocking her head to one side to hear it better. She concentrated on the sound, all other thoughts disappearing from her mind.

Now the volume increased as the pitch reached new heights. Maggie began to feel uncomfortable and covered her ears in an attempt to block out the all-encompassing sound.

It had no effect. The scream now invaded her senses. She could think of nothing except escaping from it.

Her feet failed to obey her brain's commands, and in desperation, she slid down the wall to sit on the freshly polished floorboards.

Still, the scream persisted. Strangely monotone, the single pitch rattled her brains.

Summing up every vestige of willpower, Maggie rose to her feet and ran blindly along the hallway until she crossed the doorway out onto the narrow pavement. Almost overbalancing as she stumbled off the kerb, she barely managed to keep her footing.

Maggie dropped her hands at the realisation that the scream had stopped. It ceased the moment she left the house.

Hardly daring to look, she glanced along the empty hallway. Had that been a shadow? Staring intently, she saw what appeared to be a flicker of movement close to the kitchen door, then it disappeared.

A face appeared at her side. It was Daphne from next door.

'Are you okay? You're very pale.'

Maggie tried to collect her senses.

'Yes, fine thanks. Daphne, did you hear a scream just now?'

Daphne's fears about the new neighbour returned.

'No, it's really quiet, not even a car in the street,' she said, her eyes widening as Maggie began to rub the Petrine cross around her neck, her old habit finding the cross comforting in times of stress.

To Daphne, the upside-down crucifix meant only one thing. Devil Worship.

Gingerly and not without a measure of trepidation, Maggie walked back into the hallway. Nothing. Not a sound. Whatever it was had left, or had it been in her imagination?

In an attempt to shrug off the terrifying incident, she returned to the kitchen and put the kettle on to boil. The English answer to every crisis, real or imagined, is to make a nice cup of tea.

Chapter 6

East London 1923

Gladys pulled herself together as the two boys looked down at their father's still form. They were both as deathly pale as Daisy who stood to one side, hands covering her nakedness.

'The bleeding has stopped, and we have to get him out of here before morning,' said Gladys.

'How?' echoed the boys.

'Roll him up in the carpet,' said Gladys, leaning down to begin the process, 'come along. I need your help. This is not the time to go to pieces.'

Keith and Ben kneeled beside their father's body, grabbing the edge of the carpet as Gladys rolled Ken over for the first time.

Ben, the youngest of the two boys, began to sob.

'None of that,' remonstrated Gladys, 'your father was no good. Any man that tries to rape his own child deserves no better fate.'

She attempted to comfort herself as well as the boys. Murdering her husband had never been on the cards, she merely attempted to stop him from assaulting his own daughter. A blow to the head should have merely rendered him unconscious and by morning, after the effects of the liquor had worn off, Ken would have been disgusted with his own behaviour. Or so she imagined, but it was too late now. The blow intended to stun had cracked his skull like a ripe melon. Gladys had no intention of being hanged with three children to care for.

With this thought uppermost in her mind, she, along with the boys, managed to roll Ken's body tightly into the carpet.

'Daisy, wrap yourself in a towel and get me the ball of thick string hanging on the back door.'

The girl ran to the door and fetched the string, glad to be able to take her mind off her father's assault.

Gladys cut off lengths of string and bound up the ends of

the thin and moth-eaten carpet. Ken salvaged it from the local dump, placing it in their new kitchen, much to Glady's disgust. If he hadn't spent so much time in the pub, they could have afforded a new carpet.

Now, it would be his last resting place in lieu of a coffin. In the back of her mind, Gladys thought it a fitting shroud, as worthless as her husband.

The next problem was transport. How to get him to the river, which luckily wasn't far away. The River Thames would have seen its fair share of dead bodies over the years. One more would hardly make a difference.

'Nip round to old Mr Pentley's and get his barrow. Quietly mind, we can get it back to him before he wakes.'

Keith and Ben made their way out through the back door, along the short garden path and out through the gate into the alleyway behind the row of houses.

Mr Pentley's hand cart stood in the alley, blocking the thoroughfare, and having been the subject of many local arguments, preventing others from using the lane. But the grumpy old man dismissed his neighbours' complaints out of hand.

'Bugger off and mind your own business!' his answer to one and all.

Keith and Ben wheeled the cart between them, stopping at their garden gate.

It took an enormous effort to get Ken's body, now securely wrapped in the carpet with the ends tied tightly, out of the house and onto the hand cart. With the boys on one handle and Gladys and Daisy, now donned hastily with clothes, on the other, they trundled the cart along the alleyway out onto the street. Very few ordinary people owned a motor car in 1923, so the street was empty. Little by little and as quietly as they could, the four pushed the barrow towards the East India Dock Road. Many minor streets and alleyways led to the river where they could dispatch Ken on his journey. Gladys hoped the tide had turned and, on the way out, it might carry him a little farther away before it sank to the riverbed.

Tipping the cart up by the handles, the carpet wrapped body slid off into the murky waters of the river.

They pushed the cart back at a much faster rate and by the early hours, the family were safely ensconced back in Number 15. Mr Pentley's cart stood back in its annoying position. No one noticed the brief absence.

Gladys schooled the children in what they were to say after she reported their father missing. Then they trudged upstairs to bed.

She busied herself on the lower floor tidying up, removing all traces of Ken from the previous evening. His blood had been absorbed by the kitchen carpet, now with Ken in the river. Gladys retrieved a smaller one from the front parlour to replace it. Nobody ever went into the front parlour, so it would not be missed.

The following morning, Gladys made her way to the nearest police station to report her drunken husband as missing. The desk officer smiled grimly as Gladys officially recorded him as a missing person.

She didn't know that her late husband had been well known to the police. His ducking and diving often brought him into close contact with the law, as did his part-time job as a debt collector. Several times he had been lucky to escape court appearances over the vicious beatings he handed out to late payers.

Police Sergeant Ivan Evans wrote the details into a report surmising that Ken had either fallen somewhere in a drunken state or local justice had caught up with him.

The man had been no loss in Sergeant Evan's view. Mrs Pickering looked to be an attractive woman and deserved better.

Sergeant Evans noted that fact for the future, just in case. Still single at the age of forty-three, he always looked out for a suitable marriageable companion. He unconsciously smoothed his moustache; yes, Gladys was a fine woman.

Gladys left the police station with the thought that she had done everything in her power to cover her tracks.

Five days later, Gladys answered the front door to a loud authoritative knock and opened the door to the large stature of Sergeant Evans.

'May I come in?' he asked.

Gladys tried to hide her shaking hands as she led him into the front parlour.

'What's happened?' she asked, sitting on a second-hand chair that Ken had found somewhere.

Sergeant Evans removed his helmet and sat in a mis-matched chair opposite.

'So far, we have found no trace of your husband. At this stage, we suspect foul play. Maybe some of his not so nice associates caught up with him.'

Gladys frowned.

'What do you mean, not so nice?'

'I'm sorry to have to tell you, Mrs Pickering, your husband is well known to us. He associated with members of a local gang of thugs, acting as a debt collector. An occupation at which he apparently excelled.'

Gladys looked genuinely shocked. No idea her husband had been involved in that way.

Silently, she stared at the floor.

Sergeant Evans reached over, placing a comforting hand on her knee.

'As soon as we find anything, I'll come around and let you know.'

'Thank you,' said Gladys, hoping the sergeant wouldn't notice her shaking.

Sergeant Evans did notice the slight trembling of Gladys' knee but boldly supposed it might be in response to his touch.

As she opened the door to allow the sergeant to leave, Gladys glanced up and down the street. Practically every door revealed an anxious, curious face. Neighbours were always wary when the police visited their street. The East End had been a notorious area where petty thievery abounded.

Ken was never seen again. Presumably the gas filled corpse would have been able to surface even covered with the carpet, but nobody saw anything. After the gas dissipated, the body sank back into the depths, and there it would remain until the carpet rotted away. By that time, the corpse's flesh would be gone, leaving only a skeleton gradually sinking into the soft cloying mud of the riverbed.

Chapter 7

Maggie settled into her new home. She hadn't heard the scream again or noticed any unusual activity, so put it down to her nerves being on edge due to the divorce.

She had applied for and won a position with a leading group of architects specialising in warehouse conversions and upgrading existing conversions to match the huge prices apartments now commanded in the East End, particularly in and around the West India Docks area.

Gradually, a few of her more loyal old friends began to drift back. It never surprised her that many chose to stay away, not wanting to be involved in the conflict surrounding a messy divorce case.

Her best friend, who had remained loyal even through Peter's abusive stage, sat opposite her now in the newly renovated house.

'I'm afraid it's a little down market from what we used to have.'

Penny laughed.

'Don't be silly, this area is becoming sought after. Just look at the apartments in the docklands, one million plus for two bedrooms with a view of the river.'

'I don't think these will ever get to that price,' laughed Maggie, 'they originated as homes for workers and were owned by the council. Only becoming private residences after Maggie Thatcher sold most of the country's social housing.'

'Don't be too hard on our Maggie. She is your namesake after all,' laughed Penny.

'I should make an effort to get to know my neighbours,' said Maggie, relaxing into a new leather chair.

'Brilliant,' said Penny, clapping her hands for joy like a much younger girl, 'I'll help you organise some nibbles. It'll be fun.'

Maggie frowned. Penny sometimes displayed childish traits,

and Maggie wondered if they were real or covering something Penny wanted to keep hidden.

It had been a slightly worried Maggie and a completely confident Penny who welcomed the first visitors.

Penny had, as promised, organised the event, laying on scrumptious goodies and quality wines.

Ruben and Daphne were the first to cross the threshold of Maggie's fully modernised home. They were visibly impressed and said so. Daphne walked around, staring at everything.

'This is so nice,' she said, 'it will be ages before we can do anything as swish as this.'

Ruben wasn't quite so enthusiastic.

'Yes, nice but probably not to our style, I prefer earthier tones.'

'Take no notice of Ruben. He's pissed because we can't afford to do our place up. The mortgage takes most of our wages.'

Maggie sensed a mini war brewing and withdrew in order to greet more guests.

The couple that resided on the other side but one introduced themselves as Mr and Mrs Greaves, showing their age. In their era, Christian names were not bandied about until people had been formally introduced.

Maggie made sure to introduce them as Mr and Mrs, trying to hide her smile behind a raised hand.

In the end, only four couples showed up. Two from either side. The house immediately next door on the other side of Maggie was vacant and had apparently been so for a few years. It reflected the change in society from the old days when the entire street knew each other and people seldom locked their doors. Children would wander in and out of each other's houses and neighbours would simply walk in and put the kettle on for a cuppa.

Daphne had a wonderful charismatic charm and soon had the other neighbours eating out of her hand. Ruben hung back, fearful that his size might be intimidating. He was tall, broad, and good looking. Maggie noted that the other ladies present, including Penny, couldn't take their eyes off him.

She hoped Daphne wasn't the jealous sort but doubted it somehow.

Maggie found herself cornered by Daphne in the later stages of the soiree.

'So, why do you wear the upside down cross? That's to do with the Devil, isn't it?'

Maggie automatically reached for the cross, rubbing it gently between finger and thumb.

'No, on the contrary, it's anything but to do with the Devil. The upside down cross is known as the Petrine Cross and is the Cross of St. Peter. He considered himself so far beneath Jesus that he refused to wear an ordinary cross. The upside down cross is a token of his humility. In fact, it's said that when sentenced to death by crucifixion, he insisted on being hung on the cross upside down in a final act of humility before God.'

'I see,' said Daphne, 'thank you for the explanation.'

The story sounded too well rehearsed for Daphne and she preferred instead the more common link to Satan. Perhaps Maggie didn't want to disclose her true beliefs.

Maggie extricated herself from the conversation, not wanting to be drawn any further. She had always in fact been an atheist. She had purchased the cross because the shape and design intrigued her. Owing to her natural inquisitive nature, she had researched it, finding that there were in fact quite a few variations, including St Andrew's Cross, which became the national flag of Scotland.

Daphne sidled up to Ruben and whispered Maggie's explanation to him.

'It's time for us to leave,' he said, brooking no argument. They made their apologies, thanked Maggie and left, walking the few steps to their own door.

Once inside, Daphne did have something to say.

'Well, how rude, leaving so suddenly. What will our new neighbour say?'

'I don't care what she says. Her explanation for that symbol of Satan doesn't fool me. I saw plenty of those in Haiti and they were certainly not godly.'

Back in Number 15, things were drawing to a close after Daphne and Ruben left.

After the last couple left, Maggie and Penny sat alone together, sipping wine. There were a few opened bottles and it seemed a shame to pour the contents down the sink.

'I'm sure it will keep,' said Maggie.

'Best not to take the chance,' laughed Penny, topping up their glasses.

Maggie turned down the lights and the pair sat easily in each other's company.

'I'm trying to remember when we first met,' said Penny.

'A long time ago, before Peter,' reflected Maggie.

'Yes, it would have been before you hooked up with Peter.'

A silence settled over them for a few minutes before Maggie spoke again.

'I'm going to investigate the history of this place.

It will be interesting and who knows what went on here in the past.'

Penny frowned.

'Be careful what you wish for. You might dig up something nasty.'

Maggie giggled, the wine beginning to make her tipsy.

'Who knows, it might be in the area where Jack the Ripper roamed.'

Penny shivered.

'Don't joke, didn't he kill those girls around here somewhere?'

'No, only joking. I believe he operated in Whitechapel,' laughed Maggie.

'Close enough,' whispered Penny.

Chapter 8

East London 1888

The smartly dressed man stared up at the ugly tenement building occupying the whole of his vision. It ran the entire length of Petrie Street, and the rooms that were home to dozens of families were accessed by a number of dark entryways and dingy stairwells.

He chose the middle entry and started to climb the stairs. On the second floor landing, he turned onto a narrow hallway, wrinkling his nose in disgust at the smell of the communal privy. The door stood open, waiting for the next occupant, and the stranger hurried on.

Many of the room numbers were missing, so he had to work out the location of his patient by counting the doors.

His leather gloved hand rapped sharply on a door. It opened immediately, revealing a woman wrapped in a dirty shawl.

'Doctor Jessop. I believe you called at my surgery?'

'Yes, doctor,' replied the woman, 'it's my little girl, she's too sick to leave the room.'

The doctor entered the room, which smelt little better than the privy. The room contained a narrow table and four chairs, a small coal range, and a large bed. A young girl, struggling to breathe, lay at the edge of the bed with her head on a dirty bolster.

After a cursory examination, Doctor Jessop pulled the threadbare blanket back over the diminutive form, shaking his head sadly.

'She has all the signs of consumption. There is very little I can do. To prevent the disease spreading, the child should sleep separately.'

Her mother stood forlornly, wringing her hands.

'Can you give her something to at least relieve the symptoms, doctor?'

'I can, but it will cost you another shilling on top of my fee.'

The woman went to the mantle over the range and brought down an old tin. She held out coins to the doctor, who opened out a gloved hand to receive them.

He assiduously counted the coins before dropping them into a pocket. From his bag, he produced a small bottle of powder.

'Mix a pinch of this in water and give it to her whenever she needs it.'

'Will she live?' asked the woman hopefully, tears forming in her eyes.

'She's in God's hands now,' the doctor replied, 'she will live or die as the good Lord sees fit.'

Doctor Jessop left the room hastily and hurried along the hallway, past the disgusting privy, down the stairs and out into the street. He breathed in great lungful's of fresh air before walking away, knowing full well the young girl would not survive another week. The rest of her family probably already had the disease and would not be far behind her. No one cared, it would simply leave a vacancy in the tenement.

Doctor Jessop walked the length of the building, the cloying air of human degradation settling over him. The owners of the building couldn't care less about the unfortunate tenants as long as they paid the rent. Worse, the building was owned by the Church of England, as were many in the East End. So much for Christianity, thought the doctor.

He turned away from the building and walked into an alleyway to be immediately accosted by a woman.

'Care to spend a little time with me, sir?'

Doctor Jessop stopped, looking her up and down. Her clothing, dirty and little more than rags, did nothing to stir his feelings. He was used to a better class of prostitute with no problem paying for his pleasures.

As he moved away, the woman, sensing she might miss out on some easy money, raised her skirts, revealing her nakedness.

The doctor stared at her for a second before turning away.

'You disgust me!' he exclaimed.

'A pox on you, then,' she snarled, dropping her skirts back into place.

A leather gloved fist connected with the centre of her face, and she fell back at the crunch of her nose cartilage collapsing. Blood spurted over her clothes as she sank to the ground.

Doctor Jessop continued on his way, impervious to the woman's misery.

Mary Nichols lay with her back to a brick wall, her nose still bleeding from the doctor's brutal punch. She was used to violence. At forty-two years of age, her life had been painful from the beginning.

The eldest of ten children, Mary became a second mother to her younger siblings. Her father, often drunk, began to abuse her at an early age, and her mother appeared to be helpless to prevent it. She protested once at the beginning but received a savage beating from her husband. Thereafter, she turned a blind eye to Mary's plight.

At fifteen, Mary left the family with an eighteen-year-old boy, a neighbour. She quickly became pregnant and their life soon resembled the one she had escaped.

Four children followed, and as life became harder, her husband decamped, seeking a new life with a younger childless woman.

Mary began to find solace in liquor, and needing money to fuel her new habit, she began to offer herself to any that might pay a few pennies.

Now, she lived alone, two of the four children died young and the remaining two moved out of her one-roomed accommodation.

She had sunk to the bottom, life becoming a roundabout of selling herself for the price of a bottle of gin. But she would remember this man, this so-called gentleman, who had viciously punched her. He wore a smart black coat and carried a bag identifying him as a doctor.

She made a promise to herself that the next time she met

him, she would follow him home. Maybe his wife, if he had one, would like to know how her husband treated other women.

It had been some weeks since the incident, but Mary never gave up. One frosty night, her patience was rewarded by the appearance of the same black coated, bag-carrying man. If sober, her original plan might have worked, but in her alcoholic state of mind, she resorted to verbal abuse. Her voice rose in volume to an uncontrolled scream directed forcefully at Doctor Jessop.

Such was the loudness of her scream that the doctor, for a few seconds, became rooted to the spot, his ears began to distort the sound until it became unbearable.

He reached into his bag, producing a scalpel, and without hesitation slashed her throat so deeply the blade grated against her spine. The scream ended abruptly and the doctor sighed with relief.

The experience had caused a part of the doctor's mind to snap and, far from experiencing remorse, he felt exalted at ridding the world of at least one disgusting whore.

He used the scalpel to make a deep incision from abdomen to sternum, opening the cut to expose her intestines.

Shocked to his senses by his own actions, the doctor hastily made his way from the scene, a deep burning satisfaction radiating throughout his body. However, her scream remained in his head, he could still hear her. A part of his sanity had been destroyed forever, and he would never be the same again.

Chapter 9

Maggie began searching the history of her new house. In her lunch break, she scoured the internet, looking for a site that would lead her to every owner since Number 15 Petrie Street had been built.

The original owners were listed as the London County Council. Delving further, she found the original building occupying the site had been a tenement owned by the Church of England. They sold it to the council after questions were asked in high places as to how England's principal church could not only own such squalid premises but suffer the poorer classes to pay rent for one room in which they were expected to house a complete family.

Nonetheless, a large sum of money changed hands, and the church coffers received yet another windfall.

Originally, the newly built houses were rented to tenants of the building it replaced, coming as something of a culture shock to those who previously had to make do with one room and a shared privy.

A list of tenants proved rather more difficult, and Maggie assumed there had certainly been more than one since the original build.

The house became privately owned when the Thatcher government introduced the Right to Buy in 1980. Tenants were able to purchase their homes at a heavily discounted price if they had occupied them for more than three years.

Maggie was shocked by the number of owners who had lived at Number 15. The estate agent, Julian, told her the house had been in the same family since the Thatcher era. The lying little turd!

She studied the list of owners fuming at his blatant lies, but knew she had no recourse at law for Julian's misinformation. In the fine print at the bottom of the brochure he had given her, it stated that any information the agent gave to a prospective buyer was given as a guide only and that buyers should make their own enquiries.

Later that day, Maggie sat with Penny, glass of wine in hand, venting her spleen on Julian and his despotic father, conjuring up various ways in which the devious pair should be punished for lying.

'But you like the house, don't you?' said Penny.

Maggie calmed a little.

'Yes, but why did they have to lie like that? What were they hiding?'

Maggie's search turned into an obsession. A trait that plagued her all her life. Anything she found challenging became a target.

Peter had also turned into an obsession for her. So much so that his forays into anything of a somewhat doubtful sexual nature that anyone else would find perverted, merely added to the challenge.

Momentarily, Maggie allowed her mind to drift back and she suppressed a shudder. Her screams that night were left unanswered.

Thank goodness for Google, she thought as she typed her question. Major historic events involving Number 15 Petrie Street, East London.

A newspaper clipping appeared on the screen. She could just make out the date at the top of the page, 24th December 1924.

A grainy black-and-white photograph of a terraced house leaped out at her. Number 15 Petrie Street.

The headline read: **Terror Revisits East London.**

The story under the headline detailed the apparent rape and murder of a young girl.

Maggie printed out the story to study in depth later. This would definitely be an occasion that called for company and wine. She put a call in to Penny and they arranged to meet that evening.

The thought occurred to her that Penny had, in fact, been the only one of her old friends to stay in touch. The saying: 'A friend in need is a friend indeed' came to mind.

Maybe the fact that Penny had never married was something to do with her valuing Maggie's friendship. All their peers were long since married, some remained in wedlock while others, like herself, divorced.

Since the divorce, Penny never failed to answer Maggie's phone calls, it seemed as if she were waiting for the phone to ring.

This time was no different. Penny readily agreed to meet at Number 15 for wine, nibbles, and discussion on Maggie's new information.

Penny studied the newspaper article.

'Bloody hell,' she said, 'and it all happened right here in this house.'

'Creepy, isn't it,' said Maggie, her skin beginning to crawl.

As she handed the article back, Maggie began to read aloud.

'The body of a young girl was found upstairs. She had been the victim of a vicious assault, then murdered. The killer, seen fleeing the scene, ran into the path of a truck and died instantly.'

'Would you spend the night here? I don't want to be alone tonight,' asked Maggie.

Penny hesitated for only a second.

'Okay, but I'm not staying in a bedroom alone. We don't know in which one that poor girl died.'

Maggie forced a laugh.

'Well, we'll have to share a bed.'

Maggie and Penny lay awake for hours upstairs in the main bedroom. They each had a sidelight burning, keeping darkness at bay. Sharing a bed with a woman felt completely alien to Maggie. She slept so near the edge of the queen size bed that she seemed in constant danger of falling out. Penny didn't seem to mind and talked incessantly about any nonsense that came into her head. Anything being better than envisioning the past events in the house.

Maggie began to doze off as a wayward thought crept into her mind.

'Did you ever go out with Peter before he and I got together?'

Silence hung between them like an icy veil until Penny spoke.

'We had a bit of a fling once.'

Chapter 10

East London 1923

Life for Gladys continued on at Number 15. No trace had been found of her husband and the authorities assumed he may have been dispatched by one of the many gangs in the area or perhaps simply run away to begin life over.

Sergeant Evans popped in every week at first to report on any news. Soon the visits became more frequent, and Gladys accepted that he might be rather more dutiful than necessary.

She began to look forward to their afternoon cups of tea in the kitchen, Sergeant Evans taking this to be somewhat of an affirmation for his romantic intentions.

The two boys, Keith and Ben, were not so keen. They thought about their dead father lying prone on the floor, in a position where the police sergeant's boots now rested. Guilt suffused with fear made the boys nervous and edgy.

'Come along, you two, cheer up, no point in moping around the house all day. Get out and do something constructive, like getting a job, for instance,' said Ivan.

Gladys felt for her boys, they never really liked their father, but the shock of seeing him lying dead in the kitchen and his death being at the hand of their mother did nothing to assuage their mood.

Without uttering a word, they left the house, vowing not to return until the policeman had left.

Daisy fared even worse. The trauma of being attacked by her father and then seeing him lying beside her with his skull caved in never left her, not even for a moment. Now, she had another issue to contend with. The policeman, would he be her new father?

For some time, Sergeant Evans played it cool. Three or four times a week he could be found sitting at the kitchen table. The boys began leaving the house at lunchtime to be sure of not being present when he arrived. Work might well be the answer for them, just as the policeman had suggested. They obtained work as lightermen together on the same barge. The work, while hard, didn't pay well, but anything would be better than staying in the house. Especially now that their mother visibly fawned over the policeman.

They worked the flat-bottomed barge up and down the river, both boys studying the muddy water for signs of a rolled-up carpet, fearing their father would surface and all would be revealed.

But it never happened, Ken lay quietly on the riverbed, gradually decomposing as local crabs clawed at his carpet shroud in their endeavours to get at him.

Daisy stayed upstairs while Ivan visited her mother, wanting nothing to do with him, or for any man come to that. She had decided that when old enough, she would join an order of nuns, shunning men, and the outside world forever.

The cold of winter now a distant memory, Ivan suggested they would be more comfortable in the front parlour.

'I'll get it ready for your next visit,' said Gladys, putting her hand over the sergeant's as it rested on her knee. But she made no effort to remove his hand, which Ivan saw as another good sign. He had played Gladys like a freshwater trout, gradually reeling her in without giving her cause to panic. Sergeant Ivan Evans had always been a very patient man. The front parlour would be a good spot to complete his seduction. Unfortunately, the presence of her daughter upstairs ruled out the comfort of Gladys' bed.

Ivan hated living alone, and the brief moments of solace with a local prostitute no longer held so much appeal. He never had to pay; the girls were always happy to provide him with a little pro bono service. However, now he craved for permanence in his life. Not only a lover, but a companion with which to spend the remainder of his life.

He found Gladys very attractive, and their frequent meetings were making him increasingly frustrated. He thought he must make a move soon before some other suitor pipped him at the post.

Ivan's moods were becoming increasingly malevolent.

A regular working girl found out how harsh he could be during a recent encounter. As usual, Ivan met up with her on her normal street corner. He in police uniform and she in her working clothes, an impossibly tight, short skirt and fishnet tights. Her legs wobbly on worn stiletto heels.

Delilah, certainly not her real name, rented a nearby flat on an hourly basis. A few of the girls used the same room and took turns to wash and change the bed sheets once a week. Ivan always tried to meet her at the beginning of the week.

On this occasion, he had not been his usual cheerful self. A quick romp with the police sergeant guaranteed her a get-out-of-jail-free card, saving her the inconvenience of a court appearance and the inevitable fines that the girls endured as part of their business. Delilah treated it as an insurance policy and always gave him a good time so that he might return regularly.

However, on this occasion, Ivan had been surly, allowing her to lead him upstairs to the flat. Delilah knocked on the door, checking that none of her compatriots were inside entertaining a customer.

A man's harsh voice sounded through the door.

'Fuck off if you know what's good for you!'

Without hesitation, Ivan kicked the door in with his massive size fourteen police issue boots.

He strode into the room, catching the man in bed with one of the other girls In flagrante delicto.

The man in bed quailed at the size of the uniformed sergeant. The punch took him square in the solar plexus, bending him double in agony. Ivan pulled him out of the room, naked, and tipped him down the uncarpeted wooden stairs. Flinging his clothes after him, he then turned on the girl.

'This room's taken, Flossie,' he growled menacingly.

Flossie needed no further encouragement, gathering her

clothes and running downstairs, not bothering to cover her nakedness.

Ivan turned to Delilah, who stood with her mouth slack with disbelief.

'Get your clothes off and take Flossie's place!'

What followed could hardly be described as lovemaking. More of an assault. Delilah had never seen this side of Ivan, and wondered if her get-out-of-jail-free card was worth it.

The following day, Ivan arrived at Number 15 all smiles. He carried a small bunch of flowers, handing them to Gladys with a wide grin.

'Beautiful flowers for a beautiful lady.'

Gladys flushed from the neck up in embarrassment, taking the offered flowers in one hand while placing the other on Ivan's arm.

'You have been so kind, Ivan. Heaven knows what I would have done without you.'

Ivan snatched his opportunity.

'Gladys, Ken has been gone only a short time and at present marriage is out of the question, but I'm proposing, anyway.'

'Oh, Ivan, this is so sudden, I honestly don't know what to say,' she replied nervously.

'Say, yes, and we'll deal with the rest as time allows,' said Ivan, sensing he was close to realising his dream of a real home life.

Gladys became thoughtful as she ushered him inside. Instead of the kitchen, she led him into the front parlour. It had been cleaned with a meticulous eye to detail. Nothing out of place and although only lightly furnished, the sofa looked very inviting to Ivan, long enough to lie on!

Gladys closed the door behind them and sat on the sofa, her nervousness displayed by her straight back. She tugged at her skirt, rearranging it to cover her legs. Sitting as demurely as she knew how.

Ivan sat beside her but at sufficient distance to display no immediate danger to Gladys' comfort.

Her reached for her hand and dared to utter just one word.

'Well?'

'Well,' Gladys repeated, 'my answer has to be yes, but we can't live in sin, and Ken might return at any moment.'

She bit her lip, knowing full well Ken would never return, but couldn't let on.

'Maybe we could take our relationship to the next level?' said Ivan quietly, gently squeezing her hand.

Gladys had been so lonely. Ken may have been a bastard, but that was better than being alone. Single mothers, whether through accident or misfortune, were frowned upon by society. Men thought it gave them license and wives suspected they might be after their husbands.

'I'm nervous, Ivan, I've never been with another man, Ken was my first and only,' whispered Gladys.

Ivan realised at that point how close he had come to fulfilling his wishes. Thankfully, yesterday's little episode with Delilah had curbed his desire, he mustn't blow it now.

'We can take it as slowly as you like, my dear, no pressure, I assure you.'

Ivan gently moved closer to Gladys, still holding her hand. He risked moving his face closer to hers, hoping she wouldn't pull away. Gently, he held her close and Gladys reacted as he hoped, succumbing to his embrace as he took her in his arms, and kissed her.

Sensing he had reached the limit for that day, Ivan broke away, smiling.

'How about that cup of tea?'

Gladys smiled back, getting up and moving towards the door.

'I'll put the kettle on, would you like it in here or the kitchen?'

'Oh, I think in here, don't you? This can be our very own personal meeting place in future.'

'Yes,' breathed Gladys, strangely excited in a way that had eluded her since her illicit teenage meeting with Ken when they had first made love. She felt young and alive again.

Ivan sat back on the sofa, rearranging his uniform to conceal his own true feelings. He might have to pay Delilah another visit later in the evening.

Chapter 11

At Penny's suggestion, they met at a local bar.
'You have to get out more,' she had said, 'meet new people.'

'You mean men,' Maggie said, laughing.

'Well, yes, it will do you the world of good, you can't keep sleeping with me.'

Maggie wasn't quite sure how to take that comment.

'Okay, I'll join you at the bar why not.'

The Gilded Cage used to be a local pub called The Welcome Sailor. Now, it represented a new class of patrons, the nouveau riche millennial set.

The once downtrodden area of the East End's Docklands had been transformed into a very desirable location. Warehouses once filled with imported good from all over the globe had been converted into luxury apartments with river views. Commanding price tags in the millions of pounds.

Maggie had become one of the architects responsible for designing those same sought after homes. As trade moved away from the waterfront, more warehouses became available for development. Rich pickings for adventurous developers, and their equally adventurous architects.

A small group of men and women were gathered at one end of the bar as Penny and Maggie entered.

Penny approached a forty something man smartly turned out in designer clothes and hooked her arm through his.

'Maggie, meet Stephen.'

Maggie took the outstretched hand, feeling the dry warmth of Stephen's handshake as he smiled into her eyes.

'A pleasure to meet you. Penny seems quite taken with you, and now I understand why.'

Maggie allowed her hand to drop to her side, failing to note the look Penny gave her. If she had, she would have seen the look of malevolence.

Looking around at the other patrons, Maggie saw a mixture of Millennials, those born in the 80s and early 90s to the latest generation Z, those born in the late 90s to early 2000s. Everyone looked prosperous and decked out in the latest fashion. She wished she could be more enthusiastic, but memories of Peter intruded on her judgement. How many of these people were real and not merely bull-shit artists bragging about things they did not in fact have, hoping to take advantage of their peers who might actually be someone of real substance.

Peter, dismissed from her mind, she stood beside Penny and Stephen, looking over the crowd with a glass of chilled white wine sitting comfortably in her hand.

'Anyone you could take a fancy to?' asked Penny, sliding an arm through Stephen's.

Maggie looked around for the umpteenth time before replying.

'No.'

'Never mind,' purred Penny, 'have another glass of wine, at least it will relax you.'

Penny excused herself and made for the Ladies Restroom leaving Stephen to refresh their glasses.

He returned rather quickly, holding out a fresh glass of wine for Maggie.

'So, tell me all about yourself,' he said, opening the conversation.

'I'm pretty boring really,' replied Maggie, 'I work as an architect on those old warehouses lining the river. Apart from that, a great big nothing.'

Stephen merely nodded.

Maggie thought she had better continue the conversation to avoid an awkward silence.

'And you?'

'Probably just as boring,' he laughed, 'I'm a psychologist.'

'Aha,' said Maggie, 'delving into people's minds to see what makes them tick.'

She didn't mean that to come out the way it did and immediately apologised.

'Sorry, I shouldn't have said that.'

Stephen laughed good-naturedly.

'That's okay, people usually clam up when they learn what I do. Everyone has secrets and they believe I can see into their very souls, quite untrue, of course.'

'Of course,' mimicked Maggie, 'at least one would hope that's the case.'

Penny returned, gripping Stephen's arm possessively.

'That's enough, you two, he's mine,' she said, laughing, but Maggie thought it a forced laugh. She would have to tread carefully around Stephen, although in truth she had no designs on any man after her experiences with Peter.

They left the pub, each taking a different direction. Maggie made for the office, although already getting late in the afternoon, but she had a mountain of work waiting for her attention.

Stephen paused, turning to watch Maggie walk off, completely ignoring Penny, who walked in the opposite direction.

Darkness shrouded the streets by the time Maggie arrived home. Modern street lighting brightened the area, but she shuddered as she wondered what it must have been like under the sparse, dim gas lights of the late nineteenth century.

The key turned in the lock, she pushed the door open and stepped inside, feeling instinctively for the light switch. Coldness surrounded her as her hand waved over the wall, searching for the illusive switch. A part of her wished she had opted for old-fashioned prominent light switches instead of the latest style that were flush with the wall to make them practically invisible both to the eye and touch.

Her mind began to play tricks as she imagined shadows at the end of the hall, fear increasing as her need for light increased.

At last, her hand connected with the light switch and she flicked it on. Wonderful, comforting light flooded the narrow hallway and she relaxed.

'Get a grip,' she said out loud, 'there's nothing here to be afraid of.'

Making for the kitchen, she made sure her hand found another illusive light switch before fully entering. Why did the house feel so cold?

The gas stove warmed her hands as Maggie decided coffee and leftover cold cuts would be better than starting a hot meal from scratch.

As she ate, the events at the pub that afternoon crossed her mind. She laughed inwardly at Penny's obvious discomfort about introducing her to Stephen. If she felt threatened, why make the introduction in the first place?

Maggie went over the crowd once again. No one there that aroused any interest, even if she had been looking for someone, which she wasn't. Stephen's smiling face stood out above the rest, and she quickly dismissed that image from her mind.

Her mobile phone rang, vibrating on the small table beside the chair.

'Hi, thought I'd check to see you got home okay,' said Penny, 'what did you think of Stephen?'

Maggie paused, suddenly cautious about how to reply.

'He's rather nice, isn't he? He obviously likes you a lot.'

'Yes, he does,' replied Penny, a little too quickly.

The call ended after a few inconsequential pleasantries. Maggie frowned as she put the phone down, reaching for the television remote.

'Police were called to an abandoned warehouse this evening to investigate the discovery of a woman's body. The deceased person was found on an upper floor. It is thought she may have been there for some time.'

She sat bolt upright as she recognised the building. It looked identical to the one she had been working on. If so, she had walked every floor only two weeks ago with her team.

Maggie switched the TV off and walked through the kitchen to her newly modernised bathroom. A nice relaxing hot bath with a glass of chilled white wine beckoned, then bed, she decided.

Chapter 12

East London 1888

Doctor Ralph Jessop had enjoyed a privileged upbringing. Born into money, his father a well-respected doctor and surgeon, Ralph wanted for nothing. His father put his name down for Eaton Public School the day after his birth. As an 'Old Boy' himself, he knew his son would be accepted. The system worked that way, ensuring that only generations of the 'Right' people attended the prestigious school.

They left Ralph at the gates of Eton School at the tender age of five. Merely a baby, staff ushered him away from his parents, never again to be mollycoddled by his doting nanny. Ralph received very little love or acknowledgement from his mother. She performed her duty in delivering a son. The remainder of her life her own, she made sure the experience would never have to be repeated.

The way high society conducted itself meant that his parents' attitudes were never questioned. Ralph's father, Paine, busied himself in his practice, dealing only with the upper class, while his mother Esme submerged herself in soirées to do with the arts.

Both parents had lovers. Paine employed the services of various girls in a well-known West End brothel, while Esme entertained various starving artists, who were only too pleased to shower her with compliments and endearments while receiving commissions for paintings that would never be hung.

The young Ralph endured Junior School stoically, there being no alternative. Then, he moved up to the Middle Grade and thence to Senior Grade.

By the nineteenth century, Eton became a school for the elite. A strange paradox, as when founded in 1440 by Henry VI, the establishment schooled poor, orphaned boys in order to give them a free education.

Ralph had been forced to undergo the ritual of Fagging where newcomers became Fags for senior pupils. They were nothing more than servants and were subject to corporal punishment for any perceived offences, real or imagined.

Unfortunately, when the younger Fags reached senior status, they, too, adopted the same ritual. Having been subjugated for years, they were now presented with the opportunity to enjoy the luxuries of their own personal servants, chosen from newcomers entering the system.

All kinds of abuses were perpetrated on the younger boys, including those of a sexual nature. However, very few were ever reported, as doing so would be considered Toadying and would result in the complainant being publicly flogged.

Many fine statesmen grew out of this system, but occasionally boys' minds were corrupted and they emerged as less than desirable.

Ralph eventually went up to Cambridge, where he emerged some years later as a doctor to follow in his father's footsteps.

As Doctor Jessop, Ralph took up a practice in the better part of London. Once a week, he made his way to the poorest of areas in the East End of London to attend to the sick. Not for free, however. Ralph took whatever he could from the poor, but his motives were of a different nature than mere money.

Like his surgeon father, Ralph had a keen interest in the human body. However, it had become increasingly difficult to obtain dead bodies to work with. The grave-robbers of old were no more and he now relied on the generosity of families to agree to the dissection of their departed loved ones, for a fee naturally.

As research centres grew, private surgeons found it ever more difficult to obtain specimens. The poor were easy targets. Their children often died young, and couples in these areas tended to produce many children. Families with sixteen children were not uncommon.

For one guinea, plus the cost of a basic interment, Ralph would have the child's body taken to his house. In the cellar, he set up a full-size laboratory where he could experiment on the body, packed in ice, until he arranged for a burial. Such interments were private and took place in unconsecrated ground outside the bounds of a churchyard to ensure officialdom would be kept at bay.

In order to satisfy his desires, Ralph sought out only the best brothels, except on one occasion when he happened upon the prettiest girl he had ever seen. Prostitute she may have been, but Mary Smith possessed the face of an angel. She avoided the heavy make-up of her peers and refrained from wearing the crass fishnet stockings and ridiculous high heels that were apparently attractive to men.

Mary could normally be found loitering in the better districts of the West End, an entirely different world from the East End.

However, she had to take extra care because the larger brothels enjoyed protection from gangs that extracted money from the house Madams to ensure the girls wouldn't be attacked by other miscreants or constantly raided by police.

Members of the police force received lucrative backhanders from these same gangs. However, as a streetwalker, Mary enjoyed no such protection.

Ralph passed Mary in the shadows on his way to his usual brothel. Her natural beauty captivated him from the outset, and turning on his heel he approached her.

Mary displayed an even set of white teeth, a rarity in itself for those days, especially for working girls who loved to smoke, drink, and occasionally take drugs when offered.

Ralph, at his charming best, allowed himself to be guided to an adjacent upstairs room. Once inside, Mary lost no time in stripping him of every stitch of clothing. As Ralph lay on the bed, she performed an exotic striptease for him.

'You, my dear, are quite simply beautiful,' he said, barely able to breathe.

'And you are obviously very ready for me,' Mary whispered seductively, lightly holding his penis with one hand while stroking his chest with the other.

Ralph, lost for words, remained silent while she knelt on the bed, guiding him into her.

Mary knew her trade well. Her movements were slow and deliberate. Ralph never enjoyed such delights before, and knew he wouldn't last, climaxing just minutes after she began.

They dressed together, Ralph's laboured breathing tempered by her tinkling laughter. He smiled, amazed that the sound she made appeared to be so far removed from the coarse, guttural laughter of a common harlot.

Silver coins made a jingling sound as he dropped them into her outstretched hand. He overpaid her, grateful for the experience, and pleaded with her to meet again in a few days.

She cupped his face in her hand, kissing him boldly on the lips. Again, something he was not used to. Prostitutes didn't encourage their clients to kiss, reserved for special men in their lives, sometimes husbands who encouraged their young wives to sell their charms rather than work themselves.

Chapter 13

East London 1924

Sergeant Evans surprised even himself at his ability to suppress his desire for Gladys. His patience would surely be rewarded.

It had been eight long months since the courtship began. Gladys resisted his advances, only gradually allowing him to at first fondle her over her clothes, then in stages, placing his hand under her blouse before finally guiding him to the hem of her dress.

Ivan slowly crept his hand along her inner leg until he reached the edge of her underwear. Gladys planned for this evening, and she made sure she wore her best.

As Ivan's hand slid over the cotton covered mound, he let out a groan. More than his body could bear, he disgraced himself.

Making his excuses for leaving early, he beat a hasty retreat, not wanting to reveal that his body had let him down so embarrassingly.

Gladys stood at the door, waving goodbye and smiling. She knew perfectly well what had occurred. She deliberately paced herself over the last months. If Ivan Evans wanted her, he would have to woo her properly. The first time with Ken proved too quick, with disastrous results. She loved her children, but it happened too quickly, and she doubted Ken's sincerity. In that respect, she had been proved correct.

Sergeant Evans, on the other hand, would prove to be all that Ken wasn't, or so she hoped.

The front parlour, having been designated a no-go area for the children, ensured she and her new beau would be able to canoodle without fear of being disturbed.

Owing to the fact that no trace of her husband had been forthcoming, Gladys would have to be satisfied with the legal rules pertaining to missing persons. She would have to wait seven years before applying to the courts to have Ken presumed dead before she could remarry.

She discussed this at length with Ivan.

'We cannot possibly live in sin,' said Gladys, 'what would people say?'

'The force wouldn't be too happy with the situation either,' admitted Ivan.

'We shall just have to maintain a long engagement,' suggested Gladys, 'when the time comes, we can enjoy each other's company, and I will cook you evening meals, but you will have to go home to sleep.'

They agreed it would be for the best. Ivan not so happy with the arrangement, but Gladys, who looked forward to a relationship that she could walk away from at any time of her own choosing, approved of.

Towards the end of 1924, Gladys finally gave in to Ivan's efforts at seduction and allowed herself to be fully unclothed in the front parlour. Ivan took the precaution some time before to install a small brass bolt and hasp on the inside of the parlour door, ensuring they wouldn't be surprised by the children disobeying the rule of no entry.

Ivan scrambled to divest himself of uniform and underclothes as Gladys lay invitingly on the new carpet he purchased for the parlour floor. Police Sergeant Evans ensured it was plush and of the finest quality, as he knew it would have to serve as their bed.

The fact that Gladys made him wait so long increased his desire tenfold. She insisted he wear a condom, pregnancy, the last thing she wanted.

Ivan had reached the stage where he would agree to anything and did as she demanded.

When he at last satisfied his desire, he lay beside her, breathing as if about to take his last gasp.

'Are you okay, Ivan?' asked Gladys.

'More than okay,' replied Ivan, 'can we do it again?'

Gladys laughed good-naturedly.

'Only if you promise you won't die on top of me.'

A loud knock on the parlour door startled them. Gladys put her finger to her lips, begging Ivan not to speak.

'Yes, what do you want?' she asked through the door.

'We're hungry, mum, when is dinner?'

Gladys suppressed a laugh, still lying under Ivan, trying to breathe normally under his weight. Even though he supported himself on his elbows, Ivan was no lightweight.

'Soon.' Gladys said, sucking in a lungful of air as Ivan entered her for the second time.

'Condom!' exclaimed Gladys.

'Too late,' replied Ivan.

One week later, Ivan caught up with Delilah again. Gladys may have captured his heart, but it would never be enough for him. Roughly pulling her upstairs to the shared flat, he unceremoniously threw her onto the bed, tearing at her underwear beneath the short skirt.

Due to Delilah's range of lovers, Ivan always wore a condom. He didn't care about impregnating her, but he did care about the real possibility of contracting a deadly disease.

The arrangement with Gladys continued unabated for several weeks until disaster struck.

Ivan, desperate for Gladys, called around the house in the early evening.

The children, having already eaten, retired upstairs to their bedroom as Ivan walked into the kitchen.

Gladys placed a plate of hot food on the table, but Ivan wanted more than food.

He grabbed Gladys around the waist, rushing her into the front parlour, lowering her none too gently on the plush carpet. Furiously tugging at her clothes, he forgot to bolt the door. Gladys didn't know whether to laugh or cry. A lusty Sergeant Evans would not be denied, and she lay still as he collapsed on top of her.

Neither heard the gentle tap on the door, as a face appeared around the door.

Daisy looked on in horror as she glimpsed her mother lying prone beneath the giant form of Ivan, grunting and groaning, while her mother remained silent. The night her father attacked her filled her mind and she let out a piercing scream.

The couple on the floor froze in unison.

'Daisy, it's okay,' yelled Gladys.

Ivan was not so friendly, his enjoyment being abruptly terminated.

'Bugger off upstairs where you belong, girl!'

Gladys struggled to extract herself from underneath Ivan.

'Don't be unkind, Ivan, she doesn't understand.'

Ivan, beyond caring, recommenced his labours much to Gladys' disgust. Daisy looked on, her face screwed up in horror.

Gladys looked at her daughter and began to cry, she needed Ivan to stop but he wouldn't listen to her entreaties. She began to beat him on the back with her fists, but it made no difference. What Ivan wanted, Ivan got!

Letting out a loud cry, Gladys renewed her efforts to stop his brutish rampage.

Suddenly, and dramatically, Ivan stopped. Gladys looked up to see a surprised look pass over his face.

His weight crushed her as his body relaxed completely. Gladys pinned beneath him, struggling to breathe.

The front parlour became crowded as first Daisy, then the two boys, began to push and pull the sergeant off their mother. Eventually, with much effort, they succeeded in rolling him to one side, allowing Gladys to extricate herself.

All four stared down at the supine body of Sergeant Ivan Evans. A long kitchen knife, worn to the shape of a dagger from years of use, protruded from his back.

Daisy looked down, with no sign of remorse.

'He made mum scream.'

The knife, missing the sergeant's ribcage, slid neatly into his heart, ending his life instantly.

'What shall we do, mum?' asked Ben, fingers twitching

anxiously.

Gladys, numb with shock, looked at her children.

'What have you done, Daisy?'

Daisy didn't hesitate.

'I saved you the same as you saved me, from father.'

Gladys wanted to explain that it wasn't the same at all. That Ivan and she were lovers and today, he lost control in passion. He hadn't meant to hurt her. But the pointlessness of the situation hit home. The policeman lay dead and it fell to her to protect her daughter.

'Help me roll him up in the carpet,' insisted Gladys, the irony not escaping her that Ivan bought the carpet for their lovemaking.

'The river, I suppose,' said Ben.

'When it's quiet, go and get the barrow again,' said Gladys, holding the kitchen knife that she pulled out of Ivan's back. She would have to soak it in bleach overnight to make sure all traces of blood were removed.

At a little after midnight, the four family members once again pushed old Mr Pentley's barrow towards the river. Sergeant Evans lay trussed up in the plush carpet he had been so fond of, bumping gently as the cart trundled over the uneven streets.

Down by the docks, they found the spot where their father entered the river and pushed and pulled until Ivan, the policeman, joined him.

Gladys and the children pushed the barrow back around the rear of Petrie Street and quietly replaced it in the same position. The terrace remained quiet, for which they silently gave thanks before slipping back inside Number 15.

At last, they could relax.

'Up to bed, you three,' said Gladys, looking around to make sure no evidence of Ivan's visit remained to incriminate them.

Daisy, Ben, and Keith were halfway up the stairs when Gladys let out a muffled cry.

'Ivan's police helmet, he left it on the hall stand,' she said, trying not to shout out in panic.

The three came back downstairs as Gladys stood in the hallway holding Ivan's police helmet, running it around in her hands.

Sadness enveloped her as she held Ivan's police helmet. She felt weak at the knees because she really liked him, but the rapid events of the evening had dulled her senses. Now, she began to feel the loss of both Ivan and the secure future he offered. All gone now because of her desperate cries.

'Give it to me demanded Keith,' grabbing the helmet, 'I'll get rid of it.'

Gladys called after him as he made for the back door.

'Don't get caught with it.'

Keith didn't answer, merely raising one hand in a salute.

With Keith away on his mission, Gladys and the other two retired to bed. The sheer physical effort together with stress sent all three into a deep dreamless slumber.

Gladys woke first, hurrying downstairs after checking on the children in the back bedroom. Keith had returned and the two boys lay with Daisy wedged between them. She shook her head, realising that the sleeping arrangements would have to change. Daisy, in the same bed as the boys, simply wouldn't do. Her own experience of cramped living arrangements still haunted her, recalling the nights where she had to fight off the attentions of her brothers. It was no different in any of the neighbouring households, two bedrooms were simply not enough for most families.

Breakfast came and went. Conversation remained stilted with all four concentrating on the meagre meal Gladys prepared.

'Everything go all right last night, Keith?' asked Gladys.

'Yes,' Keith replied without further explanation.

Gladys decided to let sleeping dogs lie, she didn't want to know how her son had rid them of the last piece of evidence connecting them to the disappearance of Sergeant Evans.

During the ensuing days, word gradually got out that a local policeman had gone missing. The police force were not keen on sharing any information, Sergeant Evans a well-respected copper. He lived alone with no known relationships. His immediate police friends knew of his penchant for the local ladies of the night, but nothing had come of the enquiries made in that direction. The strict code of silence amongst the locals formed an impenetrable barrier.

Delilah summed up the situation to her friends in a few harsh words.

'That's one less bastard to worry about!'

Two weeks later, the newspapers were full of the story of the missing policeman, his bloated body having been discovered off the Isle of Dogs. It washed up on the shoreline, and two of the locals, thinking they might have discovered an unwanted carpet, hauled it ashore. The smell it gave off made them vomit, and the local police were called to investigate.

An autopsy revealed the sergeant died from a stab wound through the heart with some kind of blade, and a murder enquiry quickly established.

House to house enquiries were carried out in his patrol area.

Gladys found it difficult when two detectives called around. They were speaking to everyone in the street, so she forced herself to remain calm, keeping silent about her relationship with the sergeant. The neighbours were well aware, of course, but under their code of silence, nobody mentioned it.

Newspapers love a murder, and they milked the story for all its worth. Once again, the area became linked to the gruesome murders of the late nineteenth century when Jack the Ripper roamed the East End. It became blatantly obvious that the Ripper murders bore no resemblance or connection whatsoever to the murder of Sergeant Evans, but newspapers have never been that fussy about facts. Circulation figures are all that are important to them.

Man charged with the murder of local policeman screamed the headline.

Gladys pored over the story, her eyebrows raising as she recognised the man's name.

Local petty criminal, Percy Stoppard, will appear at The Old Bailey. She read on, wondering what evidence had been discovered.

When the children came in, she showed them the paper. Daisy and Ben appeared perplexed, but not so Keith. He merely smiled.

'Where did you dump the sergeant's helmet?' demanded Gladys.

Keith sat down at the kitchen table.

'I owed that Percy big-time. He beat me up on two occasions, and always threatened me, just because I eyed off his daughter.'

'What did you do?' asked Gladys, joining him at the table and expecting the worst.

Keith smiled, but Gladys thought it a cold, mirthless smile.

'I hid the helmet in the little shed at the back of his place.'

'But surely that wouldn't necessarily mean anything to do with the murder,' said Gladys.

'I slipped back into our house that night while you lot were planning the sergeant's farewell trip and took the knife from the kitchen. You bleached the wrong one. I hid it under the police helmet. Percy's done for and no mistake, good riddance, I say.'

Gladys couldn't believe her son capable of such an act of revenge.

'Keith, you have incriminated an innocent man!'

'But we're in the clear, aren't we,' he answered with that same cold smile.

Chapter 14

Maggie watched the small television in her kitchen, ignoring the freshly toasted sourdough slices on a small plate by her side. The freshly made coffee suffered the same fate as she listened to a reporter droning on about the woman's body found the previous day.

The woman's body is believed to have been placed in the building over a week ago. There were signs that it had been interfered with post-mortem but the police refuse to clarify.

Her own recent comments to Penny about the location of Petrie Street flashed through her mind.

'It might be the old home of Jack the Ripper.'

The television reports switched to sport and Maggie began breakfast, but she couldn't get the thought out of her mind.

Detective Chief Inspector Nipper shared the same thought as he looked down at what remained of the young woman. Her handbag lay beside her, apparently untouched. Inside, documentation showed her to be one Marion Clarke. Her address on a driving licence showed her to be a local.

Nipper spoke to the pathologist, dressed from head to foot in white protective clothing.

'So, what do you reckon, Cyril?'

The pathologist looked up.

'She is, or rather was, about twenty-five years old.'

'Yes, I already know that. It's on her driver's licence,' Nipper replied tersely.

Cyril ignored the sarcasm.

'I will be able to tell you more after the autopsy, but for now I can say she has been ripped apart, literally.'

'A knife job?'

'No, I would say something smaller and very sharp, like a surgical scalpel.'

'Whoever did this certainly wasn't very neat. The poor girl has been slashed right down the middle. Anything missing?'

'I'll be able to tell you that at the autopsy. I take it you will be in attendance?'

'We'll do it at the Yard, the powers above sent me straight down here. They are afraid of the press getting hold of more detail and starting a panic. Our lovely dailies haven't published a good story since the Royals settled down.'

'You are thinking serial killer, I take it.'

'Not with only the one at the moment, but if there are more, it could be the story of the century. The newshounds will connect it somehow to the Ripper murders of the late nineteenth century, you can guarantee it.'

Cyril waited until the forensic photographers finished before giving instructions for the poor woman's body to be removed to Scotland Yard's basement morgue.

Maggie made herself ready for work, hoping she had been wrong about the building in which the woman's body had been found.

She walked to the nearest tube station, having decided to rid herself of her car. It proved to be a liability due to the lack of parking spaces, and even then she would have to apply for a special permit. Furthermore, to go into the City one had to have yet another permit and pay a fee to travel within the actual city of London.

The Tube is fast, cheap, and convenient. Slamming the front door shut, she turned to head in the direction of the station.

As she did so, she collided with someone standing very close to the door.

'Sorry, my fault, I was just about to knock on your door when you came rushing out.'

Maggie looked up into Stephen's laughing eyes.

A look of worry and doubt crossed her face as her mind whirled to take in the implications of his arrival at her door first thing in the morning.

'What on earth are you doing here? It's miles from your office.'

'Well, I don't have any appointments until 10.30, and being at a loose end, I came to escort you to work.'

'Why?' she asked bluntly, bearing in mind that this man is supposed to be involved with her friend Penny.

'Because I like you,' he said unashamedly.

'And what about Penny?' asked Maggie.

'What about Penny?' said Stephen, with the hint of a smirk on his face.

'She happens to be my friend, at present my only real friend. You're supposed to be her boyfriend and about to compromise a good friendship.'

'I'm a bit too old to be a boyfriend, don't you think?'

'Lover, then,' said Maggie, beginning to walk away.

Stephen would not be put off and followed two or three steps behind as she made for the Tube.

They didn't speak again, and Maggie began to feel threatened. Stephen's persistence worried her, and she had no idea what to do.

On the Tube Train, she sat in one carriage and he in another, smiling at her whenever she looked in his direction.

She left the train at the closest station to her office, relieved to see that Stephen stayed on, waving to her as the train whizzed noisily into the next tube.

So bothered by Stephen's sudden appearance, Maggie completely forgot the dead woman.

She quickly came down to earth when summoned into a meeting. Her associates sat gloomily around the boardroom table. Why someone chose a table in the shape of a wide coffin always bemused her. Nevertheless, she sat quietly as the chairman stood.

'You have all, no doubt, seen the news this morning. That poor woman found in our new project has forced us to put it on hold until the police release the premises from their enquiries.'

Maggie, being the appointed team leader for the luxury units that would be built within the skeleton of the warehouse, raised her hand.

'I know what your question is, Maggie,' said the chairman, 'I suggest you and your team take a week's holiday. Hopefully, we can get back to work soon. The developers are having kittens over the delay. Every lost week is costing them thousands.'

Maggie folded her papers back into the black attaché case at her feet and stood up.

'Do we know yet the identity of the dead woman?'

A gentle shake of the chairman's head answered her question.

With nothing more to do, Maggie made her way out of the building and headed back to the Tube Station, warily casting her eyes from side to side for any sign of her stalker.

Once safely home with no sign of Stephen, she called Penny. Somehow, she needed to warn her friend.

She replaced the receiver before Penny could pick up, her peripheral vision catching a movement. She turned to face the kitchen, her heart thudding. Not Stephen, surely.

However, the room appeared to be empty. She sat down heavily, the business with Stephen must be playing on her mind. Her call to Penny never eventuated.

Nipper stood to one side of the stainless-steel table displaying the woman's mortal remains. He guessed that her soul had long since departed, not that he believed in that sort of thing, although occasionally even an atheist could take comfort in old myths.

Inwardly, he remembered his late father admonishing him for joining the police force.

'You belong in the church, serving our Lord as I have all my life.'

Nipper's father, a country vicar in darkest Worcestershire, wanted his son to follow in his footsteps, but despite numerous entreaties Nipper believed his future lay with the police.

He bypassed the local Constabulary, because his father may have had some influence, fleeing to Metropolitan London. Two years on the beat had seen him qualify as a fully-fledged copper. He took the first opportunity that presented itself to join CID and became a Detective Constable. Nipper loved the job and never looked back. Successful in gaining convictions, he transferred to the Murder Squad as a detective sergeant. From there it had been Deadman's Shoes, rising through the ranks to his current rank of Detective Chief Inspector.

He had no wish to progress any further up the ladder. In that direction lay the monotonous daily grind of statistics and rosters. He would surely die of boredom within weeks. No, Nipper would stay where his talents could be used for maximum effect. At the sharp end, where he would deal with the most heinous and mysterious cases.

Now, before him, lay the remains of a young woman. Stretched out on the cold stainless steel, Marion Clarke made a pitiful sight.

The sliced body lay open, obviously pulled apart after death by whoever carried out the deed. A week inside the disused warehouse had seen rigour mortis set in, then relax. Quite quickly, decomposition set in, ruining once pretty features and leaving nothing more than a foul odour.

Nipper had become inured to the smell of rotting flesh, as had the pathologist. Their interest lay in discovering the identity of the murderer.

After beginning the dissection, the pathologist began speaking into an overhead microphone.

'Decomposition has been ably assisted by rats. This is no surprise with the river nearby.'

He carried on until all the body parts had been removed, examined, and weighed.

'Well?' said Nipper, 'any conclusions?'

The pathologist peered over the top of his frameless glasses.

'A large part of the deceased's colon has been removed. I cannot even hazard a guess why anyone would do that. Medically, the organ would be useless for transplant or anything of that nature. From the cut, better described as a rudimentary slash, I would say the killer is driven by some unknown urge.'

'Sexual?' asked Nipper.

'Well, she certainly did have intercourse prior to her death, but from the medical card found in her handbag, I would say she is likely a prostitute. The card gives details of regular check-ups for sexually transmitted diseases at a local centre frequented by both ladies and laddies of the night.'

'Bloody hell!' exclaimed Nipper, 'If this gets out, the shit will hit the fan big time. A prostitute slashed and mutilated in the East End will have the dailies ranting and raving about the return of Jack the Ripper.'

Chapter 15

East London 1924

Percy Stoppard stared up at the grilled window. Two prison officers sat at a small table playing draughts. Awake all night, they had lost count of the number of games and the score hours ago.

Percy had managed to sleep fitfully, waking with a start as he realised it would be his last night on earth. When awake, he repeated over and over.

'I didn't do it, I didn't kill anyone.'

The officers had heard that lament so many times over during their service. Guilty or innocent, the cry is always the same. I didn't do it.

'It doesn't matter, Percy, it's going to happen at nine in the morning. Nothing can stop it now.'

He knew that wasn't exactly true, a governor's pardon could stop the execution where a directive from the Home Office would be relayed to the Governor, but they doubted that would happen. One of their own had been brutally murdered, and the evidence pointed squarely at Percy.

'Some bastard fitted me up,' he snarled, thinking through the people he had upset during his career in petty crime. The list flowed through his mind and he realised he had been less than generous to so many.

One stood out. Keith Pickering. He lived quite close and courted his daughter. Percy had warned him off twice with a good kicking. But the little tyke kept coming and he feared for his daughter. Rachael was only fourteen and he didn't want her ending up in the family way at that age. He knew that's how she might end up one day, but not at fourteen. He had to admit her early development had the boys chasing her, like flies around a jam pot.

'Keith Pickering,' Percy shouted to the guards, 'it's him that fitted me up, I'm sure of it.'

The guards looked at each other knowingly. Lack of sleep and desperation often had this effect on the condemned prisoner.

'Too late, Percy. Why don't you sit quietly?' said one of the guards softly.

Percy's last meal lay on a side table, untouched. How anyone could eat a hearty meal knowing what is about to happen perplexed the two guards but the tradition had to be followed.

'I want to write a letter to my wife,' said Percy.

The guards provided pen and paper together with an envelope that would be sealed and delivered unread to his wife after 9 am.

Percy scribbled out the note, folding it into the envelope before licking the glued edge. He struck two lines over the join before signing his name between the lines.

'Nobody will open it,' said one of the guards, 'that tradition will never be broken while I'm here.'

'Thank you, thank you, both,' said Percy, suddenly at peace with himself. His time had come, and he wanted a dignified end to his life.

At five minutes to nine, the cell door opened. Percy had no idea of the time. His small cell lacked a clock and the guards were not permitted any form of timepiece. A small mercy afforded the condemned man. Watching time slowly ticking away would be torture.

The prison governor, a priest, and three others entered the small confines of his cell.

'It's time,' announced the priest, 'shall we say the Lord's Prayer together?'

Percy looked the priest in the eye.

'Why, the Lord hasn't looked after me. You are hanging an innocent man. I won't make it any easier for your conscience.'

'Very well, then,' said the governor.

At that, a side-door in the cell opened under the guidance of one of the other three. Percy, quickly ushered into the room, blanched at the sight of the already prepared noose hanging from a beam.

Led to stand over a trapdoor, his hands and ankles were quickly secured. The hangman placed the noose enclosed in a plain white cotton bag over his head, making sure the knot was located under the left side of his chin. Without any hesitation, he pulled a long lever, releasing the trapdoor, which split in the middle, allowing Percy to fall cleanly into the pit below. In a microsecond, the rope became taught, ending Percy's life instantly. The entire process had taken less than thirty seconds.

They would leave his body dangling for the statutory time before removing him in a plain pine coffin.

The letter would be dispatched, unopened, post-haste to his family.

Gladys stood amongst the people standing outside London's Pentonville prison that morning. As the prison clock struck nine, the crowd gasped. Percy would by now be hanging, dead.

Gladys turned away, tears streaming down both cheeks.

The weight of guilt pressed down on her as she walked. She could have saved the man's life but chose instead to protect her family. Gladys consoled herself with the thought that any mother would have done the same. Still, she felt the pain Percy's family must be suffering. Unable to approach them with any form of condolence even though they lived in the next street.

Two days later, Percy's widow stood in the hallway of their home reading his final letter addressed to her.

'The bastards!' she exclaimed, walking into the kitchen where the rest of the family sat still wearing mournful expressions.

'I've received this letter from your father, written on the day of his execution. Read it for yourselves.'

My dear Lil, I want you to know that I didn't kill that copper. I think the Pickering boy, Keith, planted the evidence. He wanted our Rachael, and I gave him a sorting out on a couple of occasions. Please don't think badly of me. I know I haven't always been good to you, but I'm not a murderer.

Percy.

Rachael read the letter leaning over the boy's shoulders. Bill and Fred angrily stood upright, knocking her backwards.

'Don't you worry, mum, we'll get the bastard!'

Lil remained tight-lipped.

Rachael began to cry.

'But you have no proof Keith did for him. Dad was only guessing. He must have felt terrible just before -.' she couldn't finish the sentence.

The two sons were beyond reason.

'We'll get him and his brother too if necessary. Maybe we'll do the whole family!'

Lil broke down in tears, sobbing with her head on the kitchen table.

'If you do that, I'll lose you as well. You will both hang.'

The boys' temper, soothed by the sound of their mother's sobs, sat down opposite.

'We'll think of some sort of payback!'

Fred, the oldest of the two boys and a strapping eighteen-year-old, had grown up tough; no other way in their neighbourhood. It had been a regimen of learning to take a beating and to dish one out, like his father and his grandfather before.

Fred's anger did not abate in any way as the weeks passed. If anything, he became obsessed with getting even for his dad's unjustified execution. His anger shifted from merely Keith to the entire family. He would get even somehow.

Lil became more and more concerned for Fred. He had taken to staying out late but never smelled of alcohol, unusual in itself. Like his father, he had become a heavy drinker, but now other things plagued him. The Pickering family.

Fred would loiter around the area of Number 15 Petrie Street, watching the comings and goings of the family. As Keith and Ben left the house, laughing and chatting, his knuckles would clench, turning white under the strain.

More often than not, he would miss turning up for work until his boss finally sacked him, declaring him to be unreliable, and a waste of space. There were plenty of other men more than willing to take his job.

Turning to petty crime for a source of income, he unknowingly stepped into his father's shoes. Fred became a collector. Someone feared by all. His job entailed collecting debts, usually small, that poorer families incurred in the struggle to survive. Interest rates were always high and illegal, but no one dared report the moneylenders to the authorities. Anyone who stepped out of line in that direction could, and sometimes did, end up lying at the bottom of the river. A covering of rusty chains ensuring they gradually disappeared into the sticky mud at the bottom of the River Thames.

At one stage, there were more dead bodies littering the polluted waters of the Thames than fish.

The remainder of the Stoppard family didn't ask questions. Fred threw money onto the kitchen table every Friday evening, more than they had seen before, and his surly attitude brooked no questions.

The situation carried on for a year, and Fred never ceased watching Number 15. He stationed himself close-by every day, come rain or shine.

On a particularly cold February afternoon in 1925, Fred waited patiently, as usual. Coat collar turned up to meet the back of his flat cap. The cigarette cupped in one hand against the elements gave him a tiny glow of warmth. The other hand, he pushed into his jacket pocket as far as it would go.

He guessed Keith and Ben would be at work and watched as the front door opened and Gladys stepped outside, shopping basket in hand. Smiling as Daisy laughed at some comment they shared.

Waiting until Gladys turned the corner and allowing her time to return in case she had forgotten something, Fred made his move.

The hatred he harboured for the Pickering family knew no

bounds. If he had to, he would take each one of them out over time. Percy lay dead in the cold ground, as yet unavenged. That would change today!

Chapter 16

East London 1888

The doctor had found his own piece of heaven in the form of Mary Smith. He doubted either of her names were genuine, being the most popular name in the country, from the days when every town and village had a blacksmith. Thereafter, the name Blacksmith or sometimes shortened to simply Smith grew as children were christened in the name of their father's trade.

'I want you to stop selling yourself cheaply to all and sundry,' said Ralph one evening after their coupling.

Mary laughed.

'That's all right for you, you're a rich gentleman.'

'I will pay you an allowance to keep yourself to me, and me only,' said Ralph.

Immediately, Mary could see the value of such an arrangement. Many of her friends were maintained by gentlemen and lived in modern apartments with abundant spending money.

'Will you get me somewhere nice to live?' she asked, simpering while teasing his chest hair.

'Certainly, my dear, and what is more, I shall give you a monthly allowance to spend as you wish. However, you must keep yourself for me and I shall call on you whenever I choose.'

Mary giggled like a little girl, knowing he found that particularly attractive.

Ralph, seemingly like most men, hated condoms. Since 1839, when Mr Goodyear discovered vulcanised rubber, they were easy to access by working-class men and cheap to produce. More traditional condoms made from cloth, leather, or animal intestines were expensive.

Ralph saw an opportunity to enjoy sex without resorting to

the awful things, insisting on Mary keeping herself exclusively for himself.

As a doctor, he feared sexually transmitted diseases, in particular, syphilis. At the time, the lack of a cure led to madness and eventual death.

Mary clapped her hands for joy. Her Knight in Shining Armour had appeared on his white charger. No more casual sexual escapades for a mere few pennies for her.

Doctor Jessop, for once supremely happy, had the deceased bodies of the poor to dissect and regular sex whenever he wanted.

He had once considered marriage a solution, but as all the married men of his acquaintance visited brothels, he surmised that wives were good at holding out the carrot prior to marriage but were loath to grant any marital privileges thereafter.

The doctor could see no point in pursuing any such arrangement. He had no use for children of his own, they were merely a financial burden. Ralph recalled the day he entered Eton School as a young child. He rarely saw either parent after that.

Neither Ralph nor Mary ever discussed their history or family connections, their arrangement being purely business. He had no idea about Mary's younger sister, Henrietta.

In the new spacious apartment provided for her use by Ralph, ample room existed to accommodate Henrietta. At just sixteen years old, the choices for her future were limited to the sewing rooms of vast clothing factories that were springing up in the East End, or the streets. Henrietta, like most of her class, had a very limited education.

Their mother had long since passed away from the dreaded tuberculosis, and their father languished in Brixton Prison. He, having been convicted for the umpteenth time, had no hope of an early release. In years gone by, he would have been a prime customer for the Thames Hulks, and from there, transportation to Van Diemen's Land.

Mary took it upon herself to care for her younger sister, and as soon as it became practicable, moved her into the new apartment.

The ever-present danger lay in the discovery of Henrietta by the doctor. Mary feared her much younger and prettier sister might well appeal to Ralph, and she might be replaced.

Even worse, the good doctor might choose to bed them both. Mary, even though a prostitute, possessed some morals and the latter idea would prove too much to bear.

The one fault Mary did have in spades was the propensity toward boredom. At first, sitting in her pleasant apartment had been deliriously exciting. However, as weeks passed into months, she found herself more and more frustrated with mundane things such as shopping. Even buying new clothes became a thankless chore. Mary needed excitement in her young life. Things had to change.

Henrietta thought differently and remained quite content to run the apartment. She cared for Mary by preparing meals and carrying out onerous tasks like washing and ironing. Rarely leaving the place unless the doctor put in an appearance, in which case she quickly made herself scarce.

Ralph accidentally caught sight of her one morning when he made an unexpected early visit.

'Who is she?' said Ralph, noting Henrietta's lithe young figure.

'Just a girl I get in occasionally to clean,' said Mary, dismissing Henrietta with the wave of a hand.

Ralph watched her leave and licked his lips salaciously.

'Why don't you employ her permanently, there's plenty of room and I'll gladly pay her wages.'

'I don't need her here all the time to get under my feet,' said Mary, her jealousy already on show.

Ralph smiled coldly.

'It's not a suggestion, it's an order. I shall expect to see her next time I call.'

Mary wrung her hands, she couldn't tell him her sister already lived with her permanently, Ralph would never forgive the deceit.

Ralph's demeanour changed instantly.

'I don't have long so into the bedroom with you.'

Mary complied with his every wish, smiling seductively. If nothing else, she had become a good actress.

'What!' exclaimed Henrietta, 'I'm not sleeping with him, he's an old man.'

Mary glared at her sister.

'He is not old and anyway, you should be grateful for the opportunity.'

Henrietta's face screwed up in distaste.

'I haven't done that with anyone yet, and I'm not losing my virginity to him!'

'Then, you will have to leave today,' said Mary, 'I'll make up an excuse as to why you had to go away, but it will have to be far from this area or the doctor will find me out.'

Ralph arrived two days later. His eyes were bright and Mary guessed he more than looked forward to enjoying the delights of her sister.

'Gone! What do you mean gone?' demanded Ralph.

Mary's excuse sounded pitiful, even to her.

'She had to go and care for a sick relative,' she said, toying with the ribbon holding her camisole together.

The doctor showed his displeasure. He had begun to tire of Mary, and his thoughts were already turning to others. She may have been the best girl in the world at first, but there were so many more young and willing young ladies.

Mary undid the camisole and displayed her breasts suggestively.

Ralph's disappointment, a little assuaged, squeezed them roughly.

'Ouch, that really hurts,' cried Mary.

The doctor took no notice of her complaints, spinning her

around and over to deliver a hard slap to her backside.

'I make the rules, and don't forget,' he said, pushing her down onto the floor.

Meanwhile, Henrietta used Mary's monetary gift wisely. Her sister gave her enough to survive for some time, provided she used it sparingly. Cheap lodgings were available in the East End, so that is where she headed, securing a small one roomed flat not far from the docks. Surrounded by clothing factories, it didn't take long for her to secure a job as a trainee machinist.

Henrietta obeyed her sister to the letter, and never again ventured to the West End. The thought of sleeping with the older doctor appalled her.

Mary's boredom peaked. She would have to get out of the apartment and visit the area in depth. Guessing that after his last visit, the doctor would leave her alone for a couple of days, Mary dressed up and walked out to parade along the busy West End streets.

No matter the quality of clothes the doctor bought for her, nothing could hide her obvious, lowly upbringing. Even the way she walked brought her undone. Ladies were prone to take dainty little steps when walking out, whereas Mary strode along like a common labourer.

She was soon spotted by a local man. He followed her for some time before approaching from behind.

'Looking for a little fun?' he asked jovially.

Mary turned to see a well-groomed man taller than herself and sporting the latest fashion in headgear. Ralph always wore a top hat and sober black suits from the best tailors Saville Row could provide.

This fellow looked rather dashing in a brightly coloured check suit.

Mary turned to face him.

'What did you have in mind?' she asked, immediately confirming his suspicions of her low standing.

Edgar Wimpole proved to be nothing more than a high-class pimp. His task, to round up ladies who could please the gentry in one of the better West End clubs. These establishments were strictly men only, and their exorbitant fees made sure their members were from the correct side of society.

'I can introduce you to one of the finest clubs in London,' said Edgar, 'normally they are for gentlemen only, but exceptions are sometimes made for quality ladies like yourself.'

Mary, suitably flattered and not a little intrigued, allowed him to tuck her arm through his to continue along the street.

Eyes wide in wonder, Mary walked into the Bentinck Club. The opulence together with the smell of countless coats of wax on every piece of furniture left her lost for words.

Edgar led her through various hallways with great double doors leading to who knew where.

'Where are we going?' asked Mary, at last becoming a little concerned at where this total stranger appeared to be leading her.

'Just through here,' said Edgar, opening a smaller door. The room beyond almost as posh as those they had already passed, but not quite.

A group of men stood drinking from crystal glasses and turned to watch Mary enter.

Edgar picked up an empty glass and gently tapped it with a spoon. The noise brought everyone to attention as he waved Mary into the room.

Gentlemen, allow me to introduce Miss Rosemary Smythe, a resident of the West End. He winked at Mary, who had already told him her real name.

She went along with the harmless ruse, walking among the gentlemen offering her hand. As each man bent to kiss her hand, he took time to study first her décolletage, and then her face.

Mary didn't care, this promised some fun, and she loved the attention. These men were not stinky working-class men, reeking of sour ale, and loath to part with a few pennies for a few minutes of pleasure.

These gentlemen reeked of expensive cologne, and their suits obviously hailed from Saville Row.

After introductions were made, Edgar led Mary out again. She gave a moue of disappointment when the door closed behind them.

'I enjoyed that,' she said a little too loudly. Three glasses of the finest French Champagne tends to loosen one's tongue.

Edgar silently congratulated himself on his find. Mary would be ideal for the afternoon's entertainment, and he guessed she would be back for more.

'Listen, Mary. The Toffs in there want a bit of light-hearted play, and they are willing to pay handsomely for the privilege. What do you say?'

Mary knew exactly what light-hearted play meant.

'How much will I get?' she asked, sobering with Edgar's offer. Her previous career balancing her alcohol consumption nicely.

'Five pounds for the afternoon,' said Edgar. His own reward would be one pound with the strict admonition that he would not tax any of the girl's fees.

Five pounds represented a small fortune in those days, and Mary's eyes gleamed.

'There were five gentlemen in the room, I counted them,' said Mary.

'That's right, five in total,' said Edgar.

'Well, yes or no, nobody is forcing you, but I have to know now,' he insisted.

'When do I get the money?' asked Mary.

Edgar smiled warmly.

'Right now,' he said, handing Mary a large, paper Five Pound Note.

What followed could best be described as an afternoon of unlicensed debauchery. Mary pleasured each man until all five were both satisfied and exhausted.

As she left the room, squirrelling away the five-pound note, Edgar waylaid her.

'How about a little something for me?'

Mary smiled suggestively.

'One pound, please.'

Edgar waved her away, not about to part with his entire fee. The other girls would oblige him for a shilling or less.

'Same time next week?' he suggested instead.

'Same time, same fee,' replied Mary, walking to the front door. Once again, dressed and primmed, ready to return to her apartment.

Chapter 17

Outside the Tube Station, Maggie stared at the newspaper stand. Written with a black pen, the headline add screamed for attention.

The return of the Ripper. A vicious Copycat?

She joined the queue in order to buy the paper, seldom seen in these days when smart phones and the internet usually dominate the news. People were standing around reading from open papers, oblivious to other passers-by.

Maggie thought the reporter used a great deal of poetic license in the graphic description of the poor, unfortunate victim's demise.

'Fuck!' The word came out with such vehemence that the entire office stopped in its tracks. All eyes faced the issuer of the word. Detective Chief Inspector Nipper rarely swore. The newspaper he had been reading screwed into a ball, and angrily tossed into the litter bin.

'Someone in this office leaked the story to the press, and if I find the culprit, he or she will consider the position of Traffic Warden an honour.'

Detective constable Jane Wilmot, only recently seconded to the Murder Squad, knew no better than to speak at this point.

'Maybe someone from the Path Lab blabbed,' she announced. This only increased the wrath of Nipper. Those that did know better remained quiet, knowing that once the initial rage passed, their boss would settle down and concentrate on finding the killer.

Spittle sprayed from his mouth as Nipper vented his spleen on the unfortunate new addition.

'If you cannot add something of value, kindly shut the fuck up, you moron!'

Jane literally shook in her shoes at the outburst, almost

reduced to tears.

Nipper strode into his own office, slamming the door so hard the partition window almost gave up the fight to stay intact in its frame.

Detective Sergeant Bob Wilson walked over to Jane.

'Don't worry, his bark is far worse than his bite. Expect an apology which will undoubtably be forthcoming. The Governor is a fair man, and you were not to know the office protocol. But you will in future.'

Bob smiled at her as he walked away, giving Jane a glimmer of hope that her career hadn't already ended before she managed to climb the first rung.

At twenty-seven, Jane had entered the police force as a late starter. She had recently completed her two-year stint as a probationary officer, and thereafter immediately applied for a CID posting.

As a twenty-five-year-old, she applied as a last resort to make something of her life. But the main reason was because she needed a place to hide. She read in a detective novel that the best place to hide would be somewhere in plain sight. What better place than the police force?

The initial interview proved to be the biggest trial. Her made-up list of past occupations committed to memory, she hoped the board wouldn't question her too thoroughly. All the companies she claimed to have worked for as a secretary were fictitious. The obvious question arrived, and she reeled out her prepared answer.

'I want to help people and strive to make their lives safer,' she said, rolling out the pat answer that most applicants used. The board knew that all applicants would give the same answer, but it seemed like a necessary question to ask.

'Upon checking your previous work experience, it seems that your past employers no longer exist,' said the Assistant Commissioner.

This would be her second and last interview before acceptance into the force, and the big guns were now facing her.

'The companies I worked for were all small and most went out of business during the first year of the Covid Pandemic,' she replied, hoping that the collapse of so many businesses caused by world governments and their knee-jerk reactions would be accepted.

'Quite so,' replied the Assistant Commissioner, apparently satisfied.

That proved to be the worst part of the interview. The rest was easy.

She made it! Only the medical to pass and Jane would be a member of His Majesty's Police Force, charged with upholding law and order in the land. She smiled to herself when the Assistant Commissioner welcomed her into the force. She now exalted as a member of the very people she desperately wanted to hide from.

Two days later, she attended the medical. She knew it would be strict and conducted by a police surgeon. Blood samples were taken and she waited patiently as scans were taken of her major organs. In that respect, Jane didn't worry. Her health would come up to scratch. The last year had been spent cleansing her body and building up her strength after many years of abuse.

She breathed a deep sigh of relief as she donned her clothes after the final test. The examining doctor failed to check between her toes, her fingers, or the more delicate parts of her vagina. There, they would have detected needle holes, known as track marks. She chose very carefully when injecting in the bad old days. Maybe she had an insight into the future.

Her induction progressed smoothly, and she attended the Hendon Police College, easily passing every stage.

The only glitch occurred during the self-defence course when a male instructor, teaching her how to break a strangle hold, received various blows to parts of his body he cherished the most. A three-day stint in hospital later, he confronted his student.

'That is not the accepted method of breaking a strangle hold,' he said.

'But it worked, didn't it,' replied Jane, trying hard not to sound smart.

The instructor broke into a smile.

'Yes, it certainly did, and I'll be including it in my future lessons.'

Jane smiled back, relieved. At last, she met a man she could like and trust.

The week before the end of the course, Jane weakened. It had been many months since she enjoyed any sexual contact. Self-gratification, good as a stopgap, sometimes wasn't enough. Ever since her demolition of the self-defence instructor, he made it obvious he liked her.

Brian invited her into the gymnasium for a work out. She knew where it would lead but made no objection. In the small first-aid anteroom, she succumbed to his gentle ministrations.

Jane took the initiative, pouncing on him, and satisfying herself without a shadow of thought for his pleasure.

Brian, shocked by her reaction, laid down and allowed her to use him as she wanted, thinking that sex had never been this good.

After that interlude, much to Brian's disappointment, it never happened again. Jane's attitude returned to her new found norm. She meant to make her new career work. The alternative represented the unthinkable, life in prison would break her.

Jane Wilmot became her new name after paying handsomely for a forged birth certificate. Prior to that, she had been Avril Graystroke.

Childhood should be the happiest of times. Not so for Avril and many thousands like her worldwide. What should have been a carefree time guarded by loving parents was anything but in Avril's case. Her mother gave birth to her at the tender age of fifteen. Her father, only sixteen, totally incapable of supporting a family. Avril had been taken from her mother, a mere child herself and placed in care.

So began the long and treacherous road to adulthood. She had been abused in the care home, abused by her first foster parents, and thereafter many more. By the time Avril reached her first teenage year, her life had already began spiralling downwards. At thirteen, she encountered yet another abusive foster father and resorted to running away, making a life for herself on the streets.

Already sexually active from her earlier abuse, Avril made use of her youthful appearance and sold herself to any stranger willing to pay. She considered it a bonus, at least now she could charge for what men merely previously took in exchange for a roof over her head.

Her first real boyfriend, he called himself Angel, introduced her to Heroin, and the slide downwards became markedly steeper.

Angel died with a needle still embedded in his leg. He began using his legs when his arms became hardened by repeated injections. He also shared his knowledge of places to inject that would be undetectable until she could no longer use them.

Fortunately, before that time arrived, she decided to quit. A big step in the life of a homeless teenage girl. A community drug centre became her pot of gold, helping her to first manage the addiction before stopping altogether.

However, although now free of addiction, she carried on with her old trade of prostitution. She needed to live and there appeared to be very little alternative in her eyes.

By her early twenties, Avril began to show signs of the constant misuse endured in her chosen career.

Avril's dreams were more than that. Nightmares would best describe her sleeping hours. Nightly, she would relive her experience as a victim of a serial abuser; waking to her own blood-curdling screams, wrapped tightly in bed sheets and bathed in sweat. One particular night stood out among the others.

Eddie Butcher, a married man, and like many others, brutal and uncaring, needed a little comfort on the side. His wife, Helen, would never be enough for him. There were no children, something she counted as a blessing, fearing that Eddie would not be a good father.

Their marriage foundered on the rocks of domestic violence. They slept in separate bedrooms, Helen's firmly bolted from inside.

Eddie's infidelities were many as he sought his pleasures elsewhere and that is when Avril's nightmare began.

A cold wind blew along the damp streets of the East End. A light flurry of sleet promised snow later.

Avril rubbed her hands together for warmth. Her legs, encased only in fishnet tights were chilled to the bone. Her cheap, thin, dress reached to just below her panty line affording no warmth whatsoever. Only the imitation nylon leopard-skin coat gave her any comfort but her apparel advertised her occupation. She stamped her high-heeled stiletto shoes trying unsuccessfully to generate some feeling into frozen feet.

A car slid to a halt beside her. The driver's side window rolled down emitting a cloud of cigarette smoke to mingle with the miserable weather.

'How much?'

'A tenner for a hand, twenty for a blow, and fifty for the whole way,' replied Avril. It wouldn't be very lucrative at those prices but it would get her off the miserable streets for a while.

'Hop in,' said the John. All clients were John's to the girls.

He drove down a couple of streets before pulling up at a house in the centre of a terrace. It could have been anywhere in the East End, every street designed the same.

'This your place?' asked Avril.

'While the wife's away, the mice will play,' laughed the man.

Leading the way upstairs, the man turned into a bedroom.

'Better not use the wife's room. she never comes in here. This is my domain.'

Avril noticed the untidiness of the room and the unmade bed, guessing that the couple lived separately under the same roof.

'Besides, she would smell your cheap fucking perfume a mile away,' said the man crudely.

He lunged at Avril slobbering over her, breaking the unwritten rule that you never kissed a John on the lips.

Avril backed away both from his lips and the sour breath of a heavy drinker.

She didn't see the blow until his hand connected with the side of her face, knocking her sprawling onto the dishevelled bed.

The next half-hour seemed more like hours to Avril as the man first stripped and then abused her in ways she never imagined possible.

When he finished, he threw a five-pound note at her as she stooped to gather up her clothes.

'That's all you're worth. Now, fuck off.'

With that, he pushed her along the landing, down the stairs and out onto the street.

'Keep walking and don't stop or you'll get another taste of my belt.'

Avril staggered along the street as she attempted to dress herself from the bundle of clothing under her arm. The five-pound note fell to the pavement unnoticed.

Working for Avril the following week was not an option. Nobody paid for a girl covered in bruises and with two black eyes. A couple of teeth felt loose and she hoped they wouldn't suddenly drop out. That would really make her unsaleable.

The year slid through summer and into the next winter before she saw the man again.

She stood, hand on hip in the classic hooker pose watching

as one of her colleagues bent to chat to a man through a car window on the other side of the road.

As she straightened the man's face came into view. She recognised him. The bastard is still at it!

Obviously the price given too high for him, he wound up the window, and drove slowly away.

Without thinking, Avril hailed a taxi.

'Follow that car,' she yelled at the cabbie.

'Fuck me, never thought I'd hear that,' he chuckled, accelerating after the car.

The man had obviously given up kerb crawling for the day and continued on. The taxi followed at a discreet distance until the car pulled up outside a terraced house in the East End. The man turned a key in the door of the house and disappeared inside.

Avril noted the address. Number 15 Petrie Street.

'Do you know him?' asked the cabbie.

'Oh, yes. I know the bastard,' seethed Avril through clenched teeth.

'Where to now?'

'Back to where you picked me up, please.'

'Back to work, then,' laughed the cabbie.

That broke the spell for Avril and she laughed with him.

'Yes, back to work.'

As she arrived at her spot on the road, Avril stepped out of the Taxi, handing the cabbie some notes.

The cabbie waved it away.

'No trouble, darlin', got to look after my girls.'

'I owe you one,' said Avril making a crude gesture with her hand.

'I'll hold you to that,' laughed the cabbie as he pulled away from the kerb.

From that day forward, whenever she could, Avril made her way to Petrie Street and waited at the corner where she could see the comings and goings from Number 15.

She noted the lack of children. The man and his wife

were obviously childless. Avril looked skywards thanking any invisible deity that happened to be watching for small mercies. She could imagine the life of any child sired by that beast. It would have been very similar to her own.

On one such occasion she saw a woman leave the house. She looked very pleasant, and Avril couldn't help wondering how she ended up with that horrible man for a husband.

Avril's watching became an obsession. She had no idea what she would do if confronted by the man again but her nightmares continued.

Weeks later, as she stood at her usual spot, she witnessed the same woman leaving the house, but this time carrying a suitcase.

Helen decided the time had come. If she stayed with Eddie, things would never improve and her life slowly and surely would waste away. She must get away, start a new life someplace new. The farther away from Eddie the better. His verbal tirades and lack of respect had become as unbearable as his physical abuse.

One of her old friends had come to her rescue.

Betty had suffered at Eddie's hands in the old days, and implored Helen to leave him.

However, Helen kept putting the inevitable off until Betty announced her own marriage had ended in divorce. The pair had two children and Betty told Helen she would be such a help. Her husband left for Australia with another woman so he would be permanently off the scene.

That decided Helen and she made plans to leave. With her own bank account opened without Eddie's knowledge, she had built up a considerable amount. She worked as a secretary and banked most of her wages.

Eddie would have no idea where she had gone. In any case, Helen didn't think he would care.

Avril watched the woman struggling a little with the

obviously heavy case and surmised that the wife was leaving.

Without thinking things through, she walked past the door. To her surprise a set of keys were still in the lock. She hesitated only for a second before turning the key and stepping into the hallway.

It looked different from the last time. On that occasion the man hurried her upstairs. Now, she had time to study it. No wonder the wife left this miserable place. The décor, hardly modern with old-fashioned brown wallpaper, gave the illusion that Avril might have travelled back through time to the 1940s. The place, although clean, she found depressing. Upstairs, Avril turned into the front bedroom. Obviously the wife's room because of a recent redecoration. Bright colours helped illuminate the small room, and the furniture bore the ring of quality.

The back bedroom she remembered all too well. The unmade bed made her squirm inside. The room stale and unloved.

She froze as the slam of the front door reverberated upstairs. She felt trapped, how could she explain her presence? He would surely recognise her.

Fumbling in her bag, Avril found the knife she always carried, just in case. All the girls armed themselves these days. Pepper sprays, knives, and some even managed to obtain illegal Tasers.

She held the knife behind her back, trembling as she heard heavy footsteps on the stairs.

'Keys in the door. I'll bet the fucking bitch has finally packed up and left.'

The man talked to himself as he reached the top of the stairs. His frame filled the doorway as he spotted Avril.

She became aware of her full bladder, desperate to go to the toilet, but recognised it as fear.

'What the fuck are you doing here?' snarled Eddie.

Avril couldn't answer, she had no answer.

'Saw the keys in the door and thought you could come in and help yourself, did you?'

He kicked the door shut behind him, beginning to unbuckle

his belt. The same belt he used on her before. That time he used the buckle to tear flesh from her bare back. She couldn't allow him to do that again.

He made a grab for her and she screamed as loud as she could. 'No, no, no!'

As he took hold of her hand and pulled her towards him, Avril swung her other hand gripping the knife and felt it sink into his side.

He yelled out in agony, looking down as his shirt began to turn bright red.

Still, he held her by the wrist. She pulled out the knife and struck again, this time higher, slicing into a lung.

Blood gushed from his mouth into Avril's face, and she felt sick.

At last, his grip loosened and he slowly sank to the floor. Avril stepped around him, making for the door. She stopped suddenly as in the corner of the room she thought she could make out the shape of a young girl. Avril dismissed the vision in her haste to get out, running downstairs and out into the street.

Nobody else saw her leave. The empty street a silent witness to her flight.

A few woman looked on aghast as the tartily dressed young woman stood at a sink in the public toilet, washing blood from her face and clothes. They made a quick exit closely followed by Avril as she realised that a hue and cry would soon go out and she would be caught and charged with murder.

Self-defence, surely, but as a prostitute who would believe her. Who would take her side against a man killed in his own house, in his own bedroom.

Avril had to escape before the police found the body. She would have to change her life, her profession, and her name.

Jane Wilmot now stood before Detective Chief Inspector Nipper.

'I would like to apologise for my little outburst earlier on,' said

Nipper.

'You'll get used to me. I tend to go off the deep end sometimes but I get results and that's what really matters.'

Jane allowed a little smile to pass over her face.

'Yes, sir, I completely understand. Circumstances can get to the best of us.'

Chapter 18

East London 1924

Daisy sat on the floor of the back bedroom, playing with her one and only doll. She knew she was too old for dolls, but Tinkerbelle had been with her since childhood. The doll's looks were no match for Daisy's prettiness. Very little hair remained on the head, and one eye featured a permanent droop. Arms and legs became loosely attached over years of loving attention. To Daisy, the doll wasn't only her friend, but her confidant.

'Daddy and that other nasty man have gone away. They are never coming back, so you don't have to worry. They will never bother us again.'

She didn't hear the click of the front door as it gently closed. Nor the delicate footsteps on the uncarpeted stairs. Daisy had entered Tinkerbelle's world. A place of perfect peace and tranquillity.

Fred stood in the doorway, watching her, who appeared not to notice him. She sat on the double bed, cradling Tinkerbelle and chatting with her as if the doll were human.

By stepping into the room, Fred accepted his commitment. The girl, a member of the accursed family who killed his father, must be punished.

Daisy looked up in surprise as Fred pushed her backwards onto the bed. Tinkerbelle fell to the floor as Daisy opened her mouth to scream. Fred put his hand over her mouth as he roughly wrestled her small frame. He had no plan, knowing only that each member of the family must pay for his father's untimely death at the end of a rope.

Daisy's struggles served only to spur him on. A madness enveloped his mind. Her clothes torn, Daisy bit his hand in an effort to free herself. Fred yelled in pain and slapped her hard across the face. His right hand found her throat and he squeezed hard to suffocate the scream he knew would come.

Daisy's strength surprised him, but he maintained his grip on her throat to suppress her cries. Her face turned bright red and her bright blue eyes bulged. She couldn't breathe with no way of stopping him or shouting for help.

Looking down at Daisy, lying supine on the bed, brought Fred to his senses. What had he done? There appeared to be no movement from the lifeless body. Her limbs lay askew on the bed a red smear staining the sheets. Daisy's eyes were wide open, but sightless.

All thoughts of vengeance for the death of his father disappeared in his panic. Shocked, he realised his responsibility for murdering the girl. No matter the family she belonged to, he had killed her, and he faced the same fate as his father, except for him, the rope would be justified.

Fred ran downstairs and out through the front door. He bolted down the street heedless of any direction in his panic. Neighbours looked on in alarm at the sight of the young man running, drawing attention to himself.

The truck shuddered to a halt. Anxiously, the driver left the cab and began searching underneath. He had hit something. A flicker in the corner of his eye, the only warning that something or someone ran out from the corner of Petrie Street without stopping.

A mangled body lay beneath the rear wheels. Barely recognisable as human after being crushed first by the truck's radiator, then the front and rear axles, Fred's remains lay in pieces; only his head remained intact, eyes wide in terror.

Gladys' piercing scream alerted the neighbourhood to Daisy's fate. Curious neighbours offered support to Gladys in her distress.

When the police arrived, the neighbours reluctantly left the scene, patting Gladys on the shoulder in commiseration as they passed by. She felt numb with grief, her little girl, her Daisy, lay dead upstairs. It seemed as if her fate had already been decided by some unseen force. Gladys saved her once, but fate would not be denied.

Police quickly put two and two together. The murderer, seen leaving the house and running along Petrie Street, met his own brutal fate under the truck. It seemed like God given justice to the neighbours.

Fred's mother, Lil, collapsed in tears when told of her son's crime and his ultimate demise.

'No more, this has to stop,' she cried to her daughter and remaining son, 'two wrongs will never make a right, that poor young girl suffered for the fate of your father. She never hurt anyone. Now, your brother is dead. If not for the accident, we would be waiting for the hangman to end his life, just like your father.'

Daisy's death proved to be the end for Gladys. She had to leave Number 15. It represented so much misery in her life. She had killed her husband, witnessed her daughter, Daisy, kill Sergeant Evans, and now Daisy herself had been murdered. No longer a home it had become a house of death.

Gladys and her two sons moved out of Petrie Street and moved north to Manchester. Gladys' aunt lived there and she moved in with her. Never the same again, Gladys became a recluse.

Number 15 remained empty barely one week before new tenants moved in. Unkindly, neighbours were quick to inform them of the recent murder in an upstairs bedroom. Not an auspicious beginning for the Watkins family. They were given graphic details of Daisy's murder in the back bedroom, much to Ruby Watkins' dismay, she being eight months pregnant.

Charlie Watkins stopped the idle chatter in the local pub by demolishing a local loud mouth in a flurry of punches. The neighbours were quiet after that.

However, The Watkins' were given the cold shoulder and

rarely, if ever, spoken to.

Ruby gave birth at home in her bedroom, aided by a local midwife. Little Sadie arrived promptly on time and deemed healthy, except for eyes that never stopped staring. They were crystal blue, mystifying Charley, whose own eyes were dark brown, as were Ruby's.

Chapter 19

Maggie sat at the kitchen table. Life had become mundane. She liked her job and her new home, but there seemed to be nothing else of interest in her life. Penny called around occasionally toting a bottle of white wine, which they consumed rapidly, backed up by another bottle from Maggie's own mediocre collection.

'How is Stephen?' asked Maggie.

'He's fine,' replied Penny a little fiercely. Maggie made a mental note not to mention his name too much. Penny might not have the strong hold over him that she desired.

To change the subject, Maggie nodded towards the wall separating them from the neighbours, Ruben and Daphne.

'The couple next door are selling.'

'That's a pity,' said Penny, 'he's rather dishy.'

Maggie smiled.

'Trust you to latch onto that.'

Penny giggled like a young girl.

'I wouldn't kick him out of bed.'

Maggie shook her head, whatever did Stephen see in her.

'Seriously, though, there may be more to it. Daphne seemed very hesitant to discuss the move, she mumbled something about a move to the country. And I'm not sure I believed her.'

Penny poured the last of the second bottle of wine into their glasses.

'Bottoms up,' she cried, upending the glass and swallowing the contents.

'I'm not sure you should be driving anywhere tonight, I had better call a cab,' suggested a smiling Maggie.

Penny relaxed back on the couch.

'Why don't I stay over?'

Maggie wanted to say no but didn't want to hurt her feelings.

'Okay, the back bedroom this time.'

'No way, bridled Penny, we can share your bed like before.'
Maggie admitted defeat.
'Okay, if you insist. Coffee?'
'I'd rather have a whiskey,' purred Penny.

Maggie, beginning to feel uncomfortable with the whole idea of sharing a bed with a tipsy Penny, brought out an unopened bottle of Chivas Regal.

'Now you're talking, said Penny.'

A good measure poured into a glass, Maggie handed it to Penny, figuring if she imbibed enough she might collapse until the morning.

An hour later, Maggie helped Penny upstairs, who promptly flopped onto the bed.

'You'll have to undress me,' she slurred.

Maggie helped her off with her top clothes but stopped there, covering her with the top sheet.

'Now you,' said Penny, her eyes drooping.

Maggie paused, guessing that Penny would be asleep within seconds.

Snoring loudly, Penny succumbed to the evening's alcohol. Maggie made her way quietly out of the room and went into the back bedroom. Problem solved.

Maggie sank into the new bed, loving the fresh scent of her new linen. She had matched Penny drink for drink and relaxed instantly into a deep sleep.

In the early hours of the following morning, Maggie sat bolt upright. The deafening scream had been tortuous and loud, very loud.

Her bedroom door burst open and Penny staggered in.

'What's the matter, you near scared me to death, screaming like that.'

'Not me, it woke me up too,' said Maggie.

'I know your voice and I'm telling you it was,' insisted Penny.

Perplexed, Maggie sank back into her pillow.

'It must have been a nightmare.'

'A pretty loud bloody nightmare,' said Penny, sliding into the bed beside Maggie, 'it scared the crap out of me.'

Maggie felt Penny's hand slide over her midriff and tensed.

'Go back to sleep,' whispered Penny, 'I'll look after you.'

As soon as light crept into the bedroom window, Maggie climbed out of bed. Penny slept on while she gathered her clothes and went down to shower.

Convinced that nothing untoward had happened in their shared bed, Maggie began to relax under the hot shower.

As she towelled herself dry, she became rigid with fear as a scream sounded from upstairs.

Clad in only the towel, she rushed out to meet Penny hurtling downstairs.

'Get my clothes, I'm leaving,' she yelled.

'Did you cry out?' asked Maggie.

'Yes, I bloody well did. There's a man up there and he tried to touch me,' sobbed Penny.

Maggie fumbled for the phone and called the police, dragging a shocked and shaking Penny out the back door and into the small back yard to await their arrival. Maggie in nothing more than the towel and Penny still dressed in fancy underwear.

It took only minutes for the police to arrive. Maggie had left the front door ajar, hoping the intruder would leave after Penny's scream. The police entered and immediately began searching the house.

Minutes later, a young constable ushered the two women back inside.

'There's nobody upstairs. He must have fled,' he said.

After a thorough search, the police officers assured Maggie there were no signs of a forced entry. Maggie began to believe they had both been dreaming under the influence of wine and whiskey.

The patrol car pulled away with an audience of interested neighbours looking on. Not least of whom were Ruben and Daphne.

'You had better get dressed,' said Maggie.

'I'm not going back up there, you'll have to fetch my clothes,' insisted Penny.

Maggie climbed the stairs, listening for any sounds, but she met only silence.

Gathering Penny's clothes and a fresh set for herself, she made her way back down.

Penny dressed without washing, refused the offer of breakfast, and slammed the front door shut on her way out.

Maggie smiled in spite of the frightening night. No longer would she have to worry about Penny's night time intentions towards herself. The scenario unlikely to be repeated.

Later that day, Ruben sat at Julian Yates' desk.

'I want to lower the price. We want it sold quickly.'

'Certainly. If we list it as a bargain, it may well be sold sight unseen on the internet. What price would you consider?'

Ruben looked the young man in the eye.

'All offers considered. Put up a sign, do anything you have to. You can sell it fully furnished, we just want out!'

Maggie spotted the For Sale sign in next door's window and noted the addition of a sticker. All Offers Considered.

'They must be in a hurry,' she pondered, I wonder why.

As she closed her door, Daphne emerged from hers. Too late to turn back inside, she had to say something.

'Good morning,' Daphne said timidly.

'Must be something good happening in your life to make you sell so quickly,' said Maggie.

Daphne once again stared at the upside down cross around Maggie's neck.

'Yes, we have to move quickly,' she said, quickly returning to the sanctity of her house.

The screaming the night before had finally broken the Haitian couple. They had clung to each other in bed after Penny and Maggie had finished their drinking spree, hiding beneath the covers, not knowing what to expect.

'We have to move, Ruben,' said Daphne, 'I will not stay here another minute. I'll go to my mum's while you sell the house.'

For Ruben's part, he didn't fancy sleeping alone with all the goings on next door, and decided he would take any offer to escape.

Thankfully, after the last incident, all appeared quiet next door, and Ruben began to relax in spite of the fact the sale was taking longer than expected. Daphne would not even consider returning to Petrie Street, so he had to accept living alone for the time being. He no longer wanted any of their furniture. They had spent hours looking in stores until they had found exactly what they both wanted. However, it had been tainted by the goings on next door, and Ruben didn't want to take anything in case the curse travelled with their belongings to their new home.

Chapter 20

A gentle tap on the front door summoned Maggie.
'Stephen, fancy seeing you here,' she said.
'Just passing,' he laughed.
'Liar,' she replied, smiling, 'you had better come in.'
The greeting kiss seemed to happen naturally, and Maggie allowed the kiss to linger a little longer than necessary.
'How is Penny?' she asked.
'I don't know what happened between you two, but she goes quiet every time your name is mentioned,' replied Stephen.
'Nothing happened between us. I have a suspicion it's this house. She seems to believe it's haunted.'
'That's interesting. Do you think the place has a ghost?'
'No. of course not. I don't believe in ghosts. If they existed, there would be more concrete proof by now instead of a bunch of loonies gabbling on about what they saw or heard.'
Stephen laughed at the same time, producing a bottle of wine from his overcoat pocket.
'Drink?'
'I'll get glasses,' said Maggie.
They sat side by side on the couch, sipping the chilled white.
'So, what really brought you here tonight?' asked Maggie, already suspecting she knew the answer.
'Can't get you out of my mind,' said Stephen, clinking glasses in a toast.
Maggie knew where this would probably lead but admitted to herself that she felt very lonely, there had been no one since Peter. Maybe this was the spark she had been eagerly waiting to lift her spirits.
'What about Penny?' she said quietly.
'To be honest, Penny and I aren't hitting it off too well at present. I'm sure we both realise our relationship has reached a point of no return.'

Maggie had been wondering about Penny ever since she insisted they share a bed. Maybe Penny's preferences were changing. With the inevitable second bottle of wine opened, Stephen relaxed, and Maggie felt warm and fuzzy.

The next kiss seemed natural and lingered far longer than their original greeting.

Maggie began idly playing with the buttons of Stephen's shirt and he took that as consent that she wanted to take it further.

Their slow lovemaking reached its climatic conclusion in the bedroom. Both lay exhausted. Maggie chuckled.

'My goodness, I needed that! It's been a long time.'

'Happy to oblige,' laughed Stephen.

'On a serious note. I hope this isn't a one-night stand,' he added.

'You have to finish completely with Penny first. I don't want her to be hurt,' said Maggie, sincerely, not wanting to make an enemy of the only friend that stuck by her during her messy breakup with Peter.

'I'll see her today,' said Stephen, kissing her shoulder. Maggie lay back, welcoming his attention.

The week passed swiftly for Maggie. Stephen called around every evening, and she began to wish he would give her some time alone. Life by herself had been difficult at times, but also advantageous. Like not having to look prim and proper all the time. Maggie began longing for an evening where she wouldn't have to make an effort to look her best.

Penny stopped calling, which saddened Maggie. However, she dared not phone her because of Stephen. Nevertheless, she worried about her friend.

The old saying, 'hell hath no fury like a woman scorned,' proved accurate for Penny. In her eyes, Maggie had stolen Stephen, exactly like she had Peter.

Maggie had no idea that Peter and Penny were an item before she appeared on the scene. Peter had been captivated by

Maggie and within weeks, he unceremoniously dumped Penny in favour of her. Never revealing that fact took a great deal of effort on Penny's part, but she would wait and watch. She swore to herself that sometime in the future, her turn would come, and vengeance was better served cold.

She had been more than happy when Peter and Maggie split up and made a special effort to always be there for him, but he once again spurned her advances. Instead, she maintained her friendship with Maggie, looking for any opportunity to bring her down.

Twice she encouraged her with overt sexual advances, but Maggie didn't take the bait. Now, she had stolen Stephen away in the same manner.

Why did this always happen to her, what had she done to deserve such treatment?

Penny Pickering. How she hated her name. Her mother and father no doubt found it cute to give their only daughter a rhyming name, but she hated it. Constantly ribbed at school by other children, she quickly built a reputation. Girls were slapped and beaten while any boy that made fun of her name received a kick where it hurt most.

School became a lonely place for Penny. With no friends, she spent a solitary time in classes that held no particular interest for her.

She had been born in Manchester to parents both born there themselves. She believed her grandfather, Keith Pickering, originated from London, but he never talked of his past. He always kept to himself, as did his brother Ben.

Keith married Irene, a local Manchester girl, and they had a son, Colin. He stayed at home until well into his thirties, eventually marrying Agnes, a local spinster, already past her prime.

Colin had been shocked when his wife told him she was expecting. They believed Agnes would have been past childbearing age but were thrilled at the news.

The birth hadn't been easy. Agnes' age made for a difficult confinement and it had been touch and go for both mother and child.

They mused over names for some time before agreeing on Penny. To them, Penny Pickering had a musical ring to it, but like most parents, they failed to take into consideration what other children would make of it.

In later years, Penny became involved in seeking out her family tree. She became obsessed with her new fad and diligently sought out her history.

When she delved into the London side of her antecedents, she had been shocked to discover that her grandfather's sister, Daisy Pickering, had been brutally murdered in her own home.

The exact location where the murder took place so far eluded her, but only a question of time, she told herself. One day, she would find out.

In her apartment, Penny sat drinking yet another glass of wine, recalling her time with Peter.

Still very much a loner, she met him one night at a club in the West End. Penny often sat in noisy clubs watching her garrulous peers, seemingly enjoying themselves, while she sat by herself in a darkened corner.

'Why is such a pretty girl sitting alone?' Peter asked.

Penny, never having been approached before, couldn't think of anything to say.

'Can I buy you a drink?' he persisted.

'Sure, why not,' replied Penny, rather more forcibly than she intended.

She, by her attitude, already presented herself as an irresistible challenge, and Peter returned with the drinks.

Penny grimaced at the taste of the brandy and champagne concoction.

'It's called a Wicked Lady,' laughed Peter.

Penny drank it down, not wanting this young man to best

her.

Peter went to the bar before Penny could protest and brought back yet another Wicked Lady. He carried another whiskey for himself, and she guessed there would be more to follow.

After the second drink came a third, and Penny began to feel a mixture of bonhomie tempered with a strange feeling of giddiness.

'Come on, let's get out of this shithole and go somewhere nice,' Peter suggested, sliding one hand along her leg.

Penny giggled her agreement and they left together, weaving across the small dance floor hand in hand.

Peter appeared to be familiar with all the clubs and disappeared downstairs from a narrow doorway set in Greek Street, Soho. Penny had no alternative but to follow with Peter's hand firmly holding her own.

In the gloomy smoke laden air of the basement club, he led them to a table set into an alcove. From a small dimly lit stage, three musicians played modern jazz. Two couples danced inelegantly on a minuscule area set aside for that purpose.

Penny thought it to be more of a shithole than the last place, but accepted the Wicked Lady Peter placed on the table.

After another two drinks, Peter suggested moving on.

'Where to, another shithole?' laughed Penny, slurring her words.

'Come on, don't be a spoilsport,' urged Peter, pulling her by the hand upstairs into the garish neon-lit Soho street.

Penny almost lost control of her limbs, concentrating wholly on keeping on her feet. She barely noticed descending into the London Tube system or boarding a train.

She decided that seeing double must be the worst effect of drinking too much. But closing her eyes made it even worse. Her spinning head threatened imminent vomiting, so she kept both eyes open. Closing one eye caused much the same effect as closing both.

She vaguely recalled stumbling upstairs on bare boards in a

building that reeked of boiled cabbage until Peter propelled her through a doorway.

'Home, sweet home,' he laughed, falling onto an overstuffed settee, and pulling her down beside him.

Penny, disorientated, hardly noticed the liberties he began taking. He kissed her passionately, fumbling with her clothes while she tried to keep both eyes open and focussed on the wall opposite in order to avoid vomiting.

Why did her head hurt so much? Penny stared at a grimy, uncurtained window through slitted eyes as the early morning sun attempted to burn them out of her head.

She lifted the sheet and stared first at her own naked body, then at the man's lying next to her.

'Morning sweetie-pie,' murmured a voice next to her.

She looked sideways into Peter's eyes.

'Did we do it?' she whispered.

'Several times,' he said, grinning back at her.

'I need to pee,' she said, starting to get up.

Peter pulled her back.

'In a minute.'

That inauspicious beginning led to a more regular relationship in which Penny became more and more comfortable. She left the loner side of her character behind and began to join in at functions. Becoming just as garrulous as those she once spurned for being empty-headed.

That Peter wasn't every girl's dream she came to accept. His love of gambling kept him poor, together with heavy drinking. Peter's idea of lovemaking was the epitome of boorishness.

Penny purposely ignored his faults. She had a boyfriend and that meant everything to her.

The day arrived when she introduced Maggie to their circle of friends. Peter couldn't take his eyes off her, even when Penny held his arm and cuddled him. She noticed his eyes were still fixed on Maggie.

What happened later served the bitch right. Penny bore no regret about being part of it.

Chapter 21

East London 1925

Ruby lay in bed at Number 15, feeding her baby daughter. The child's eyes were fixed on her own as she suckled. The warm glow of motherhood became tinged with a faint feeling of fear. The as yet unnamed baby engendered this feeling with cold blue eyes together with a slightly vicious sucking motion, culminating in a hard toothless bite as she finished.

Ruby smiled down at her firstborn and kissed her forehead. Her innate motherly love overcame her fears, but the baby's stare continued to concern her.

Charlie stood at the foot of the bed, watching.

'I can't understand where she got those baby blues from,' he said, meaning her eye colour.

Ruby answered awkwardly.

'A freak of nature, I suppose.'

Charlie nodded.

'I suppose so, but odd just the same.'

Ruby knew only too well from where the eyes had come. Ted bloody Richards, Charlie's supposed best friend.

He had been the best man at their wedding, and a frequent caller afterwards.

He would call in at any time he pleased, not the best idea for a newly married couple.

He never thought to knock before entering their house and on occasion walked in at an intimate moment. Charlie didn't seem to mind and merely laughed.

'Bad timing, Ted, you nearly put me off my stroke,' Charlie would say vulgarly.

The fact that Ruby neared her time didn't seem to bother Ted, either. She doubted whether he gave a second thought as to how the baby might turn out.

Ruby counted the weeks and days carefully. It would be nine months to the day when Ted won the local darts tournament. It had been the highlight of his life to date. A hard-fought contest going right down to the final three darts. Ted had been crowned champion of the area, and drinks flowed freely well into the small hours. The landlord closed the pub doors at the normal closing time, declaring it now to be a private party, an easy way around the strict closing times imposed by the liquor licensing authorities.

Ruby had been seeing Charlie for only a matter of weeks, and they barely progressed past first base. In those days courting ran along strict unwritten guidelines. The boys made to toe the line and court a girl before any intimacy took place.

Charlie reached the third and final base only the week before, being very careful to ensure Ruby would not fall pregnant. He really liked Ruby, but maybe not enough to marry her. Ruby, not aware of his true feelings, thought he might as well go all the way as they were bound to end up married.

Then came the darts tournament. Everyone in the pub wanted to buy Charlie a drink to celebrate his popular win. Ted egged him on, matching him drink for drink.

Ruby hung back with the other girls, sipping at their port and lemonades. However, as the night progressed through to the wee small hours, the girls became rather tipsy.

At one point, Ruby left the bar as inconspicuously as possible, making for the rear door. The room had been spinning and she needed fresh air.

She only just made it outside when the fresh air she craved pulled the oldest trick in the book. It made her vomit uncontrollably.

As she leant against a brick wall, she tried to regain her composure but failed miserably.

She felt arms encircling her and a head burying itself in her shoulder and neck. Thinking it to be Charlie, she responded in kind.

'Not here, someone might see,' she slurred.

But her entreaties came too late. She felt her skirt slide up and busy hands adjusting her underwear.

Over very quickly, she reached for the head on her shoulder, turning the face so she could kiss Charlie.

Even in the inky darkness, Ruby knew it wasn't her boyfriend. She pushed him away and in the gloom saw Ted's face, and his satisfied smile.

She tried to call out, but Ted clamped a hand over her mouth.

'Now, now, you wouldn't want Charlie to know how free you are with your favours,' he sneered.

Ted's breath reeked of sour beer, and she pushed him away roughly.

'Not a word, not one bloody word!' she exclaimed as she staggered back through the door to re-join the party.

Ted sidled back inside and joined his best friend in another drink. As they toasted each other, he managed a sly wink at Ruby, who looked away in disgust.

A few weeks later, Ruby missed her monthly.

'But we were so careful,' protested Charlie.

'Mistakes happen all the time,' sobbed Ruby, 'what will we do?'

'Get married, I suppose,' said Charlie without much enthusiasm.

'Ruby's pregnant,' announced Charlie to Ted.

'Bloody hell, you going to marry her?'

'I'll have to or face her father and brothers. You know what they'll do to me if I don't marry her.'

'You'll need a best man,' said Ted.

Charlie at last managed a smile.

'You, of course, I wouldn't want anyone else.'

Ted vaguely recalled the night of the darts tournament. Smiling to himself as he remembered Ruby's welcoming body, he never thought for a moment that the impending marriage might be entirely his fault.

On a cold miserable day, Ruby and Charlie were married in a

civil ceremony with Ted acting as best man.

Happily, Ruby left the registry office hand in hand with her husband, followed by Ted.

'Let's go to the pub,' he announced.

Nothing changes, thought Ruby, rolling her eyes.

'What are we going to call her?' asked Charlie, looking down at his daughter.

'I thought Sadie would be a nice name,' suggested Ruby.

'Sadie, it is,' replied Charlie. Ruby wished he would show more enthusiasm and guiltily wondered if he doubted Sadie's fatherhood.

To her, the real father appeared to be demonstrably obvious. Ted, with fair hair and deep blue eyes. Surely Charlie would put two and two together, or maybe Ruby's guilty conscience clouded her judgement.

Ruby's guilt had a companion when Ted called around to welcome the new arrival. Charlie absent when he walked in unannounced as usual. Ted would have been sure to notice the look of horror that passed over Ted's face.

'Shit!' exclaimed Ted after staring at little Sadie for a few moments.

'Not as clever as you thought you were,' said Ruby.

'What are we going to do?' said Ted, panic colouring his face.

'We are not going to do anything,' replied Ruby, 'you'd better make yourself scarce before others begin noticing the similarities. Move away, tell Charlie you have a job opportunity up North. I don't care what you say as long as you bugger off.'

Ted left the house before Charlie returned, knowing his guilty looks would reveal all.

'Ted's gone,' announced Charlie.

'Gone, where?' asked Ruby.

'He said a good job opportunity had come up in Manchester.'

'Did you manage to see him before he left?'

'No, the bastard simply upped and left.'

'That's sad, he might have at least said goodbye.'
'Have you seen him?'
'No, and he didn't even get to see Sadie.'
The conversation ended there. Charlie often lamented that his erstwhile best friend deserted him, but Ruby never commented.

Life carried on as usual for the new family. Charlie, Ruby, and Sadie spent the following years in Number 15. Charlie hadn't changed his habits and still frequented the same pub.

Ruby settled into motherhood, welcoming into the world two more children: a boy, Horace, and another girl, Florence. Both children inherited their father's features and dark brown eyes.

Unkind neighbours pointed to the three children and wagged their heads.

'Something not right there,' they would say.

Years passed, and Sadie became even more beautiful while her young sister, Florence, developed into a stocky young lady without Sadie's good looks. Horace became a smaller mirror image of his father.

A knock at the front door sent Sadie scurrying to answer.
'Hello,' she said, 'can I help you?'
Ted couldn't reply, struck with her beauty.
Ruby approached the door, standing beside Sadie.
'What are you doing here?'
'I wanted to say hello,' said Ted stiltedly.
Ruby glanced up the road and almost cried out in dismay as she spotted Charlie ambling along, heading for home from the pub.

Ted turned to leave, thinking that his obsession with seeing the child who might be his daughter might not have been the best idea.

'Ted,' shouted Charlie.
'Hello, Charlie,' said Ted meekly, 'long time no see.'
'Come in, don't stand here on the doorstep. We have a lot of catching up to do,' laughed Charlie, pushing his old friend inside.

Ruby thought she might have a heart attack as she stood in the kitchen. Her three children stood in a line to greet Ted.

The difference in the three children became startlingly obvious to anyone except the blind.

Charlie looked at Sadie, then turned to look at Ted. His expression grim. His words spontaneous.

'No wonder you left in such a hurry. I've always known Sadie's not mine, especially after the other two arrived.'

Sadie burst into tears.

'What are you saying?'

Ruby stepped in.

'You men go into the front parlour to talk. You're upsetting the children.'

Charlie, fresh from the pub, bridled.

'Don't tell me what to do! I should never have married you, how many others did you have, before and after we were married!'

Ted interjected.

'It's not Ruby's fault. At the darts tournament I got drunk, we all were, it's not her fault.'

Charlie's hands formed into fists. He had suspected since the day Sadie's birth, but to be confronted with the truth hurt more than he could bear.

'Get out while you can still walk, Ted. I'll deal with my wife in my own way.'

'You are not to hurt her,' pleaded Ted.

'Get out, I won't tell you again,' hissed Charlie, his eyes turning completely black.

'Leave, Ted, please go,' said Ruby quietly.

Ted made his way outside, followed by Sadie.

'Are you my real dad?' she sobbed. None of the conversation had escaped her quick mind.

Ted looked at her, knowing that here stood his daughter, but all too late.

'You better go back inside, you'll make him even angrier if you don't,' said Ted, turning and walking away, resisting the urge to turn around. Knowing Sadie stood watching him leave.

Sadie walked back into the house, tears clouding her vision. She became aware of loud screaming from upstairs together with angry words from the man she called father.

Horace and Florence stood cowering in the kitchen, their eyes raised to the ceiling, listening to the noise coming from above. Sadie put her arms around them, saying that everything would be all right.

Leaving her two siblings downstairs, she raced upstairs, bursting into the back bedroom to catch Charlie in the act of punching her mother. Ruby's face already showed the results of where other punches had landed, and she lay on the floor screaming for him to stop.

Charlie, beside himself, yelled at the top of his voice that his wife had always been a whore. His florid face and staring black eyes made him almost unrecognisable. He looked like the Devil incarnate.

Sadie yelled at him to stop, but with Charlie's shouting and her mother's screams, her voice could not be heard.

Charlie delivered another punch to Ruby's face.

'I'll kill you, you unfaithful bitch!'

Sadie felt herself go cold. Her fear disappeared, replaced with pure hatred for the man beating her mother.

She picked up the dressmaking scissors, used by their mother to make their clothes, and plunged them into Charlie's back with such force that only the rounded handles protruded. They penetrated his ribcage and entered his heart, killing him instantly.

Once again, Petrie Street became a crime scene. Sadie, had been duly arrested and charged with patricide, the murder of her father.

However, being a minor, and in view of the fact she had been protecting her mother from a savage beating, Sadie received special dispensation from the court. The evidence of events leading up to Charlie's death suggested she had acted in defence of her mother's probable murder. Sadie returned home to her mother and siblings.

Standing in Number 15, Sadie held her mother's hand.

'He will never hurt you again, mummy.'

Ruby stared at her daughter in disbelief, with a tinge of fear. Sadie's words had sounded cold without the least hint of regret, her crystal clear blue eyes displaying no emotion.

September 3rd, 1939. Britain had declared war on Germany and expected that London would be a major target for the Luftwaffe.

Ruby, lost for words, looked skywards as a siren sounded its mournful sound. Her heart sank, and she held out her arms for Sadie.

'We have to go to the shelter, it's started.'

Rushing through the streets with Sadie, Florence and Horace, Ruby glanced skywards, expecting at any time to see the diminutive shapes of aircraft appear overhead.

They reached the Underground Station, their closest shelter, as the All Clear sounded. The same mournful sound droned through the air, but this time brought relief to the listeners.

Ruby turned around, making for home.

'False alarm,' she said, trying to remain calm but failing miserably.

The air-raid siren sounded twice more that day, each time a false alarm.

Whether the government sounded the alarm three times on the first day of war to prepare the population of London for what would undoubtably come, or if a genuine administrative error didn't matter. People now knew what to expect.

Ruby remained in Number 15 for a while after the war had been declared. Horace and Florence were evacuated in Operation Pied Piper along with 800,000 other children over a period of four days. The preparations having been ongoing for a year prior to the beginning of World War ll, the government well aware that the country would soon be involved in an inevitable war with Germany.

Sadie, volubly refusing to be evacuated with the other children, occupied the back bedroom of Number 15 as before and revelled in her newfound independence. No matter that the room, always icy cold, could never be warmed.

Sometimes, Ruby could hear Sadie talking to someone, even though her mother knew she was alone. occasionally, she would laugh out loud, sending chills through Ruby's entire body.

Something wasn't right with her eldest daughter. Sadie never talked about the day Charlie died, the man she had called her father.

Ruby tried on occasion to broach the subject in case Sadie harboured some unseen mental trauma, but the girl merely dismissed the incident with a shake of her head.

'It doesn't matter, he won't hurt you again.'

Chapter 22

East London 1888

Mary fidgeted. Something down below had been irritating her for weeks. At first, it had been an itch which she constantly scratched, sometimes at the most inopportune moments.

Lately, she noticed small blemishes appearing around her vagina that itched even more. Still, she kept it to herself. Her income from the West End soirées steadily increased as word got around about the promiscuous genteel lady willing to supplicate herself to any gentleman of means. She now served groups of as many as seven or eight gentlemen at a time.

Edgar Wimpole assured Mary that the high-class gentlemen at the club never strayed to the poorer part of town where they might encounter unclean girls.

'They are all clean and safe,' he assured her.

Sometimes the meetings became rather confused and out of hand. Mary feared becoming pregnant but could do little about it with so many men crawling over her naked body.

Finally, Mary sought out a doctor, certainly not Ralph, in the posh West End of London.

'I'm afraid you have the pox, my dear lady,' announced the doctor.

Mary couldn't speak.

'It's the worst kind, I'm afraid, Syphilis,' added the doctor.

That brought Mary's power of speech back instantly.

'Can you cure it?'

The doctor shook his head.

'There is no known cure, although I can give you various tinctures of mercury that may ease the symptoms.'

'How bad will it get?' asked Mary, knowing that many of her peers in the East End suffered from the disease.

'As bad as is possible,' answered the doctor, 'you will be able to hide it for a time until it becomes obvious with rashes and the like. In time, your sexual area will become sore to the touch and may demonstrate weeping sores. Eventually, the disease will spread to your brain and you will be driven insane. After that, death.'

Mary left the doctor's rooms walking mindlessly, uncaring and lost. She knew Ralph would have to be told. He would know she had been unfaithful and would insist on knowing the man's name. How could she reveal that fact with so many lovers?

Ralph stared down at his penis. Through a magnifying glass, he stared at the red blemish that marked the shaft. As a doctor, he lost count of the times he witnessed the identical sores on others, both men and women. Not painful to the touch, even more worrying.

He decided on a second opinion, discretely visiting another colleague of good standing.

'I'm afraid the news is not good,' began the doctor, 'It is undoubtably Syphilis, and I dare say you are aware of the prognosis.'

'Treat me as you see fit,' insisted Ralph, knowing that the usual mercury treatment in itself could and often did prove fatal.

'Very well,' said the doctor, 'however, by the accompanying rash on your shoulders, I would say the disease has already taken hold. It may well travel to your brain, and you know what comes next.'

'Madness, then death,' said Ralph.

'Indeed,' replied the doctor.

Ralph left the surgery in a daze. His future once assured now shattered beyond hope.

He would certainly take the mercury treatment, but knew it would only extend his life, at best, for a few months.

The mad house beckoned. He had witnessed inmates screaming as they smashed their heads against the brick walls.

Taken possession of their bodies after death, paying the gaoler a small fee. They were good subjects for dissection. Now, he would join their ranks, perhaps even becoming the subject of a dissection himself.

Doctor Ralph Jessop waved away the cab, deciding a walk would do him good, it might temper the rage he felt building inside.

He had been so very careful not to expose himself to the virulent disease so common among the poorer classes, especially cheap whores.

Mary had proved to be his salvation. Naturally, he would never marry her, her obvious low class would never stand up to the scrutiny of his peers. However, it must have been Mary. He felt the rage building again as he entered the door of her apartment. Wonderful, pretty, sensual, Mary.

'Hello,' said Mary quietly as Ralph entered the room.

Ralph steeled himself.

'How are you?' said Ralph between clenched teeth.

'I'm well,' replied Mary, suspecting that, from his demeanour, Ralph had discovered her ailment.

Ralph strode across the room and, without any warning, tore Mary's dress from her shoulders. The fabric ripped unevenly as the garment fell away.

'How long have you carried that rash?' Ralph demanded.

Mary quailed before his staring eyes.

'Not long, I'm sure it will clear up on its own.'

'Why didn't you show it to me? I'm a bloody doctor, after all.'

'I didn't want to bother you, it's a mere trifle.'

'A mere trifle, you say. I wouldn't call Syphilis a mere trifle!'

Mary turned cold, he knew, but how did he know, unless….

She began to sob and Ralph knew instinctively the origin of his disease.

'Who gave it to you, who have you been seeing?'

Mary sobbed even more, shaking her head.

'I don't know who.'

'You mean there has been more than one?'

A nod of her head, affirming the truth, sent Ralph into an uncontrollable rage. His hands clenched and unclenched as he thought of how she sought to dupe him. His precious Mary now signed his death warrant. He would be doomed to spend what little time remained waiting for the onset of madness, waiting for the constabulary to cart him off to the madhouse, where class meant nothing.

The ignominy of the situation dealt a harsh blow to his personal pride with nothing left to live for. Ruined by a prostitute, how he hated them, despised them!

Mary remained quiet as he silently fumed, his pallor turning red as his insides railed from the injustice of the situation.

'We are going out,' he suddenly announced.

'Where to?' she asked fearfully.

'Back to where you belong, the back streets of East London, where I found you,' said Ralph, an eerie quietness settling over him.

A hansom cab carried the pair to the edge of the East End, where Ralph paid off the cabbie. Already dusk when the cab picked them up, it was now even darker with a cold mist creeping up from the River Thames, reducing vision to a few feet.

Ralph, holding Mary firmly by the elbow, walked briskly, turning into Buck's Row, a quiet byway flanked by warehouses and dingy two storied cottages.

Mary didn't know what the doctor intended. She assumed he would beat her, something she had been accustomed to in the old days, but nevertheless feared.

Stopping suddenly, the doctor released her. Mary staggered, falling to the cobblestones. Ralph grabbed her by the hair and, as she looked up pleadingly, he slashed a blade across her throat, not once but twice. Blood gurgled from Mary's throat, but Ralph had not finished. The rage inside him still boiled uncontrollably. Roughly pulling her dress up to expose her lower body, he slashed downwards through her abdomen, exposing bloody entrails as they slithered from the wide gash.

Ralph looked into Mary's startled eyes as they slowly misted over in death. The imprint of her killer's face, the final vision to register on her dying brain.

Coming to his senses, Ralph tore the ring he had given to Mary off her finger, pocketing it before beating a hasty retreat towards the West End. Racing through the darkened streets with his cape streaming behind him. At that time of night, nobody witnessed his haste.

In the safety of his home, Ralph washed Mary's blood from his hands and stripped himself of the clothes now tinged red with her blood. The scalpel he washed and put back in his instrument case. The satisfaction he felt in dealing with the whore who consigned him to a lingering, ignominious death still gave him a warm feeling. They were all whores, no matter their class. All women were now whores in his mind, but particularly those in the East End. He would find further use for the scalpel, and soon. For Ralph, the clock already ticked.

A few days later, he left his home and once again headed towards the East End. The misty darkness descended as he entered Whitechapel, and he walked slowly, his black cape and top hat signalling to the local prostitutes the possibility of a man with a shilling or two to spare.

'Evening Guvnor,' said Annie Chapman.

Poor Annie had been left destitute when her ex-husband died, leaving her to care for their two surviving children. Even though their marriage had long since fallen apart, the husband always supported her financially. Now, Annie, having no other means of support, resorted to prostitution.

Although Mary's murder attracted the attention of the press, a girl still had to work. Annie took hold of Ralph's hand, pulling him towards the dingy room she used for clients.

Once in the room, Annie quickly stripped and lay down on the filthy mattress, devoid of even a single sheet.

Ralph swept off his cape and top hat, putting them carefully on the only chair in the room.

'Cor, you aint half a toff,' giggled Annie, her grimy body revealed in the dim yellow light shining through an equally grimy uncurtained window from a street gas light.

She lasciviously looked up at the man approaching the bed, her sultry look changing to horror as she saw the long-bladed scalpel arcing down towards her. The scream died in her throat as the instrument twice slashed her viciously from ear to ear. The blade cut through to her spine, almost severing her head.

Once again, Ralph drew the blade down her abdomen, spilling her entrails onto the bed, making a mockery of her once feminine body.

Meticulously donning hat and cape, Ralph quietly left the building, disappearing into the night.

A photo of Annie's body appeared on the front page the following day. An intrepid photographer followed police into the room and before they could stop him, took the shot.

The newspaper headings told of two mysterious killings bearing the hallmark of a possible serial killer, but that all changed when both they and the police received an anonymous letter which included facts that could only have been known by the murderer.

The letter bore the signature, 'Jack the Ripper', and from that day forward, Jack the Ripper became an infamous part of Whitechapel history.

On the night of September 30th, Jack struck again, but this time killed two women.

Elizabeth Stride, a prostitute in her homeland of Sweden, inherited some money from her late mother, and moved to London to begin a new life. After marrying John Stride, the couple managed several coffee shops in the East End. Unfortunately, the marriage eventually soured taking the business with it and culminating in John's untimely death from natural causes.

Elisabeth returned to the only thing she knew, prostitution.

On the darkened streets, she made enough to survive using her pronounced Swedish accent and her natural blonde hair to gain popularity among clients.

Her life reached its dramatic conclusion when her throat yielded to Ralph's scalpel. Elisabeth's body, having been discovered only moments after her killer had struck, led police to believe that her murderer had been disturbed before he could complete his work.

Only one hour later, the body of another woman was discovered next to a warehouse. Catherine Eddowes, again a local prostitute, had recently been released from a local police station before meeting her killer.

A local passer-by saw her body just 10 minutes after her murder. However, the killer had the time to cut her throat to the bone, slice through her abdomen, and bizarrely decorate her using her entrails to wrap around her body. He also removed her kidneys and uterus, leaving those organs stacked on her chest. The skill of this operation led the police to believe the killer must have some medical and surgical experience.

The police began to think they were dealing with some deranged doctor. Jack the Ripper's exploits had taken a new twist. Perhaps not some low-class murderer but a professional gentleman of means who for some reason took a keen dislike to working girls.

October passed with no new killings. The various working girls suffered the usual assaults with stoicism. It went with the business. Black eyes and bruises were common among the women and worn almost as a badge of office.

That all changed on November 9th.

Mary Jane Kelly, a pretty twenty-five-year-old girl, obliged to take to the streets after her husband, Joseph, lost his job. He hated her new profession, even more so when she began to bring men back to their room. Obliged to wait patiently outside while his wife satisfied her clients, Joseph eventually moved out, although they stayed in contact. He, unable to secure another job, remained tethered to Mary for financial support.

That night, Mary had been seen with a well-dressed gentleman making their way to her room.

On the morning of the following day, her mutilated body had been discovered by her landlord. Attempting to peer through the grimy window, he had been confronted by a gruesome scene. Mary's breasts were cut off, as were her thighs, and her throat cut in the same manner as the other victims. Due to the savagery of the attack, the room was awash with blood. The most vicious attack so far, and the police still clueless as to the identity of the assailant.

Strangely, there were no more murders in the same vein. It seemed that Jack the Ripper finished his work with that final terrible flourish. Maybe he had sated his bloody desires, or could he have possibly been arrested for something else and locked away? The case grew cold and police, although keeping the case open, appeared to leave it to history. Their work load increased as the years went by and Jack the Ripper passed into folklore.

Doctor Ralph Jessop's career as a sadistic murderer of East End prostitutes ended at the same time when his father, the elderly Paine Jessop, committed him to an asylum in Colchester, some sixty miles to the east of London.

Paine, although elderly, guessed the truth. He followed the newspaper stories of the Ripper, and, after paying his son a visit, quickly put two and two together. Ralph greeted his father in what had been a neatly kept home but now resembled an uncared-for slum. The domestic staff had long since departed, either fleeing the wrathful tempers of a fast mentally declining employer or been sacked without a reference for the merest trifle.

Ralph's mental state suffered from the spread of the disease, and he became incoherent.

Paine recognised the sketch of Mary, Ralph's first victim, in a newspaper and although it gave her real name as Mary Ann Nichols, he recognised that the likeness represented the same Mary Smith his son bragged about in the club where they were both members.

He thanked God that Ralph's mother, Esme, died the year before. She would have been crushed with the revelation that her only son could have been the serial murderer, Jack the Ripper.

Paine Jessop went to great lengths in order to protect both his own reputation and the family name. As his son sank into increasing depths of insanity, Paine had him quietly committed to the Eastern Counties Asylum for Imbeciles and Idiots at Colchester in Essex.

Ralph, placed in a padded cell, ranted and raved during his waking hours. He often screamed manically through the small, barred hatch in the door.

'I'm Jack the Ripper. I killed them all, the whores!'

Warders ignored his rantings. However, other inmates swiftly caught on and joined in, screaming, 'I'm Jack the Ripper.'

Ralph's brain, infected with syphilis, turned him into a slobbering, incomprehensible idiot, and after eighteen months of madness in his solitary cell, he died.

For years after Ralph's death, staff swore they could still hear his rantings against prostitutes, damning them all to Hell.

Inmates placed in the same cell quickly descended further into madness, talking to themselves and occasionally screaming for no apparent reason. The warders began to suspect the cell was haunted, believing that maybe the mysterious private patient had been the Ripper after all.

Although the killings ceased, the inhabitants of Whitechapel and the surrounding areas of the East End of London walked the nights in fear. Prostitutes in particular constantly glanced over their shoulders, wondering if Jack might one day return to seek them out. After all, his victims had all been working girls from the same area.

Over time, redevelopment reshaped the area more than once. It was in the 1920s, on the spot where Mary met her brutal demise, that a row of terraced two-story homes were built.

The old byway known as Bucks Row had been widened and its name changed.

The exact place where Mary Ann Nichols' blood-spattered body had been found now formed part of the hallway of Number 15 Petrie Street.

Chapter 23

Maggie slammed the door behind her as she left for work. The sign in the next-door window stopped her in her tracks. A large Sold banner had been placed diagonally across the For Sale sign. So, her neighbours were no more. She wondered who had bought it and how likely they would become friends. The Haitian couple had been strange, to say the least, almost as if they were scared of her. She laughed to herself at the thought. Surely she wasn't scary.

Arriving at her office, she was surprised to see the detective inspector there with a young woman detective.

'What's going on?' she whispered to a compatriot.

'They are here about that dead woman they found in the warehouse we are redeveloping,' said Simon, a junior draughtsman.

The general hubbub of conversation stopped as Detective Inspector Nipper cleared his throat to bring everyone to attention.

'I'm afraid there has been another murder.'

Nobody spoke, the silence absolute.

'Found early this morning in the same place as the first,' said the inspector.

Still, nobody said a word, waiting for the inspector to go on.

'The young woman suffered the same style of death as the first unfortunate victim, but I won't go into details.'

At last, the head of development spoke.

'I assume the crime scene will once again preclude any further work on the site?'

'Yes, I'm afraid the area has been cordoned off.'

The inspector turned to leave, the young woman detective following. Maggie managed to catch her eye and she stepped to one side.

'Do you know the identity of the victim?' asked Maggie.

'No, not yet, but we think she might have been in the same profession,' answered the young detective.

Realising what she had said, the young detective put her finger to her lips.

'I'm not supposed to say that, please don't say anything. If it gets out, I'll lose my job.'

Maggie grinned.

'Just between us.'

Detective Constable Jane Wilmot let out a sigh of relief.

'Thank you, I owe you one.'

The decision had been taken to move onto another project. The warehouse would be put on hold.

Maggie couldn't wait to tell Penny of the latest incident. That is, if Penny had forgiven her for seeing Stephen.

Penny at first seemed a little reserved as she sat with Maggie in Number 15. However, as Maggie began telling the story of the latest murder, she became more and more interested. Stephen, for the moment, had been put to one side.

'Gosh!' she exclaimed, 'perhaps the Ripper has returned.'

'Don't say that,' replied Maggie, 'if anything, it's some nutter committing the ultimate in copycat killings.'

Maggie leaned in closer, conspiratorially.

'I'm not supposed to say, but I believe the latest woman is also a prostitute.'

'There you are, then,' said Penny, 'Jack's back!'

The pair looked at each other before Penny burst out laughing.

'Only joking,' she said, 'I think.'

After finishing their bottle of wine, Penny got up to leave.

'Be careful,' urged Maggie.

'I'll be fine,' Penny assured her. 'I have my pepper spray here in my bag.'

Maggie reluctantly watched her disappear around the corner of Petrie Street, heading for the tube station, before stepping back inside and securely locking the front door. Their conversation had made her nervous, and she re-checked the back door to make sure it was secure.

Heading upstairs, Maggie hesitated at the sound of a soft wail coming from the back bedroom. The skin crawled on her back as a cold shiver ran down her spine. Telling herself not to be stupid, she continued up, turning into the front bedroom.

A welcome quietness settled over the house as she switched off the bedside light.

Then it happened again. It sounded like a young girl in distress.

Maggie hurriedly switched the table lamp back on and the sound disappeared.

Eventually, she managed to sleep. However, the bedside light burned brightly for the remainder of the night.

Penny felt less confidant than she portrayed as she left Maggie's house. As she turned the corner, she stopped momentarily to listen for any footsteps that might be following. She sighed in relief, realising there were none.

Penny walked as fast as she could towards the tube station, where there would be plenty of people. She would be safer being part of a crowd.

She shivered as the night turned colder. It seemed to be a damper cold than usual, and a mist had appeared swirling around her feet. She assumed it must be coming off the Thames river, although the days of the legendary Pea Soup fogs that were a regular occurrence before the city cleaned up its act and banned the use of coal fires had long since been confined to the past.

She found her vision limited as the mist rose around her, and the cold intensified. Barely able to see more than a few feet ahead, Penny began to tingle with panic. She quickened her pace even more, although risking bumping into a street lamp. She stopped, looking around in amazement. Where were the street lamps? There must have been a power failure. Only the odd dim light could be seen through the mist.

Her heart almost stopped. A dim figure approached her. By

its size it must be a man, but cloaked in a swirling cape-like garment, difficult to tell.

If she turned and ran in the opposite direction, he would almost certainly catch up with her in a few strides. With no alternative, she walked on in the same direction to pass him by.

He spoke as he approached.

'Excuse me, my dear, what's a pretty little thing like you doing out in this foul weather?'

With her heart in her mouth, Penny touched the can of pepper spray at the bottom of her bag. Fumbling, she pressed the button, aiming at the man's face.

He cried out in pain as the spray entered his eyes. Unable to see, he disappeared into the misty gloom as Penny ran for her life.

The one hundred yards to the tube station seemed like one hundred miles as she staggered to a halt at the tube station entrance.

As she looked around, Penny stared at the overhead lights. They lit up the street like daylight. And where had the mist gone?

Safe in her own flat, Penny breathed a sigh of relief. The business with the man in the mist had taken away the pent-up anger she had when talking to Maggie. However, she still seethed at Maggie's deceit in taking Stephen away from her.

She knew she should dismiss Maggie from her life, but something made her want to keep in touch.

For Maggie, the apparent thawing of her relationship with Penny came as a welcome surprise. Penny still remained her only true confidant.

'Be careful,' said Stephen as he accepted the glass of wine from Maggie, 'she can be spiteful at times.'

'That's hard to believe,' said Maggie.

'People aren't always what they seem,' insisted Stephen.

'How do you mean?'

'Penny has a darker side that she rarely shows but once seen, never forgotten.'

'I don't understand.'

'Come with me and I'll show you.'

Stephen led the way outside to where his parked car stood.

'There, see for yourself.'

Maggie looked shocked as she saw the side of his car. A late model Mercedes, the shiny black duco had been viciously keyed along one side along the length of the car from front to back. Underneath the scratch an emoji with a downturned mouth stared back at her.

'How do you know Penny did that?' asked Maggie in disbelief.

'Have a look next time she writes you a note or messages you on the phone. She always finishes with a smiley face emoji, indicating her mood.'

'Stephen, that could have been anyone. Vandals hate people with nice cars and take out their insecurities by defacing them.'

'Or in Penny's case, an act of vengeance,' said Stephen.

Two nights later, Penny once again sat at Maggie's kitchen table. She couldn't wait to relate what had happened the last time she had left Maggie's house.

'I thought he was going to attack me!' she exclaimed.

Maggie listened to Penny relate the story, thinking that maybe Stephen had been correct in his observations. Penny did appear to be delusional.

She found it difficult to believe the story of the mist and the lack of street lighting, and the poor man Penny had attacked.

'What do you think happened?' asked Maggie.

'I don't know but it scared the hell out of me,' said Penny, 'it must have looked that way in the old days when Jack the Ripper killed all those poor women.'

Maggie unsuccessfully tried to conceal a yawn that didn't escape Penny.

'I'm not crazy,' said Penny, 'misty, dark, and cold. I've never seen anything like it.'

Maggie sensed her anger.

'I'm sure it happened just the way you said, I'll be very careful in future when I go out at night.'

That seemed to appease Penny, and Maggie poured her another drink.

'Let's change the subject. Next door has sold, I wonder who my new neighbours will be?'

They chatted for another hour until Penny said she should be on her way.

At the front door, Penny hesitated.

'I don't suppose you fancy walking me to the tube station?'

Maggie, sensing her fear, agreed.

'I'll get my coat and we can walk together.'

As they walked, Penny rambled on about any subject that came to mind. Maggie didn't want to join in the conversation; she knew Penny only talked to take her mind off the previous occasion.

The street lights shone brightly, chasing away any shadows, and the mist didn't make an appearance. They parted at the tube station entrance with a wave, and Maggie turned for home.

Nervously, she retraced her steps, at any moment expecting the overhead lights to suddenly disappear and a mist begin to creep over the streets.

Nothing happened, she arrived at her front door and went inside, wondering if her friend should seek professional help. Maybe the sudden break-up with Stephen had affected her more than she realised.

Clearing away the used glasses, Maggie stopped in her tracks. She could hear a girl sobbing, not a grown woman, the voice thin and tremulous.

The glass fell from her hand, smashing into pieces on the kitchen floor. She stood stock still, listening as the voice continued to keen from above.

Maggie stood at the bottom of the stairs, afraid to ascend as the sobbing continued.

She fumbled with the phone and had to dial the number three times before it would connect.

Stephen answered, but before he could even say hello, Maggie began talking.

'Please come, there's something happening upstairs and I'm really scared.'

'Go outside and wait for me, I'm on my way,' said Stephen, sounding alarmed.

Maggie dropped the phone and mechanically unlocked the front door before going outside. From the open doorway, she could still hear the girl.

Stephen arrived in his car and approached Maggie, who had lowered herself onto the pavement beside the door. She greeted him with a face devoid of colour.

'There's someone upstairs. I think it's a girl and she's crying.'

'Wait here,' he instructed.

Climbing the stairs slowly, Stephen listened for any sounds. The house appeared quiet; nothing to suggest anyone there and certainly no crying.

He searched both bedrooms to find them empty. Downstairs, searching each room thoroughly, he found nothing out of the ordinary.

Outside, he knelt down beside Maggie.

'The place is empty, Maggie, nobody, upstairs or down.'

'But I heard the girl crying, I didn't imagine it.'

'Tell me what you did this evening.'

'Penny came around and we talked about her strange experience she said she had after leaving here last time.'

Maggie retold the story about Penny, the mist, and the stranger she had pepper sprayed.

Stephen smiled, trying not to laugh.

'Sounds to me like you two are scaring each other into thinking things are there that actually don't exist.'

Maggie looked into his eyes.

'Stay with me tonight, please, I don't want to be on my own.'

He led her by the hand and climbed the stairs to the front bedroom. Everything looked normal and Maggie sank back onto the bed, relief sweeping over her.

'Come on, let's get you into bed,' he smiled.

Stephen stayed at Number 15 for the remainder of the week. Maggie revelled in his company, it seemed like being in a relationship again, a good one this time. She felt comforted to no longer be alone, especially at night.

The following week, they decided that Maggie should be a big girl. Stephen would return home, but he would always be a mere phone call away.

'Your car looks as good as new,' said Maggie, standing in her doorway as Stephen climbed into the black Mercedes.

'I picked it up on the way here last night, thank goodness it's insured. I filed a police report for the insurance company but nothing will come of it. Criminal damage is taken for granted by the police these days.'

Maggie put up her hand to wave, but Stephen continued speaking.

'Hey, look. Next door has been leased.'

Maggie stepped outside to look at next door's window. A Leased sign had been stuck across the Sold sign.

She smiled back at Stephen.

'A new neighbour, I wonder who it will be.'

Maggi contemplated this as the Mercedes drew away, still a little insecure as her erstwhile bodyguard departed.

That night, she slept peacefully. No untoward sounds disturbed her and she woke up pleasantly refreshed.

Perhaps the whole business had been in her mind? Not helped by Penny's vivid imagination.

Later in the week, Maggie left for work as usual, closing the front door behind her.

'Hello, fancy seeing you here,' said a voice at her shoulder.

Maggie turned, surprise turning to laughter as she recognised the owner of the voice. there stood Jane Wilmot, Detective Constable Jane Wilmot.

Before Maggie could venture a reply, Jane spoke again.

'I'm your new neighbour, this house came up for rent and I swooped on it immediately. The owner offered to rent it at a very reasonable rate, and it's fully furnished.'

'Yes,' said Maggie. 'the previous owners appeared to be in a mad rush to sell. I did wonder about the furniture. I didn't see a removalist.'

'Well, I'll see you later, then,' said Jane, climbing into an old Mini Metro, adding:

'Can I give you a lift?'

Maggie shook her head.

'No, that's okay, I'll get the tube.'

Thinking about the strange coincidence of her new neighbour and how the world seemed to be shrinking in size, Maggie felt nonetheless heartened by the thought that she now had unofficial police protection. It would give her a new sense of security in Number 15 with her detective neighbour living next door.

Chapter 24

East London 1940

London lay in darkness each and every night. The city waited for the expected attacks from the German Luftwaffe with bated breath. It would happen, they knew, more a question of when, and how vicious.

The citizens were about to find out. On Saturday, 7th September 1941, it began. London sustained intense bombing throughout the night.

In the bleak morning light, Londoners emerged from shelters to find a scene of utter desolation. Having never experienced such a thing, people stood and stared at that which had once been their beloved city. Now, thick smoke hung everywhere, with seemingly endless clouds of dust permeating the air, making everyone cough and splutter. To add to the confusion, the architecture of the area, now so altered, it became difficult to find a way home. If that home still existed!

Miraculously, Petrie Street remained untouched. Not even a shattered window greeted Ruby and Sadie as they walked into their home.

'We've been lucky,' remarked Ruby, 'but it can't last, we have to get away.'

Sadie didn't want to leave. She enjoyed her newfound freedom of having her own bedroom and showed her reluctance to give it up. Besides, she felt comfortable in the area despite what that nasty Mr Hitler had done the night before.

'I don't care, Sadie, we have to leave,' insisted Ruby.

Sadie ran up to her room without replying, slamming the door in anger.

'She can't make me,' Sadie said to the shadowy figure at the foot of the bed.

'I'll miss you when you've gone,' whispered the shadow.

'Well, I'm not going!' exclaimed Sadie, clenching and

unclenching her hands in frustration, but it looked like anger.

'Find a reason for her to stay,' said the shadow.

Sadie stared at the shadowy figure. A youngish girl stared back at her, the feeble light of early morning partially illuminating one side of her face.

'Are you a ghost?' asked Sadie.

The shadow laughed almost soundlessly.

'Perhaps, but I am your friend.'

'Why are you here in the first place?'

'This is the last place I remember.'

'Did you die here?' whispered Sadie, round eyed.

'Yes. I died here in this room.'

The shadowy figure of the girl appeared to gain height as anger replaced her previous timidity.

'Fred killed me. He wanted to punish me for the death of his father. He ripped my clothes and held me down but didn't even notice when I stopped breathing.'

Daisy paused before continuing.

'Funny, really. After he came to his senses, he ran away in panic, but somehow I could watch him. I followed him outdoors and along the road, trying to push him to run faster. I don't know if I succeeded, but he ran in front of a truck and it mangled his body into a bloody mess. That made me smile, it took some of the hurt away from being dead I suppose.'

Sadie sat on the bed in silence. She had her own personal ghost. How could she leave now?

'What's your name?' she asked.

'Daisy,' replied the shadow.

'That's what I'll call you, then,' said Sadie.

'You'll stay here?'

'Yes, I'll find a way to make mum stay here.'

'Get her a man, they always stay for a man.'

Night after night, the bombs fell around them. It became a regular routine to make for the tube station at dusk before the air-raid warnings made their inevitable fearful drone. Arriving early meant finding a reasonable spot to lie down and sleep.

Latecomers were reduced to sleeping between the steel rail lines. The deadly current from the third rail would have been switched off before the evacuation began, but there was still something bizarre about resting your head so close to a steel line that through the day carried enough electric current to kill you instantly.

Ruby and Sadie returned night after night to the same spot until others began to save their spot for them. A regular community developed and as the bombs rained down overhead, cheerful voices joined together in popular songs of the era. Mostly women and children and some older menfolk inhabited the safety of the deeper tube stations.

Up above, the fire brigades and ambulances worked tirelessly in the dangerous conditions. Buildings burnt, falling to the ground in a blaze as brave men and women attempted to quell the out-of-control firestorms, rescuing the injured where possible. All the time, bombs continued to fall around them.

Incendiary fire-bombs fell with the high-explosive bombs to further enhance the living hell perpetrated on those below.

On one such occasion, Sadie noticed a man sitting against the tiled wall of the underground station. He didn't look that old and she wondered why he wasn't up above with the other fit men.

She plucked up courage and dared to approach him.

'What are you doing down here with the women and children?' she asked, not bothering to curb her rudeness.

The man at first showed annoyance at the impertinent question but instead of replying, pointed to his leg.

'Yes, I can see it's a leg,' said Sadie, 'so what!'

The man slowly raised the leg of his trousers and Sadie saw only a crude wooden pegleg instead of flesh and bone.

'It's temporary until I can get a better one,' said the man.

Sadie stared at the false leg.

'Sorry, I didn't realise.'

'How could you? It's covered up.'

'How did it happen?' asked Sadie, being more forthright than she intended.

'Dunkirk,' replied the man, adding, 'on the beach.'

Sadie, not really interested in how it happened, saw an opportunity to ensnare her mother.

'Are you married?' she asked.

The man looked hurt.

'Not anymore, my wife found comfort elsewhere while I languished in France.'

'Oh,' said Sadie, 'that's a shame.'

Ruby had been observing her daughter talking to a stranger and considered it time to interject. She approached and squatted down beside her daughter.

'Everything all right?'

'Mum, this man lost his leg at Dunkirk and his wife ran off with someone else,' said Sadie undiplomatically.

'Sorry,' said Ruby, 'my daughter can be a bit jolly blunt sometimes.'

'That's okay, my name's Frank, no harm done.'

Sadie moved back slightly, so Frank faced Ruby.

'Tell us what happened,' said Sadie, 'we've plenty of time, the bombing hasn't started yet.'

Frank leaned back against the wall and looked at Ruby.

'You sure you want to hear?'

Ruby nodded enthusiastically.

'Yes, go on, tell us what happened.'

Frank, eyes beginning to glaze as the memories of Dunkirk Beach overtook him, began his story as the first bombs began to fall overhead, adding to the drama.

His regiment had been posted to strengthen the French battalion on the Maginot Line. A line of impenetrable fortifications built in the 1930s along the border with Germany to deter any hostilities.

Unfortunately, the advancing German forces simply went around them through The Netherlands and Belgium.

Within hours of the start of the German invasion, French and English troops were on the run pursued by tanks and harried from overhead by the Luftwaffe.

Frank found himself fleeing in the face of the German onslaught, and with thousands of others, made for the coastal town of Dunkirk, where they hoped the navy would be able to rescue them.

Hundreds of thousands of soldiers descended on the town, eventually making their way to the beach. Soldiers faced an agonising wait to be ferried out to ships which could not get too near the beach. Instead, they relied on smaller boats to carry them out.

The famous fleet of Little Ships, numbering some 850 from the Cinque Ports of Kent and Sussex, made numerous trips across the channel to help evacuate around 330,000 troops.

Standing in line with so many others in long lines tailing down the beach to the water's edge, Frank felt like a sitting duck. The wail of Stuka dive bombers overhead made them fall to the ground every few minutes. The planes streaked towards ships to release the one bomb they had attached underneath their fuselage. Then, aiming for the troops on the beach, they raked the area with machine guns.

Frank lay flat as yet another Stuka roared overhead. He saw from his position lying flat on the sand, the high plumes of sand being kicked up by bullets. Terrified, he saw a long line making its way inexorably toward him. He had nowhere to go, but in seconds, the plumes of kicked-up sand passed over him.

With a sigh of relief, Frank looked around for his mates, wondering if any had fallen to the Stuka's bullets. He spotted the gruesome sight of a leg lying only inches from his body and wondered about the poor sod it had once been attached to.

The pain struck mid-thought. A searing excruciating pain emanating from his leg made him look down and, to his horror, he realised the mystery leg had been his own. The machine-gun bullets severing it completely.

Fortunately, a medic had been lying next to him and without hesitation applied a tourniquet to his upper leg, halting the gushing blood pouring from the stump just below his knee.

Frantically, the medic, helped by his friends, lifted him bodily and propelled him down the beach to the water's edge. A Little Boat no more than twenty feet long carried the rescue party to the side of a ship where Frank had been hoisted aboard. The ship's doctor did all he could to seal the shattered blood vessels, and Frank remained on deck as the ship, already overloaded, began to pull away from shore.

With the blessed peace of unconsciousness covering him, Frank saw and heard nothing of the planes diving overhead.

He came to his senses, choking on the bitter taste of seawater. The numbing coldness helped dull the pain from his leg, but at the same time, he felt himself sliding further down into the water until it splashed over his face. The ship had received a direct hit from a Stuka and slowly sank as men tumbled over the sides. Frank slid off the deck into the water, chaos surrounding him as he regained consciousness with the shock of water entering his mouth. He had no idea how many times he changed from conscious to unconscious until willing hands dragged him from the sea and into a boat.

Some kind soul covered him with an army greatcoat as he lay on deck. As his lucidity began to return, he managed to look around. The Little Boat seemed overfull. Not one smile illuminated the company. Nobody spoke.

Sleepily succumbing to the gentle motion, Frank slept or slipped once again into unconsciousness. Waking up, he could see the wonderful sight of Ramsgate's coastline. He had made it home.

Someone pushed a lit cigarette into his mouth, and he sucked the smoke down into his lungs gratefully. Around him, a few quiet cheers broke out, quickly rising to a crescendo as everyone realised they had made it.

Eager hands lifted him from the boat to a stretcher and thence to a waiting ambulance. Around him, other wounded soldiers lay or sat as the vehicle bounced its way out of the docks.

Frank slid into another faint as the ambulance began to

disgorge its customers into the arms of waiting doctors and nurses.

Two days later, he regained consciousness to find himself in a crowded ward of soldiers. Some appeared to have minor wounds, others were covered in bandages from head to toe.

Frank lifted up a blanket and looked down at his legs. One complete, one missing a bit. He allowed the blanket to drop down, covering his disability, a single tear escaping down one cheek.

The following week passed in a blur of pain and instant relief. Pain when the stump needed to be dressed for the umpteenth time and relief when an injection of morphine entered his bloodstream.

By the end of the second week, Frank began to feel almost human again. A doctor stood at the end of his bed as he asked the same question that many other amputees asked.

'Why does my leg hurt when it's not there?'

'It's a natural phenomenon, your brain thinks the limb is still intact. It will take a while for it to get used to the idea that the leg below the knee simply isn't there,' replied the doctor.

Puzzled by her lack of visits, Frank wrote three letters to his wife, Doreen. All three were returned unopened with return to sender written across the address. They had occupied the flat in London's East End for two years. Frank only spending one year together there before he had to go abroad.

Finally, after weeks of recovery, he had been able to leave the hospital, the bed needed for other wounded soldiers. Part of the continuous flow of war casualties.

They fitted him with a wooden prosthetic, promising that after the war he would receive a specially moulded one. No mention having been made of what would happen to him if Britain lost.

As soon as he could, Frank boarded a train and headed home. He left behind the chaos of the Liverpool Train Station in the East End and painfully limped to his old flat in a large tenement.

Surprisingly, it had escaped damage from the nightly bombings so far.

Four flights of stairs became a lengthy business, as, one step at a time, he made his way up.

Eventually, he reached his own front door and knocked. Naturally he didn't have keys of his own, they lay somewhere on the beach at Dunkirk.

A middle-aged woman answered with a curt, 'Yes?'

Frank stumbled over his words.

'I'm looking for my wife, Doreen.'

'There's no Doreen here, luv. I've been here for a year. Perhaps the last tenant? The place was empty when I moved in, cheeky buggers took everything that wasn't nailed down, even the light bulbs.'

Frank looked down as he thanked the woman and turned away. She noticed he walked with difficulty and stopped him.

'Fancy a cuppa? I've just put the kettle on and it looks as if you need one.'

Gratefully, Frank sat in a hard-backed chair in his former front room while Edna, the new tenant, brought in the tea.

'There you are, luvvy, get that down yer.'

He sipped the mug of hot tea and began to regain some composure.

'My wife and I lived here for a year before they sent me over to France.'

'Is that where you got that?' Edna asked, pointing at his legs.

Frank shyly lifted one trouser leg to reveal the false leg.

'The stump hurts like hell,' he said, gently rubbing the part where his leftover lower leg entered the new leg.

A knock sounded at the door and Edna left to answer it, returning with another woman.

'Ivy's from next door,' she announced.

Frank smiled in recognition.

'Hello, Ivy, remember me?'

'Course, I do,' said Ivy, her eyes sparkling with excitement. Her dull life needed an outlet, and Frank fitted the bill nicely.

'You're looking for your wife, I suppose?' she asked.
'Yes,' said Frank, eagerly, 'do you know where she's gone?'
Ivy sat down as Edna placed a mug of tea in front of her.
She leaned across the table, looking directly at Frank, waiting for his reaction.
'She left after you went away with the army.'
It had the desired effect, Frank jolted back in his chair.
'What do you mean, she left?'
'Buggered off with that slimy git from the pub, him what's always got money but never did a day's work in his life.'
With names spinning around in his mind, Frank leaned with elbows on the table, the confused look on his face telling Ivy that he had no idea.
'Him with the fancy clothes and the thin moustache. Thinks he looks like a bloody film star, that one.'
'Harry Hewitt,' whispered Frank, 'the sleazy bastard always gave Doreen the eye.'
'She's getting more than his eye now,' said Ivy crudely.
Frank looked shocked but Ivy carried on, this being her chief form of entertainment and knowing her audience wanted more.
'I reckon he had his leg over your missus before your bleeding train left the station,' she said, hardly able to suppress her glee.
'That's enough, Ivy,' said Edna, recognising Frank had suffered more than enough hurt from Ivy's acid tongue.
She had pushed him over the edge. A low growl from deep inside his throat increased in volume and pitch until his cries rent the air, scaring both women. Edna placed a hand on his shoulder, shaking him gently.
'There, there, never mind luvvy, she's not worth it.'
'Where is she, do you know?' Edna mouthed silently to Ivy.
'They moved up to Islington, Seven Sisters Road, I think,' blurted Ivy, with Edna shaking her head violently.
'I didn't mean for you to tell him,' hissed Edna, 'the poor bloke has suffered enough.'

The sound of the All-Clear sounding overhead brought Frank's story to a close. The shelters population began to file out, up the escalators, to the early morning light of a new day.

Outside, the results of the previous night's raid greeted them with unholy organised chaos. Fire engines still played jets of water onto still burning buildings while rescuers searched amongst the ruins of collapsed houses for any survivors. Mostly, they recovered dead bodies, to be laid in black painted vans for the short trip to the nearest morgue. Autopsies were unnecessary. The cause of death, more than obvious.

Fred breathed in dust laden fresh air, glad that the siren had sounded. He didn't want to share any more of his story.

A dainty hand slipped into his. Sadie began tugging him in the direction of Petrie Street.

'You can come home with us if you like, can't he, mum?'

Ruby hesitated, she didn't know this stranger and her daughter invited him so eagerly.

'Well, maybe for something to eat and drink before he gets on his way.'

Fred allowed himself to be guided, Sadie still clasping his hand as if she dare not let go. She had plans for Frank, he would do. Exactly as Daisy said.

Chapter 25

East London 1888

The murders stopped for a while. Jack the Ripper had left the area or maybe died, at least that remained the consensus of local opinion.

However, a year later, girls began to meet with a similar fate, and the old fears returned. Was he back? The police suspected the new murders were the work of copycat killers. Certain elements of The Ripper's methodology were missing. Some of the girls were stabbed and slashed with knives, but a few were simply bashed to death, leading the police to believe that there were now several killers at large. All the victims were prostitutes, but that had been established as the only thing in common.

Police failed to secure even one arrest until the murders simply stopped, as if the perpetrators had grown tired of their sport. The public continued with their business as usual. Nobody cared about the welfare of prostitutes, and demand had not decreased as the years marched on towards the twentieth century.

The frightened screams of a girl in distress hardly caused a ripple in the misty, darkened, narrow streets of the docklands areas of the East End. Girls were constantly being beaten up by clients and pimps alike. It came with the job.

On odd occasions, reports of a mysterious man began to surface. Apparently never involved in any of the murders, he merely walked the same areas. Dressed as a gentleman in a black top hat, cape, and carrying a silver-topped cane, he could be seen walking slowly through the mist under spluttering street gas lamps.

Girls, plying their sordid trade, ran for their lives if they spotted the lonely figure. Nobody tried to follow him, all were too afraid to meet the same fate as the others.

Paradoxically, he only appeared when the mist swirled around the darkened streets during colder months of the year. Most girls dismissed him as a mere figment of a working girl's imagination. However, none dared test the theory.

Chapter 26

Maggie returned home from work, unlocking the front door and stepping inside. Before she could take a step towards the kitchen, a sharp rap at the door summoned her.

Jane stood at the door, bottle of wine in hand.

'I thought we might celebrate my good fortune together,' she said, laughing.

'Good fortune?' asked Maggie, puzzled.

'At getting this rental so cheaply and as a bonus having you as a neighbour.'

'I believe the bonus is mine,' laughed Maggie, 'It will be good having a detective as a neighbour.'

Relaxed in Jane's company, Maggie told her of the mysterious events occurring in the house since she moved in.

'Scary,' said Jane.

'Not really,' replied Maggie, 'It's probably all imaginary. I've never believed in ghosts. There's usually a logical explanation for every so-called bump in the night.'

'Funny how the bumps in the night never happen during the day,' laughed Jane.

'Our imagination is enhanced by darkness. Being unable to see clearly makes things far scarier than they actually are,' agreed Maggie.

Conversation slowed as Maggie opened a second bottle of wine. The two sat quietly for a while, comfortable with their own thoughts.

'I don't suppose you can comment on the murdered woman in the building I'm supposed to be redesigning?' Maggie asked.

Jane sipped her wine, taking her time.

'I'm not supposed to say, but both women were on the game.'

'Prostitutes, you mean,' asked Maggie innocently.

Jane giggled.

'Yes, the posh people use that name. Us Plebs tend to call it being on the game, and the participants, Toms and Johns.'

Maggie joined in the laughter.

'I never consider myself as being posh.'

'Trust me, you are on the posh side of the social class,' said Jane.

A noise from upstairs stilled the conversation.

'What's that?' said Jane.

'Here we go again,' answered Maggie, 'it's what I spoke about earlier. Strange utterings and the odd shout.'

Jane got to her feet and walked towards the stairs. They could hear a soft keening sound, like a young girl moaning.

Maggie stood behind Jane, feeling a layer of protection between herself and whatever or whoever made the noise.

'Hold my glass,' said Jane, passing it back to Maggie.

'Be careful,' whispered Maggie.

Jane didn't answer, climbing the stairs slowly as the moaning continued.

Maggie shivered as Jane disappeared at the top of the stairs, pushing open the back bedroom door and entering. The click as the door closed sounded unusually loud in the still surroundings. The moaning had stopped.

Inside the bedroom, Jane confronted the shadowy silhouette of a young girl.

Smiling, she reached out and touched the outstretched hand of the girl. As their fingers met, a soft blue light travelled between them.

'I wondered when we would meet again,' whispered Jane.

Turning on her heel, she opened the door and lightly descended the stairs, holding out her hand for the glass of wine.

'It must have been the wind howling through the bottom of the window. I've closed it now.'

Maggie sighed with relief, pushing aside the thought that she hadn't left any windows open.

Jane led the way back, grabbing the bottle of wine to top up their glasses.

'Anytime you hear those mysterious cries from upstairs, just give me a call.'

'I thought you said it was the wind,' said Maggie, again feeling unsettled.

Jane laughed, upending the glass to finish her wine.

'Yes, but you seemed so concerned. I'll be happy to check for you anytime.'

With that, Jane rose to leave. Maggie reluctantly showed her to the door, her feelings of insecurity returning as she was once again left alone. She shivered, glancing upstairs, knowing she would have to go up to her own bedroom soon.

Maggie never made it upstairs, preferring instead to make up a bed on the settee. As morning broke, she stretched, sighing in relief at the lack of any disturbance during the night. Not for the first time, she mused, whether buying the house had been a good idea.

Upstairs in the back bedroom, shadowy figures faded as the morning light crept into the room.

Chapter 27

Peter Trowbridge had been drinking. Nothing new in that or the maudlin feeling that normally accompanied it. His thoughts turned as usual to Maggie, and he poured yet another whiskey. He began going over their time together at university. A common theme for the end of an evening's drinking, and a descent into the hell of his own making. But not in his opinion. No, it was Maggie's fault that his life had turned to shit!

His mind drifted back in time to the first flush of their love. Initial shyness led to a more comfortable friendship, and they were rarely apart. Their friends accepted that the two had become a couple, more so when it became evident they had crossed the sexual boundary.

For the first six months, Peter wallowed in the sexual delights. In his own words, Maggie and he went at it like rabbits. He accepted that she wasn't a virgin when they met. Maggie showed him how to satisfy a woman in every way. Shocked at first at the level of intense intimacy, Peter soon became adept, and caught on very quickly, realising that his previous experiences with girls had been amateurish.

At first he didn't worry about the fact that Maggie had known other boys in the past but began to wonder just how many. Gradually, resentment grew and Peter thought it unfair. He began to crave other women as a form of catchup. After all, university abounded with young women, many unattached.

His first foray happened by a twist of fate that left him alone with a girl he often admired from a distance. Rachael begged him for a lift in his ancient Ford Consul. The end of a college dance, which he attended with male friends, finished, and his friends drifted off in different directions. Maggie cried off attending due to upcoming assignments but encouraged Peter to go to the dance with his friends.

Now, with the crowd dissipating rapidly, Rachael approached.

'Hi, Peter, you don't know me, but I'm stuck for a lift,' she said.

Peter listened hard because she slurred the words and he guessed she'd been drinking. He had also been to the pub prior to the dance but could handle the alcohol due to years of practice.

'Sure, I recognise you from uni,' he said brightly.

Settling into the old Ford, Peter turned the key, grateful that the engine turned over smoothly. On occasion, it refused to start altogether and required the assistance of a few friends to push it.

The heater sprang into action and it soon became cosy. Rachael slid across the bench seat and snuggled up to Peter as he drove towards her home, following directions, she giggled into his ear.

Peter began to enjoy the experience of being close to another girl and slowed the car. He wanted to prolong the experience as long as possible. Glancing down, he couldn't fail to notice Rachael's impossibly short skirt.

'Would you like to stop for a while?' he asked, throwing up a quick prayer to the heavens.

'Okay,' she giggled, moving even closer.

Peter's heart began to thump loudly, certain Rachael would feel it through his chest. The excitement built as he pulled into a quiet lay-by screened by tall bushes.

He left the radio on as he turned off the engine, pushing her gently to the passenger side of the bench seat. She, ready for his kiss, responded savagely, taking him by surprise. Her wide mouth covered his and he at first baulked at the strange sensation of being kissed in that fashion. Her probing tongue followed, and he felt himself being dominated for the first time.

His hand dropped into her lap and the short skirt proved no obstacle. The more he fondled, the more passionate Rachael became, and both were soon partially unclothed. Peter sighed as he entered her. Different to being with Maggie, he found he liked that, and decided there should be more experimentation.

That had been the first time he strayed, and the level of

excitement overruled Peter's conscience. He knew he would do it again given the opportunity, but his impatience led him to begin making the opportunities happen.

Other girls at uni appeared to be as obliging as Rachael, and Peter began to question Maggie's faithfulness. He reasoned that she, already an experienced lover when they first met, might be continuing her old ways.

His conscience, at first placated by Maggie's possible infidelity, quickly led to pangs of jealousy. The soup of human emotions soon became so murky that Peter transformed himself into a victim, convinced that Maggie did have other lovers.

It all came to a head one night as they celebrated their graduation.

Deliriously happy, they had retreated to a fellow student's flat to drink as much alcohol as humanly possible.

Penny was also there having befriended one of Peter's friends. Anything to get close to Peter.

The night continued into the wee small hours, everyone very drunk by that time. Peter sat opposite Maggie, separated by a low coffee table. He had consumed so many drinks his emotions were running from high to low in an instant.

Maggie sat next to one of Peter's friends, one of the Four Musketeers. Another Musketeer slid down beside her on the other side, the third stood behind the couch, gently playing with her hair.

Penny looked on, ignored by the others, their attention solely on Maggie.

In Peter's drunken state, he saw Maggie being far too familiar with three other young men, and it confirmed his worst fears. Without thinking, he yelled across the coffee table.

'I knew you were having it off with other guys!'

Maggie heard the yell but couldn't make it out, Peter's diction so impaired by the vast quantity of consumed drinks.

Maggie laughed good-naturedly. In doing so, she innocently placed her hand on one of the Musketeers' legs.

Peter's face turned purple with rage.

'If you act like a slut, you should be treated as such.'

Maggie still couldn't clearly hear what he said but picked up on his mood. Her laugher died as Peter struggled to get to his feet. The coffee table upended as he lurched clumsily toward the couch.

The other three Musketeers, as drunk as Peter, at first shied away but began to join in enthusiastically when they realised Peter's ire wasn't directed at them.

Grabbing Maggie roughly by the arms, Peter threw her to the floor.

'Hold her, she needs a lesson,' he shouted, fighting to undo his belt.

The others were quick to catch on in their drunken state and grabbed hold of Maggie, pinning her to the floor as she began to cry out,

'Get off me, you bastards.'

That made them laugh even more, sensing the night might be about to become even more exciting, raising their passions to the limit.

Peter knelt on the floor and pulled off Maggie's underwear, exposing her to the leering three Musketeers holding her down.

With a mixture of emotions from love to downright hatred, Peter entered her accompanied by the cheering of his accomplices.

When he finished, Peter sat back on his heels, a stupid smile illuminating his features.

The smile turned into a snarl as one of the others attempted to take his place. Peter appeared to wake up, as if from some terrible nightmare. He saw the other three laughing as they all removed their underwear. The sight snapped him out of his drunken stupor, realising the enormity of what he had done.

'Enough! Bugger off all of you,' he shouted, lashing out with a fist at the Musketeer attempting to take his place with Maggie, who lay defenceless on the floor.

Penny smiled, she had done nothing to prevent the assault on Maggie. The bitch deserved it!

That proved to be a night Maggie would never forget. The following day, Peter spent hours apologising. Crying as he blamed the drink.

'I'm so sorry, Maggie, but jealousy overcame me when I saw you touching Neil. I love you so much I couldn't take any more.'

'You have a strange way of showing your love,' said Maggie coldly.

'I promise I'll make it up to you,' whined Peter.

It had been a classic case of a victim marrying her rapist. Maybe Maggie considered some of the blame should be apportioned to her? However wrong that might be, she chose to believe Peter and married him.

Maggie noted with relief that none of the other Musketeers had been invited to the wedding. She met them individually in the course of her continued relationship with Peter, but when she stared at them, they looked away, their guilt evident. Nothing came out about that fateful night, they all shared the secret, including the victim.

Their marriage had been doomed from the outset because neither could forget that night. They struggled on for what seemed ages. Maggie continued on to earn critical claim for her work while Peter found mundane jobs with little prospects for advancement. He continued his heavy drinking and began to gamble. Maggie not interested in joining him on his nights out because she had better things to do than drink and play the tables.

Peter carried on womanising, only the women became older and less attractive the lower down the ladder he tumbled.

Divorce became inevitable and he began to blame all his woes on Maggie. After the final decree nisi, Peter's anger grew as he tried to come to terms with the settlement. In his view, paltry.

He knew where she lived now, and as his resentment grew, he began following her. Waiting for her to justify to him what he always suspected. She is a slut and never deserved to have him as a husband.

Determined to get even somehow, Peter watched and waited for any opportunity that might present itself.

Chapter 28

Penny had walked as far as Maggie's front door. She missed her company despite the fact that in many ways her loathsome feelings towards Peter's ex-wife remained intact.

Her fist, held up to knock at Maggie's door, slowly unclenched. She couldn't bring herself to do it. Feelings of missing her erstwhile best friend were still tinged with an innate hatred for the woman who had robbed her of the love of her life, twice.

Turning to retrace her steps, Penny failed to notice the shadowy character observing her from the darkened doorway further along the road.

She walked quickly along Petrie street and around the corner, making her way to the tube station. Her heart skipped a beat as mist began to coil around her ankles in wispy tendrils. Fearfully, she recalled the last occasion, and picked up the pace, almost breaking into a run.

From behind, she thought she could hear footsteps. Turning as she walked, she couldn't see anyone, the mist had now enveloped the area, and strangely, the street lighting appeared dimmer than normal. Almost colliding with a green cast iron decorative post, she looked up to the glass box perched on top, staring at the incandescent yellow light of an ancient gas mantle struggling to compete with the mist.

Fear invaded her senses and she began to tremble, what is happening?

The footsteps behind her still rang out on the pavement, and she began to run blindly in the direction of the tube station. Horrified, Penny heard the pace of the following footsteps increase. Soon, they were both running.

Reaching into her handbag, she felt for the small pepper spray cannister, and dragged it out, holding it at chest level. As the footsteps behind caught up with her, she reached behind with the cannister and squeezed the little button. The entire contents of the can emptied in one long spray, surely, it must have enveloped her pursuer.

She ran blindly in the thick mist but didn't notice the uneven path, falling headlong. Her bag slipped from her grasp as she splayed out both hands in an attempt to protect herself.

Penny must have passed out because when she came to her senses, she found herself lying on the cold pavement. The mist had disappeared and the overhead street lights blazed white, completely illuminating the scene.

Propping herself against the brick wall of a house, she looked down at her knees. Both showed the damage caused by her fall and were still bleeding. Her handbag lay a little way from her, together with the exhausted pepper spray cannister.

At that point, Penny dissolved into tears, closing her eyes in abject misery.

Beside her, a door opened and a voice called out.

'Is anyone there?'

Penny looked up, unbelievably she recognised Maggie's voice.

'I'm down here,' she cried miserably.

'Whatever is wrong?' asked Maggie, kneeling beside her, 'let's get you up and inside, it's freezing out here.'

'I wanted to knock at your door but chickened out at the last moment,' began Penny as she sat in the warm kitchen.

Maggie had bathed both her knees and applied a salve before binding them with a bandage.

'Now, let me see your hands,' she said, getting to her feet.

Penny held out both hands, exclaiming as she saw the beginning of dark blue bruising beginning to show.

'How did this happen?' asked Maggie, gingerly holding Penny's hands.

'I don't know,' replied Penny, 'I remember walking away, back towards the tube station, when a mist began to form.'

'Same as last time?' interjected Maggie.

'Yes, exactly the same, but this time I heard footsteps behind me. As the mist thickened, the footsteps seemed to get closer, so I ran. I must have tripped on the bloody pavement, but not before I emptied the pepper spray behind me.'

'How did you get back to my door?' asked Maggie.

Penny's face contorted into sobs.

'I didn't. I sat against a wall next to where I tripped and you opened your door.'

Penny stayed, but once again refused to stay in the back bedroom. Maggie reluctantly agreed to share her bed, spending an uncomfortable night lying beside her restless friend.

The following morning, Penny left. She had cheered up from the previous evening and Maggie wondered not for the first time if she suffered from bi-polar disease. The story about the stranger in the mist seemed far-fetched, and even more so with the dawning of a new day.

A knock at the door soon after Penny had left announced the arrival of the next-door neighbour.

'I don't want to alarm you but there have been reports of a man loitering in the area,' said Jane, 'a neighbour reported the matter to the local bobby who forwarded it on to us in CID.'

'Any ideas?' said Maggie, recalling the events of the previous evening.

'Only that he has been seen hanging around not far from here, might be better if you didn't walk alone, especially after dark.'

Maggie didn't mention Penny's experience, fearing it would seem too far-fetched to be creditable.

'Anymore bumps in the night?' asked Jane, laughing.

'No, all quiet on the Western Front,' Maggie replied, joining in with Jane's laughter.

Detective Chief Inspector Nipper sat at his desk chewing the end of an HB pencil. For some reason, he enjoyed the flavour of the inside. The graphite core differed in hardness and Nipper opined that HB tasted better than 2H and especially better than the harsh 5H. He bought them by the pack, keeping spares in his desk. None of the pencils were ever used for their intended purpose. A trusty Biro far more efficient, but the plastic casing too awful for words.

His habit had begun the day he gave up cigarettes. After being a fifty a day man for many years, the wrench of giving up led to intense eating. Sugared donuts were his preference, and his expanding waistline bore testimony to the amount he could digest on a daily basis. Mrs Nipper began to worry about his health and to placate her, he promised to give up donuts as well as cigarettes.

HB pencils were a substitute, but at least they didn't cause cancer or heart disease. Mrs Nipper had no idea about the new habit. Nipper squirreled a few away at home and retreated to the toilet for a secret chew when the occasion arose.

He began seriously gnawing the latest pencil as Detective Constable Jane Wilmot entered his office.

'Morning, Guv. You wanted to see me?'

'There's been another one,' said Nipper, crushing the end of a new HB with yellowed teeth, the product of his former habit.

'Where did they find this one?' asked Jane.

'In an empty house at the end of Petrie Street. Bloody nasty by all accounts. I'm about to attend the scene, get your coat.'

Jane was of the opinion that bloody nasty may have been the understatement of the century. The body had been discovered by workmen engaged in renovating the terraced house. They stood outside with the local uniformed police as Nipper and Jane entered.

'What's that horrible smell?' asked Nipper as he passed over the threshold.

'One of these blokes threw up everywhere,' replied one of the uniformed officers.

Nipper applied a large white cotton handkerchief over his nose, glancing at Jane in wonderment as she remained apparently unaffected by the obnoxious odour.

The body, or what was left of it, lay in the hallway. Closer inspection revealed it had been a young woman, maybe in her twenties. Her clothing had been removed and discarded haphazardly. The face might once have been pretty, but a long cut down one cheek exposed the inside of her mouth and bare cheekbone. The chief inspector's eyes were drawn to her midriff. A sharp instrument had been drawn vertically downward from her breastbone to navel and her inside organs now lay piled beside her on the floor.

Nipper, a man with considerable experience of the gruesomeness murders can present, turned away.

'Fuck this!'

He left to walk outside as the pathologist and his team arrived. Jane stayed by the body, studying the scene before pinching the woman's cheek together and using her smartphone to take a photo.

'Don't touch,' said the pathologist, 'you should know better.'

'Sorry,' said Jane, 'I wanted to know what she looked like before.'

Outside, Nipper shuffled his feet.

'Bit close to home for you, isn't it? I understand you live around here.'

'Yes, sir, the same terrace at Number 17,' answered Jane.

'I don't want to scare you, but there has been another murder,' said Jane.

Maggie poured the wine as the pair sat in Maggie's kitchen.

'Whereabouts?' she asked.

'In the same terrace as us, a few doors down,' said Jane, sniffing the wine before sipping the cold nectar.

Maggie sipped her own wine, trying to remain as calm as Jane appeared to be.

Jane continued.

'A young woman in her twenties. I can't give you her name just yet, but she was apparently on the game around these parts.'

'A prostitute?' breathed Maggie.

'Yes, I'm afraid there are quite a few in the area, oldest

profession in the world and all that.'

Maggie looked in consternation at Jane, who smiled.

'Sorry, it's the job, you get used to the seamier side of life and the bad things that happen. It makes us appear cold and unfeeling, but without that defence, being a police officer would be impossible.'

'I understand, at least I think I do,' said Maggie.

A huge bang came from upstairs, like a door being slammed shut.

Maggie rose, but Jane beat her to it.

'I'll go and check,' she said, making for the stairs.

'I thought it might be you,' said Jane quietly.

The barely discernible outline of a girl stood in the centre of the back bedroom.

'He's back,' whispered the girl.

Chapter 29

Nipper raised his eyes in a question, no words needed.

'Alice Morgan,' said Jane.

'Age?' asked Nipper.

'Twenty-eight. She's been on the game since her teens. The local girls all liked her, and apart from the odd pull by the local plods, she has a clean record.'

'Who looks after her?'

'A local ponce, Kyle Stringer. Apparently, he is one of the gentler ones. Looks after the girls and isn't too mean to them.'

Nipper continued chewing his pencil.

'Don't we have any clues at all? We have bodies stacking up in the fridges. Surely one of you lot has an idea.'

'Nothing,' Jane admitted, 'not one trace of DNA at any of the crime scenes. Whoever is doing this has the expertise to leave no traces of themselves.'

'Could it be a copycat killer?' added Jane.

'Copying who exactly?'

'I know this is going to sound a bit outrageous, but the current murders have a lot of similarities to the Ripper murders of the late nineteenth century.'

Nipper grimaced.

'Not that old tale again, surely. Jack the bloody Ripper seems to pop up every few years and it always ends up with some local nutter doing the deed.'

'But it's the right location and the victims fit the bill. They are all prossies and all have been mutilated.'

'Like I say, it's all happened before. A maniac trying to emulate his bloody hero.'

Jane remained silent while Nipper continued to chew before looking up sharply at her.

'I hope you're not going to suggest it's something to do with the supernatural. The bloody ghost of the Ripper is all I need!'

'No, sir. I wouldn't dream of suggesting that,' Jane murmured.

'I should bloody well hope not. You'd better get back to the brains trust and see if something in the real world pops up. We need to catch this bugger, whoever it is, and soon.'

Maggie took an early mark and arrived home in the mid-afternoon. She had been putting off doing the laundry for days, but knew she had to make an effort. Lately, she had been feeling tired, even though she had been sleeping soundly enough. Her entire body had become drained of energy.

First, she stripped her own bed and carted it down to the kitchen, feeding the sheets and pillowcases into the washing machine. Trudging back upstairs, she opened the door to the back bedroom.

'Bloody hell, it's freezing in here,' she said to the empty room.

Her eyes swept the room, coming to rest on the bed. Someone or something had torn the sheets to shreds. They had been slashed with something sharp. Long cuts travelled in every direction until the material barely resembled a bedsheet.

Maggie idly began removing the remnants, piling them up on the floor beside the bed.

'At least I won't have to wash them,' she said, once again addressing the empty room. Or was it empty? Maggie felt her skin crawl with the sensation that someone could be watching her. Walking over to the window, she pulled the curtain aside to peer out into the street. Her eyes caught a dark shape, ducking back around the corner opposite her house and along the street. She continued staring at the same spot and, sure enough, a head slowly appeared around the corner. She couldn't see who because they wore a wide brimmed black hat and as they spotted her, the head rapidly withdrew.

Maggie, angry now, raced downstairs and out into the street. Her bare feet stinging on the road surface, she made for the corner, heedless of who might be waiting.

Nothing. The next street proved to be completely empty as

far as the eye could see. Whoever it had been was quick to make themselves scarce. Maggie thought it might have been someone who lived in the street. They could never have run the length of the street before she had rounded the corner.

Her feet suddenly reminded her of their recent abuse as Maggie hobbled back home, still pondering the identity of the mystery spy.

Peter struggled to regain his breath after running in sheer panic. He had seen Maggie storming out of her door and heading straight for him. Turning on his heel, he ran pell mell along the street, knowing he would never make it to the end without her seeing him, or at least the back of him as he receded into the distance. Still, it might be enough for her to recognise him and he didn't want to give his ex-wife the satisfaction of catching him stalking her. The law had strict penalties for that sort of thing.

As he ran, a door ahead clicked open, and without hesitating, Peter turned sharply and slammed into the doorway. The door crashed open, hitting a wall with a sharp thud. A woman lay at his feet, out cold, stunned by his sudden entry into her hallway. Peter's head spun with fright as he closed the door. At least Maggie would no longer be able to see him.

The woman, Peter noted, appeared to be quite young and not a bad-looking sort. She lay prone on the floor. He knelt down beside her to feel for a pulse at her neck and breathed a sigh of relief when he realised she proved only to be unconscious.

Peter's heart raced with a mixture of panic and sheer excitement. The combination of both stirred his emotions.

Peter, never being burdened with any particular morals, revelled in the excitement. He knelt beside the young woman whose skirt had ridden up to her waist by the impact of him charging through her front door and began to explore.

Nipper stood over his team, glowering.

'There's been another one, and in the same area. A young

woman by the name of Rita Hemsworth.'

'Same as the rest?' asked a detective constable.

'No, this one is different. The young lady was certainly not a prostitute. She works for the local branch of St. Vincent de Paul, the Catholic charity organisation and is beyond reproach.'

'Who found her?' asked the same D.C.

'Her poor bloody husband when he came home from work this afternoon. The local plods attended and called it in. We should get there at the same time as the forensic team.'

A small crowd of onlookers had gathered outside Number 41 Elton Street, together with two vans from the media. Uniformed police managed to keep everyone at bay as Nipper entered the premises.

'No further, if you please,' shouted the leader of the forensics team, 'you'll need to suit up for this one.'

Another officer handed Nipper a plastic coverall and shoe covers.

'What a bloody mess!' Nipper exclaimed.

The scene resembled the previous one in that the woman's body had been horribly mutilated. Rita lay naked in a sea of congealing blood, her organs once again having been torn from her body.

'Do what you can,' Nipper instructed the forensics team, 'hopefully you might find some alien DNA this time, we need a break.'

Back in his office, Nipper spoke to Jane.

'This one is different in that the victim is not on the game. However, the injuries are similar to the others.'

Jane remained silent, finding nothing to add.

Much later that evening, Jane knocked lightly on Maggie's door, bottle of wine in hand.

'Mind if I come in for a bit?' she said as the door opened, holding out the bottle as an inducement.

'I understand an incident occurred around the corner today,' said Maggie once they had settled in the lounge with wine in hand.

'That's what I came around for,' answered Jane, 'I thought I'd better warn you not to venture out alone, especially after dark. There have been two particularly gruesome murders in this direct vicinity and I'd hate for you to be number three.'

Jane carried on to explain, as much as she dared without breaching police protocol, the circumstances surrounding the latest murders, carried out so close to where they both now sat.

The hour being late, Jane didn't linger long and made her way towards the front door.

'Any strange bumps in the night?' she joked.

Maggie frowned.

'No, but when I went into the back bedroom to change the sheets, I found the ones on the bed torn to shreds. Perhaps slashed to shreds might be more accurate.'

'Mind if I take a look?' asked Jane, already half way upstairs.

'Be my guest,' said Maggie, as Jane disappeared into the back bedroom.

Studying the torn sheets Maggie had left there, Jane whispered.

'Are you here?'

There being no response, Jane quickly returned downstairs.

'I'd say you have a serious rat problem up there,' she laughed.

Maggie tried to join in but failed miserably.

Chapter 30

Nipper smiled, a rare sight these days, thought the team.

'At last, forensics found DNA on the body. Now we have a chance.'

Detective Sergeant Tim Wilks, new to the team having recently been promoted to sergeant, spoke for everyone.

'Solid DNA or merely a touch?'

'As solid as you can get,' replied Nipper, 'the bastard left his semen all over her.'

Jane piped up.

'That's unusual. None of the others showed any evidence of sexual contact. Why is this one different? Don't tell me we already have a copycat!'

Nipper stared at Jane long and hard.

'Don't bugger up my day, get onto records and see if you can cross match the bugger.'

Leaving the others to do the research, Nipper made his way to the morgue.

Nipper stared down at the woman's body, he grimaced. The stripped-out organs still lay on the outside of her torso. At the completion of the autopsy, they would be shuffled back inside and sewn up.

'Anything else I should know?' asked Nipper.

'Only that the traces of semen were on the outside of the body. None inside where you would expect to find it.' answered the pathologist.

'That's odd, this one must be a right kinky bastard.'

The pathologist nodded his head sagely.

'Seen it all down here, nothing surprises me anymore.'

'Do we have a positive identification?'

'Not until I've made the poor girl decent. The husband will identify her, but I'll shove this lot back inside and lace her up first. He will only get to see the face after I cover her with a sheet and put the ruff around her neck.'

'Poor sod,' said Nipper, 'we'll have to ask him for a DNA sample for elimination purposes.'

'He won't appreciate that,' commented the pathologist.

'They never do,' answered Nipper.

By the end of the following day, they reached another impasse. The husband reluctantly agreed to provide a sample of DNA. Still in a state of shock, especially after viewing his wife's body, he railed at the suggestion he had anything to do with his wife's murder. But in the end, rushing the sample through the lab, it proved to be a negative match.

Nothing came up on the database either, so the team once again gathered in the inspector's office.

Nipper's previously elated mood disappeared.

'Someone must have seen the bugger. It happened in daylight. Question everybody in the area.'

'All the others were committed at night, none had any signs of sexual contact and in fact there wasn't any trace of alien DNA. Are we sure this isn't another sadistic killer?'

'Well done, professor fucking Wilks, trust the new boy to come up with the obvious!'

The newly promoted Tim Wilks glared at Nipper, how dare the supercilious bastard show him up in front of the others?

For once, Nipper felt contrition. He knew he had overstepped the mark. To publicly deride his new sergeant meant undermining his authority with the lower ranks.

In a barely discernible voice, Nipper made a rare admission.

'I'm sorry, sergeant, my comments were completely uncalled for. You are quite right on every count, we may well have another nutter to hunt down.'

Wilks' relief washed over him, his position had been secured, and he needed not to add to the conversation.

That evening, Jane sat in Maggie's kitchen, a freshly opened bottle of red decanted into two glasses.

'What a day,' breathed Jane.

'What a day, indeed,' rejoined Maggie, 'so it looks like there is another killer on the loose. What are the odds!'

'Either a copycat or the original killer has completely lost it,' said Jane, 'in any event, you had better err on the side of caution whenever you leave the house. Before, they happened at night, but it's not safe at any time now.'

The following morning, Maggie slammed the front door shut as she made her way to the tube station. Whatever the drama surrounding her street, she still must go to work. The street appeared different. There were no other pedestrians and the whole area appeared to be unnaturally quiet, as if even the street itself expected more unrest.

As soon as she left the immediate vicinity, the number of people increased. When she reached the tube and the normal hurly-burly of the early morning London rush hour, she became absorbed in the crowds of commuters and relaxed.

That comfort suddenly disappeared as she caught a glimpse of someone who, apparently, wanting to avoid being seen, ducked down behind a newspaper display stand. It wasn't very high and the person would have to almost kneel down to avoid showing their face.

Maggie paused, not sure what to do. Should she approach and confront them or walk off quickly in the opposite direction?

Steeling herself, she headed straight for the stand.

'You!' she exclaimed, 'what the hell are you up to?'

Peter slowly got to his feet, his face reddening with embarrassment.

'Hello, Maggie, fancy seeing you here,' he mumbled.

'You were following me, weren't you?'

'No, really, it's sheer coincidence.'

'Then why did you hide?'

'I bent down to tie my laces,' he replied, his voice becoming stronger as he defended his actions.

Maggie glance at his shoes.

'Did you forget you're wearing slip-on shoes?'
Peter's voice returned to a mumble.
'Silly me, of course I am.'
'Stop following me or I'll report you to the police as a stalker.'
'Oh, that's a bit harsh,' said Peter, offended, 'I never meant you any harm.'
'After what happened in the next street, I'm not sure of anybody,' said Maggie defensively.
Peter looked puzzled.
'What happened?' he asked.
'Surely you must have heard about the horrible murder in Elton Street, it's the street adjacent to mine.'
Peter couldn't control his emotions, his face turned deathly white.
'What murder?' he managed to say.
'Are you okay, you're awfully pale?' said Maggie, showing genuine concern.
'Yes, I'm fine,' said Peter before walking away and leaving Maggie confused. What the hell was he up to?

After the excitement of the other day, Peter had gone to ground. He raced home after the incident with the woman in Elton Street and submerged himself in the depths of a bottle of bourbon. He had not heard the news about the murder, and Maggie's revelation came as a shock.

At the first opportunity, he bought a newspaper and studied what facts had been released to the press. Sketchy details outlined the vicious murder. The hard facts having been suppressed to save the immediate family any further distress.

Collapsing in a chair in his dingy flat, Peter opened another bottle of bourbon. Between glasses of the amber fluid, he went over and over what happened after he cannoned into the woman, knocking her down inside her own hallway.

Barely escaping the attention of his ex-wife brought on an acutely excited state, and he couldn't take his eyes off the woman's underwear showing beneath her skirt.

Peter, trembling with excitement, and not thinking of the possible consequences, ejaculated over her.

Immediately coming to his senses, Peter opened the front door, looked left and right and bolted down the street, leaving the door wide open. He only touched the woman, certainly didn't kill her. What could he do now? Peter watched enough cop shows to know he left clear evidence of his presence. Not only had he been there, but he left evidence of the sexual nature of his presence. Before passing out in yet another drunken stupor, he consoled himself with the fact that the police didn't have a record of his DNA, and so long as he never found himself in a position whereby he had to give it, he would be safe.

The figure, dressed entirely in black and sporting an expensive silk top hat, stared at the figure lying in the hallway. The front door having been left open by the man running away in the distance.

Stepping lightly into the hallway and closing the door, the black figure looked down upon the unconscious woman spreadeagled on the floor.

With a sneer of disgust, the shadowy shape produced a sharp-bladed instrument, and leaning down, sliced open the woman's throat. The shock and pain momentarily brought Rita out of her state of unconsciousness, and she stared in horror at the face above her before the light finally dimmed in her eyes. The scream she so wanted to release died on her lips, ending in a mere whimper.

Swift strokes with the blade reduced her to a bloody mess of entrails. The figure looked down with acute satisfaction. Another whore sent to Hell!

Chapter 31

Penny raised her fist to knock at the door but hesitated. Should she or shouldn't she? This man had rejected her for another and even though that relationship failed, it still galled her to come begging on bended knee to the man who forsook her so lightly.

As she heard movement through the door, she panicked, turned and descended the stairs. Penny wanted this man badly, had always wanted him, but she lacked the courage to face possible rejection yet again.

She walked around the block, determined to pluck up the courage. Twice more she walked the same route. Finally, she prepared herself. This time, she would do it to hell with the consequences.

Penny meant to knock softly, but with her mind made up, the loud knock reverberated through the door.

Nothing happened, so she knocked again, even harder. One minute of waiting seemed like an eternity, but the door opened the merest crack. She stared at a bleary red eye, studying her.

'Peter, let me in. Please.'

The door opened to reveal her ex-boyfriend, Maggie's ex-husband, barely able to stand. He reeked of alcohol and cigarettes, and she doubted he had seen the inside of a shower for some time.

'What do you want,' Peter asked harshly.

'I'm worried about you,' Penny replied, 'can I come in?'

Peter opened the door wide and Penny witnessed the shambolic way in which he now lived. Stepping inside, she wrinkled her nose at the stale smell of the place. Curtains were drawn so that the merest sliver of daylight permeated the room, and the coffee table couldn't hold another empty beer can or overflowing ashtray.

Peter slumped on the settee, knocking empty beer cans off the coffee table.

'Why don't I run you a bath?' Penny suggested, 'then I'll clean the place up a bit.'

Peter had been drunk for three days, substituting sleep for yet more alcohol, and he could barely stand. The events of the horrendous murder at Elton Street finally hit the airwaves and he drank himself into oblivion while watching the news on television, knowing he would be the prime suspect if any connection could be traced to his DNA.

He cursed himself loudly. What began as an erotic, and in his eyes innocent, interlude, now blossomed into a full-scale murder hunt. It wouldn't have been the first or even the second time he had performed the secret rite over some woman who passed out with the effects of too much drink. Peter never missed an opportunity in the past. The victim would wake with no memory of the incident, and Peter's strange obsession satisfied.

This one proved to be different. Some deviant had butchered her after he left. He cursed again, remembering how he had left the front door wide open. Easy access for the killer, the woman already partly naked and lying in the hallway.

The bath steamed in the tiny bathroom as Penny struggled to get Peter out of his clothes. She would put them into the washing machine while he bathed and sort more clothes from his bedroom. She had never been inside this flat, so as yet unfamiliar with the layout.

Returning to the bathroom, she studied Peter's body. What she remembered as a well-developed physique had declined into the pale rather flabby vision that met her gaze. Still, she found the sight attractive but acknowledged that part of the attraction, the fact she had lost him to another, and she could now seize the opportunity to reclaim him for herself.

Peter struggled to get out of the bath and needed Penny's help. She dried him like a child. He stood while she patted him dry, taking extra care around his genitals but unable to resist the temptation to linger longer than necessary.

Peter, all thoughts of his present predicament cast out of his mind by Penny's suggestive ministrations, began to react.

The old Peter came to the fore and he unceremoniously pushed Penny into the bedroom and onto the bed. At first, she welcomed his amorous attention but as his manner became more aggressive, began to object.

'No, Peter. Let's talk about this first.'

'No time for talk, do as you're told,' he snarled, ripping off her underclothes in his haste.

Penny looked up, frightened that he appeared more than ready for her.

'Please, Peter, you're scaring me.'

Her cries were met with raucous laughter as he applied his full weight and entered her.

'I'm so sorry!' Peter's face creased into a sob.

Penny quickly dressed after he had finished with her.

'You scared me, you never used to be like that,' she said, nervous that he might once again change into the manic animal that had used her so coarsely.

But Peter, the old Peter, had returned and sat before her, contrite. The knowledge of the recent murder and the fear of imminent pursuit by police came crashing back into his mind the moment he ejaculated.

'I don't know what to do,' he whispered feebly.

'Do about what?' asked Penny.

Peter sat up straight, his manner changing abruptly.

'Nothing, forget what I said,' he spat.

Penny reached for his hand.

'I hope we can rekindle our romance now that she's gone.'

Peter pulled his hand away.

'Maggie hasn't gone, we are merely having a break from each other. You'll see, we'll soon be back together.'

His words jolted Penny, how dare the bastard say that after basically raping her only moments ago.

'That will never happen, she already has another boyfriend, and he's quite the lover, apparently.'

She couldn't resist gilding the lily with the final comment, even though Maggie never discussed her private life.

'Tell me more,' asked Peter in a voice that barely concealed a threat.

'He's a psychologist,' said Penny. Very handsome, too.

'Where does he work and what's his name?' Peter demanded.

Penny felt unsettled again. The old Peter, her old Peter, had vanished again.

'Stephen Pendle, and he has an office quite close to where Maggie works.'

Peter finished the glass of scotch and slammed it down on the coffee table.

'You had better go.'

Penny didn't object, in fact, she left gladly. The look in Peter's deep, sunken eyes didn't fill her with confidence.

She slammed the door and walked downstairs out into the street, a welcome air of freedom encapsulating her. The flat felt like a prison cell. What had gone wrong with Peter?

Maggie sighed in relief as Stephen walked in.

'Am I glad to your here.'

Stephen laughed, brandishing two bottles of her favourite wine.

'Now, that's a welcome worth getting used to.'

They sat close together as the first bottle of wine disappeared.

'Tell me what happened in the next street?' Stephen asked.

Maggie shook her head.

'Murder, that's what happened.'

'Any details?' Stephen asked.

'I got all the gory details from my new next-door neighbour, Jane. She is working on the case. Apparently, it's not your average run-of-the-mill murder either. A young woman has been butchered in a way too harrowing for the media to touch. They reported it as a mutilation, but that's an understatement, according to Jane.'

'Yes, I read the headline: Is the Ripper back?'

Maggie finished her wine and reached for the second bottle.

'Typical bloody media. Anything to grab the attention of the buying public. Next thing, there will be a hue and cry and fingers will be pointing at anybody out of the ordinary.'

'From a psychological point of view that is to be expected,' said Stephen, relaxing into a subject close to his heart. 'People are afraid and fear is the real enemy.'

'I thought it was the Ripper,' laughed Maggie, realising she had drank the first bottle of wine far too quickly.

'Sorry, that was uncalled for,' she added.

'That's okay, I tend to climb on my high horse sometimes. You merely unseated me,' he joked.

Maggie needed to soften the tone of the evening.

'I hope you're staying,' she said, unbuttoning her blouse daringly.

Stephen reached over to help her with the last button.

'How could I not?' he laughed.

Later, after making love, the couple lay entwined in each other's arms.

'Let's not talk about the outside world with all its horrors,' Maggie murmured, 'It's nice, safe, and comfy here.'

Stephen answered with a quiet snore, already fast asleep.

Maggie drifted off to join him, a deep sigh of contentment escaping her lips.

The illuminated bedside clock showed three a.m. The scream began as a distant moan, gradually building into a piercing crescendo that reverberated throughout the house. Both Maggie and Stephen woke at the same moment. Maggie sunk beneath the covers, holding her hands over her ears in an effort to quell the sound. Stephen leapt out of bed. The scream came from the back bedroom and close enough to muddle the senses with its volume.

Stephen opened the back bedroom door and stood back. He could see nothing in the darkness, but the scream emanated from the centre of the room. The volume pierced his eardrums painfully as he felt something brush past him and descend the stairs. A fleeting glimpse of something resembling a young woman registered in his brain, the noise tailing off as she left the house. He heard the scream tailing off as it travelled along the street outside, disappearing around the corner into Elton Street.

As he sat on the bed beside Maggie, Stephen reached for her hand.

'Whatever just happened, I didn't like it,' he said.

Maggie shook her head.

'When I bought this house, I made the biggest mistake of my life.'

Chapter 32

Jane frowned.

'What noise?' she said, looking back at Maggie.

'Surely you must have heard the scream last night. It must have been about three in the morning.'

'No, not a thing, maybe I slept through it?' said Jane.

Maggie laughed grimly.

'I don't think anyone could sleep through that. It was ear shattering.'

'Have you tried next door? Perhaps they heard it,' suggested Jane.

She took Jane's advice and walked next door.

The front door looked as if it had been seldom opened, and Maggie gave a tentative knock. She had never bothered to find out who lived next door. So often in crowded cities, neighbours rarely communicated.

She knocked again a little harder and stood back expectantly.

'What do you want?' said an unseen person behind the door. It sounded like an older woman, but the gruffness of the voice made it difficult to pick up on the gender.

'Hi, I'm Maggie from next door. We haven't met yet and I thought it would be nice to introduce myself.'

The door, sadly neglected and in need of a coat of paint, opened enough to enable the occupant to peer out at Maggie. The stale odour emanating from inside made her take an involuntary step back.

'Hello,' said Maggie cheerily.

The face, severely lined with old age and dominated by watery eyes, didn't change expression.

'What do you want?'

'Only to say hi,' said Maggie, forcing the smile to stay on her own face.

The old woman appeared to be thinking, then,

'You can come in if you want, we don't get many visitors.'

'Thank you, that would be nice,' said Maggie, regretting her decision to knock in the first place.

The door creaked open, allowing the exit of stale air as if the house actually breathed a sigh of relief.

Maggie steeled herself and stepped forward, crossing the threshold.

The old lady violently slammed the door shut behind her.

'The door sticks,' said the old lady by way of explanation.

Her shoulders gradually sank back down as she relaxed from the sound of the door crashing back into its frame. Maggie stepped further into the hall, closely followed by the old lady shuffling close behind.

The smell became more atrocious as she passed through the hall into the rear kitchen, and she felt the hairs on her arms stand erect as cold shivers ran up and down her spine.

An old man sat in an ancient wing-backed chair in front of what must have been the original coal fired black kitchen range. Cobwebs hung over the range, and it clearly hadn't been lit for some time.

As Maggie approached, he gradually turned his head to face her.

'Who have we got here?' he asked through a mouth dotted with the odd yellowed tooth. His bare gums moved up and down in a chewing movement, his mouth clearly empty.

'This is our neighbour,' shouted the old woman, startling Maggie. 'He's as deaf as a post is my Ernie,' she added, speaking normally.

Maggie put out her hand, speaking loudly.

'Pleased to meet you, Ernie.'

The hand that reached for her own made Maggie cringe inwardly. Ernie's hand bore both the signs of old age and perhaps some chronic illness. She shook his hand, having the idle thought that it might come off, so released her grip immediately.

The old lady sidled around to stand by Ernie's side.

'I'm Ada.'

'Nice to meet you,' said Maggie lamely.

'I can't offer you tea, we don't have any,' said Ada.

Maggie allowed her eyes to wander around the dimly lit kitchen and took in the dust laden surfaces. Cupboard doors stood partially open and she could see they were all empty.

She recalled the original purpose of her visit and faced the old couple.

'Were either of you aware of a loud scream last night?'

Ada and Ernie glanced at each other before Ada answered for both.

'We often hear screams. You get used to it after a while.'

Comforted by the fact that at least one neighbour could attest to last night's screams, Maggie smiled with relief.

'How long have you lived here?' she asked.

'Such a very long time,' answered Ada, 'such a long time.'

Ernie nodded gently in acquiescence.

Maggie turned to leave, beginning to feel distinctly uncomfortable.

'I'll see myself out,' she said, beginning to walk along the hallway.

The old couple didn't move, and Maggie tried to hurry, her nervousness making her panicky.

However, her pace actually slowed as she became aware of something in front of her pushing back. It clearly didn't want her to leave the house.

Panic settled in as Maggie pushed back at the unseen force.

'Let me go,' she cried, louder than she had intended. But the force wouldn't relent and she came to a standstill.

A loud, commanding voice rang out from behind her.

'Let her go!'

Maggie stumbled, whatever held her back disappeared in an instant.

She reached the front door and turned the handle, pulling with all her might. The door reluctantly gave way and opened enough for her to slide through.

Ada's thin, reedy voice followed her outside.

'Mind how you go, dear.'

The door slammed shut violently as if it had a life of its own, leaving Maggie standing on the narrow pavement, shaking.

Maggie returned to Jane and relayed what happened at the old people's house.

'Well, so much for the neighbours, they're straight out of a horror movie.'

Jane chuckled, 'I'll run a rates check and see who they are.'

'I'm not going near them again, no matter what,' said Maggie.

That evening, after Maggie had attended to business in the real world, she sat in her kitchen with Jane, who waved a sheet of paper like a magic wand.

'Guess what?' she said.

Maggie glared.

'That has to be the worst intro to any conversation.'

Jane chuckled, 'Annoying, isn't it?'

Maggie grabbed the sheet of paper from Jane's hand and set it down on the table, her eyes taking in every line. It proved to be a printout from the local council records department. However, the words clouded in council rhetoric, meant nothing.

'Nobody lives next door,' said Jane, taking the paper and explaining its contents.

'What do you mean nobody lives there? I talked to them, the old couple next door,' said Maggie.

'Nobody there,' repeated Jane, laughing.

Maggie became irritated by Jane's attitude.

'Okay, you're the copper, let's go next door right now and you'll see.'

The old door shuddered in protest at Maggie's insistent knocking, but nobody answered.

Standing back, Maggie set up to shoulder charge at the

offending door.

'Whoa, hold on a minute, you can't break in. As you said, I'm a copper,' said Jane, holding up a hand in protest.

Maggie stood, catching her breath, her shoulders heaving with the effort. Her face showed anger and Jane witnessed another side of Maggie, the not so sweet Maggie.

Finally, Jane convinced her they should return to Number 15. As they walked away, a loud click sounded and, amazed, they witnessed the door creak open.

'Bugger this!' said Maggie, it's getting too creepy for words.

Her dander, well and truly up, she walked to the door and pushed it open, looking into the darkened hallway.

'Come on, it's open, so we aren't breaking in, are we.'

'I suppose not,' said Jane, hanging back.

Maggie strode through the door, calling out to Ada and Ernie, 'Yoo-hoo, it's only me, your next-door neighbour.'

Silence greeted the two women as they made their way slowly along the hallway to the kitchen.

The place had a deserted air about it, but Maggie had noticed that before with the old couple.

She pushed open the kitchen door, and they walked in.

'It's like the bloody Mary Celeste,' said Jane.

Maggie nodded her head in agreement.

'These cups weren't here the last time and the plates of untouched food weren't either.'

'Are you sure?' asked Jane.

'Yes, I'm sure. The old lady, Ada, said she couldn't offer me a cup of tea because they didn't have any.'

Jane studied the plates of food.

'This has been here for years,' she said, 'it's covered in mould.'

'What about upstairs?' asked Maggie.

Jane went to the foot of the stairs and looked up. As she raised a foot to the bottom stair, a figure appeared at the top of the stairs, holding up one hand in a way that could not be mistaken for anything but an order to stop.

'I don't think there will be anything up there,' she said, 'there are cobwebs everywhere.'

Maggie approached and looked upstairs, but the figure had disappeared.

'Come on,' said Jane, 'back to our wine. There's nothing here.'

Maggie reluctantly agreed.

'But I'm sure an old couple live here,' she mumbled, beginning to doubt her own sanity.

Chapter 33

Jane sat in the kitchen going over her past. For some time, she had been aware that she could see dead people. The expression stuck in her mind ever since seeing the movie about a young boy who also, 'saw dead people'. It summed up beautifully her own experiences.

At first she ignored it, blaming a trick of the light, but since that horrific encounter in the back bedroom of Number 15 Petrie Street, she noticed more tricks of the light. It seemed ironic that she now lived right next door to the same house.

Eddie's body lay undiscovered for three months. He hadn't shown up for work, but nobody cared. Never popular, they assumed he left and his workmates sighed with relief. Noted for being a bully, he wouldn't be missed.

The method of his dispatch had been obvious even after so long lying on the bedroom floor. Rigor mortis came and went and by the time someone reported a foul stench in the street. His major organs were almost liquefied.

With nothing to act upon, the police soon consigned the case to the unsolved drawer. The coroner recorded death by person or persons unknown and basically Eddie had been forgotten.

Paradoxically, two women were relieved. His wife, Mary, once informed, placed the house on the market for immediate sale, fully furnished. She wanted nothing from that place. Everything in it would be tainted by Eddie, both when alive and certainly now that he lay dead.

Avril maintained a low profile after the killing, fearful at any moment of a heavy knock at her door from the police. After three months, she began to wonder if Eddie's death would ever be reported.

She even risked revisiting the street, walking slowly along the side where Eddie's house stood. Wearing a dark, long, hooded coat, she doubted if anyone would remember her.

When she drew level with Number 15, she noticed a foul smell, and wondered why nobody else had reported it. She assumed that, as in all cities, people tended to mind their own business. Avril decided to report it herself, anonymously, from a public telephone, covering the hand piece with a piece of cloth to disguise her voice.

Waiting for two weeks, she again walked along Petrie Street, but this time the front door of Number 15 had been criss-crossed with police tape with a Do Not Enter - crime scene sticker stuck across the door.

As she paused beside the door, she noticed the thin outline of a figure standing against it. She immediately recognised Eddie, and he mouthed something to her, looking angry. Avril hurried off and never returned. Not as Avril anyway.

Now she lived next door as Jane. She looked every day but never saw Eddie again, for which she remained very thankful.

However, her visions of the departed didn't stop with him. In the deserted warehouse, the scene of the first murdered woman, she saw the victim as well, standing beside her own body, with head downcast. Jane deliberately stared at her and she seemed to notice, looking up and returning Jane's look.

It had been the same with the next victim. Jane could see her outline as well, but clearer now.

In the back bedroom of Maggie's house she saw Daisy, dead for so many years. She felt so real that Jane reached out to touch her, but her hand passed through thin air.

As she spoke, Daisy paid attention and quickly relayed what had happened to her. She, too, had been murdered in the room.

Jane accepted the 'gift'. What else could she do? She heard the screams that terrified Maggie and saw the old woman next door, standing at the top of the stairs.

Jane wondered if she could channel these dead victims and somehow bring their killers to justice. It seemed far-fetched, like something out of a movie, but her visions were real.

'Bugger, bugger, bugger!' exclaimed Nipper. The detective sat at his desk chewing on an HB.

'We have DNA from the body, but no bloody matches.'

Detective Sergeant Wilks, loathe to make a point after being chewed out by Nipper once before, cleared his throat.

'Maybe we could suggest to the media that we might be conducting a DNA search in the immediate vicinity?'

Nipper frowned, missing the point entirely.

'Have you any idea of the cost that would entail to say nothing of the bleeding hearts brigade going on about desecrating our freedom?'

Wilks cleared his throat again.

'No, sir, I merely suggested dropping a hint to the media. The mere thought that it will happen might flush out the killer.'

Nipper remained tight-lipped for a few seconds.

'I underestimated you, sergeant. I'll give Tommy Tompkins a call and suggest a lunchtime pint.'

Tommy held the position of chief crime reporter for a major daily paper and would be only too pleased for the tip.

'What area are you intending to test?' he asked over his beer.

'I would rather you leave that to the reader's imagination,' replied Nipper.

'I wouldn't like to be caught out publishing false information,' said Tommy.

'Say, it is rumoured,' replied Nipper, 'that should cover you.'

The following morning and true to his word, the front-page banner read, Murder latest. Mass DNA testing to identify the killer.

Peter read the headline and immediately made for the toilet. His bowels could no longer cope with the anxiety. He was done for. They were bound to catch him now, he left his DNA all over that poor woman.

After some time in the toilet, Peter emerged, sitting once again amongst empty beer cans and bottles, looking into space.

An idea came to mind. It might not do any good, but at least it would stir up Maggie's new lover-boy. Lover, how he hated to think of him with Maggie. She would always be Peter's, he never gave up on his conjugal rights, and meant to take them back whenever possible.

Sergeant Wilks knocked at Nipper's office door.

'Excuse me, Guv. We've just had a tip off. Some bloke suggests we question a Stephen Pendle about the most recent murder. Apparently, he's been seen in the area, around the corner from the victim's house.'

Nipper frowned.

'Did the informant give his name?'

'No, only a brief message, then hung up from a public telephone.'

Nipper had been around too long to believe it might lead anywhere. It was probably some loser trying to get back at this Pendle fellow for some reason. However, it ought to be followed up.

'Trace him and invite him in for a routine interview but watch for his reaction. You had better take Sergeant Wilson with you, he has more experience in the field.'

Stephen sat in his office when his receptionist showed the two detectives in.

He, having no idea what it could be about, cheerfully invited the officers to take a seat.

Sergeant Wilks opened.

'We wonder if you wouldn't mind coming down to the station to answer a few questions, it's routine. Nothing to worry about.'

Stephen's mood changed abruptly.

'About what, exactly?'

Sergeant Wilson spoke softly, with a hint of kindness in his voice.

'Nothing to worry about, sir. Only a few questions about a recent incident. We think you might be able to help.'

Stephen glared at them.

'You might have read on the door that my profession is psychology. This sounds awfully like the good cop, bad cop routine. Just tell me what it's about and I can clear it up.'

'Down at the station would be better, sir. Less embarrassing.'

'For whom?' said an exasperated Stephen.

'For all of us, don't you think,' said Sergeant Wilson.

Stephen summoned his receptionist and told her to cancel his appointments for the rest of the day while he went with the detectives to clear up an obvious mistake. Nevertheless, it felt to him as if he were being arrested and no doubt Amanda, his receptionist, felt the same way.

While Stephen and the two officers descended the stairs to the waiting car, his receptionist became busy on the phone. Amanda belonged to a circle of fellow office workers and they loved sharing juicy gossip.

'Mr Pendle has just been carted off by two detectives,' she said to one of the group, 'I've no idea what it's about, but they were not leaving without him.'

At the station, Nipper looked across a table at Stephen. They were in an interview room and they told him everything would be recorded on video tape.

'Do I need to call my lawyer?' Stephen asked.

'I don't know, do you?' replied Nipper, the beginning of a smile touching the corner of his mouth.

'No, of course not. I haven't done anything,' replied Stephen, 'now what's this all about?'

Nipper calmy asked Stephen's movements at the time of the assault and murder of the housewife at Number 41 Elton Street.

The significance of the crime shocked Stephen.

'I wasn't anywhere near there on the date of the murder!' he exclaimed.

'Yes, but you are familiar with the area, aren't you?' said Nipper in the well-practiced manner of the experienced inquisitor.

'Certainly, I am seeing a lady in the next street,' he replied.

Nipper made a point of picking up his pen and sat, pen poised.

Stephen gave Maggie's address, his mind working furiously, trying to remember where he had been on the date of the killing.

'Call my receptionist,' he insisted, 'she will know exactly my appointments on that day.'

Nipper nodded to Wilks, who quickly left the room to issue instructions.

When he returned, Nipper smiled.

'Cup of tea?' he asked Stephen.

'Yes, please,' replied Stephen, having suddenly gone very dry in the mouth.

Nipper paused the tape, noting the time.

In a matter of minutes, a knock came at the interview room door and Sergeant Wilson walked in.

'A word please, Guv.'

Nipper left with him and as the door closed behind them, spoke.

'Well?'

'It's not him,' said Wilson, 'his appointments covered the entire day. He didn't even go out to lunch. The bugger must be making a mint.'

Nipper shrugged.

'I wonder if he knows who might have fingered him for the murder. Not a friend, that's for sure.'

'We're sorry if we have caused you any embarrassment or inconvenience,' said Nipper when they returned to the room.

Stephen felt relief wash over him like a cleansing warm wave.

'I wonder if you can think of anyone who might want to make an accusation against you?' asked Nipper.

'The caller, man or woman?' asked Stephen.

Nipper nodded his head slowly.

'Well, I shouldn't really say, but they appeared to have a low voice, if you get my drift.'

'If I think of anybody, I'll be bloody sure to let you know,' said Stephen.

As he left the office, Wilks made a comment to Nipper.

'The informant might be the one. He's trying to muddy the water.'

Nipper sighed.

'I love it when they get flustered and try to cover their tracks or point us in the wrong direction. It means he's worried, and a worried man is vulnerable.'

'Someone tried to pin that murder on me,' said Stephen.
Maggie went cold.
'I wonder who it could have been,' she replied quietly.
'If I ever find out.......' muttered Stephen.

Maggie stood in the light rain, watching the entrance to Peter's flat. She didn't want to confront him inside, she knew how violent he could be.

From the shelter of a brolly, she saw him come out. He wore a raincoat with a hat pulled low down, partially covering his face as if he feared being recognised.

She crossed the road and stopped, barring his way.

'You low mongrel,' she hissed, 'how could you, and did you believe for one moment I wouldn't guess.'

'What?' said Peter, trying to bluff it out.

'Stephen, that's what.'

'I don't know what you're talking about.'

'You called the police and gave them Stephen's name.'

Peter decided that attack would be the best form of defence.

'So what, you're still my wife as far as I'm concerned, and you shouldn't be seeing him.'

'Peter, we are divorced, get that through your thick skull. You have no more rights over me, not that you ever did. Marriage isn't ownership.'

Peter stared at Maggie.

'I still want my conjugal rights!'

At that moment, she knew he had crossed some line, his logic becoming skewed. He could no longer face reality.

'You're crazy!' she exclaimed, 'keep away from me or I'll be the one calling the police.'

Peter sensed his control slipping away. Anger began bubbling to the surface.

'You will always be mine,' he said.

Maggie knew it would be a waste of time arguing any further and turned to leave, adding, 'You've been warned.'

She didn't see the blow arrive. Peter's bunched fist caught her on the side of the head, sending her crashing to the wet pavement.

Stunned, Maggie lay still in a pool of blood gushing from her head, diluted by the still falling rain.

Shocked by his own actions, Peter ran off down the road. But not unnoticed. An elderly man walking in the opposite direction witnessed their confrontation and had already called for help on his mobile.

He knelt beside Maggie, not sure what to do. But she began to come to her senses and tried to get to her feet.

'Stay where you are miss, I've called for an ambulance and the police.'

Maggie sank back onto the wet pavement, grateful for the kind words and pleased that Peter had left.

Beyond caring about protecting Peter, Maggie gave the police a full account of her meeting with him, including the fact that she believed he phoned the police about the murder on Elton Street.

The young, uniformed constable duly reported the incident to his sergeant, who, in turn, sent the information upstairs to the detective section.

Eventually, it reached the ears of Detective Chief Inspector Nipper, who slapped his desk with glee. A rare occurrence that quickly attracted the attention of the rest of the team.

'Pull Peter Trowbridge in for questioning over the assault on his wife. Ask him for a DNA sample and see how he reacts.'

'You need to come down to the station over an alleged assault on your ex-wife,' said Sergeant Wilks to an apparently confused Peter. He hadn't been expecting a visit from the police, but when they appeared at his door, his insides turned to jelly. His greatest fear stood at the door in the shape of two detectives.

'She's lying, I never touched her, she won't leave me alone. I've told her countless times to stop, but she won't accept that our marriage is over.' Peter's tirade of bluster didn't impress the detectives.

'All the same, sir, it would be better if you came with us,' said Wilks, 'alternatively, we could simply arrest you if that's what you want.'

Peter quietened, picked up his coat and left with them, still mumbling about his ex-wife, who simply wouldn't take no for an answer.

Nipper sat in the interview room opposite Peter, calmly contemplating a shiny new HB pencil, turning it over and over.

'We have a witness who saw you strike your ex-wife, knocking her to the ground,' he said at last.

Peter maintained his silence, realising he for once had to stay calm.

'Did you make an anonymous call to the police about the recent murder in Elton Street?'

'No,' replied Peter, surprising himself with his own composure, 'I want a lawyer.'

'But you haven't been arrested, you're here helping us with our enquiries,' said Nipper, still delicately twiddling the pencil between thick fingers.

'Not anymore, I want a lawyer,' insisted Peter.

The pencil snapped with a loud crack. Nipper had been playing the good cop role, meaning to slip in the request for a DNA sample, but Peter had gone to ground too soon. He could hardly request a sample now.

Switching off the tape and noting the time, Nipper got up to leave.

'Cup of tea while you wait?' he asked.

'Thank you,' replied Peter, grateful for the lull in proceedings.

Nipper left the room.

'Get him some tea and a fucking lawyer. Try to get that weak twat we saw last week. He's new and we don't want anyone too smart on his side.'

Before the lawyer arrived, Peter's empty mug had been removed. Nipper insisted it be carried with one of his pencils through the handle.

'Get that off to the lab and check for DNA.'

Wilks popped the mug into a plastic bag but frowned with concern.

'Even if we get a match, we won't be able to use it. The courts won't accept evidence obtained illegally, and he hardly gave consent, did he?'

Nipper smiled,

'He will never give his consent after reading the article in the paper. This way, at least we'll know him to be at the scene of the murder and can lean on him a bit heavier.'

The lawyer arrived and, as Nipper hoped, it proved to be the young man recently admitted to the bar with the accompanying lack of experience.

'Mr Nopes, how nice of you to join us,' said Nipper with a smirk on his face.

Rodney Nopes shuddered. The presence of Detective Chief Inspector Nipper at the interview indicated something serious.

Chapter 34

Maggie tried to cover the bruise on one side of her face and the graze on the other where she had struck the pavement, but Stephen insisted on knowing what had happened.

'Silly bugger that I am. I slipped on the wet path, cannoned into a street sign and knocked myself out. When I came too, I found myself on the pavement, bleeding.' Maggie laughed.

Her cavalier attitude didn't fool Stephen.

'How about you tell me what really happened?'

'I did, that's what happened,' said Maggie in a voice that brooked no further discussion.

The couple spent the evening together, but things were strained. Maggie spoke lightly of mundane things while Stephen struggled to come to terms with the fact that Maggie had obviously been the victim of an assault but refused to come clean.

'Are you staying the night?' asked Maggie.

'No, I have an early morning appointment, so I had better make tracks,' replied Stephen.

The couple kissed at the door and Stephen left, the mood not being as convivial as normal.

He walked away with a worried frown, while Maggie's face darkened as she closed the door.

'What do you mean, you won't press charges?' said a bemused Detective Sergeant Wilson, 'you that made the original complaint.'

'Well, I don't want it to go any further,' insisted Maggie.

She stood at the front desk of the police station with the detective.

'Where do I have to sign?' she asked.

'You don't have to sign anything,' said Wilson, becoming

angry. They had wasted their time.

He couldn't resist adding, 'I suppose your ex may be right, he still expects his wife to obey.'

Maggie sensed the argument about to erupt and cut it short.

'Goodbye, sergeant and thank you for your understanding.'

'She's fucking crazy,' said Wilson in Nipper's office, 'the ex-husband bashes her and she lets him off.'

'They're all fucking crazy,' commented Nipper, 'are you married sergeant?'

'Yes, sir.'

'So am I, so we both understand, right?'

Wilson left the office, only to return seconds later, his face beaming.

'The DNA on chummy's mug came up trumps, it's a match.'

Nipper continued chewing on a pencil.

'He's in the frame, but we can't pull him in based on DNA that we obtained illegally.'

'That is so frustrating. We have the killer but can't touch him!' exclaimed Wilson.

'Detective Constable Wilmot appears to be chums with Maggie Trowbridge, get her in here for a word.'

'I believe you know Maggie Trowbridge,' said Nipper.

'Yes, sir, as a matter of fact, I'm renting the house next door,' said Jane.

'You know her ex-husband bashed her and she has now withdrawn the complaint. The trouble is, he's in the frame for the murder at Elton Street, and we can't lay a finger on him until, for some reason, he gets himself arrested.'

'So, you want me to try to convince her to press charges against him,' said Jane.

'Exactly,' replied Nipper, 'and the sooner the better.'

That evening, Jane appeared once more at Maggie's door with two bottles of wine.

'You'll turn me into an alcoholic at this rate,' joked Maggie, beckoning Jane inside.

After some time, Jane broached the question.

'Why did you drop the charges against your ex-hubby?'

Maggie, in spite of the amount of wine they had both consumed, became defensive.

'Because it would mean he's back in my life and that's the last thing I want.'

'I understand, but there is another reason why we would like you to proceed.'

'Which is?' said Maggie.

'Can't say,' said Jane, 'but it is important.'

Maggie thought for a while before speaking,

'No, I'm sorry, but I don't want to go there. I'm free of Peter and I intend for it to stay that way.'

'But he tried to implicate your friend, doesn't that make you mad?'

'That's what I mean. The more I involve him in my life, the harder it will be to break away.'

Jane played her ace.

'How about if he were in prison for a very long time, you would be free?'

Maggie stared at Jane across the table.

'Is that the other reason?'

'Yes, we can put him away so that he would never bother you again.'

The following day, Maggie walked into the police station and asked to see a detective.

Nipper almost tripped over his wastepaper basket in his eagerness to meet her.

'I've changed my mind, I want him charged, but you have to promise me I will be protected. My ex-husband can be extremely violent. He's hit me on more than one occasion, worse than the one I'm reporting.'

Nipper smiled, sensing victory.

'I'll have him arrested, charged, and detained in custody.'

Jane signed a complaint and followed through with the witness statement procedure. She embellished the facts with a little poetic license, making sure that Peter would be damned in the eyes of the police and, hopefully, the courts.

Peter opened his door to two detectives and two uniformed constables. Lost for words, he backed into his room, hotly pursued by the four officers. In moments, he stood securely handcuffed while one detective read him his rights. They were arresting him for grievous bodily harm, or GBH as the offence is known in police parlance.

Silent throughout the journey in the back of a police car, Peter finally found his voice at the police station.

'I suppose my bitch of an ex-wife put you up to this?'

Nipper ignored his jibes and proceeded to read out the charge.

'I want my lawyer again,' Peter's only reply.

Lawyer Rodney Nopes sat beside Peter in an interview room.

'The charge, I believe, is grievous bodily harm, so why did you take a sample of my client's DNA?'

Nipper stared at Nopes across the table, his eyes boring into the hapless lawyers own.

'It's customary for a charged offender to be photographed and fingerprinted. Your client also agreed to a DNA swab.'

'Is that what you did?' said Peter nervously, knowing the possible consequences.

Nopes turned his head to face Peter.

'Did they or didn't they ask if they could take a DNA swab?'

'I can't remember,' muttered Peter, 'I'm confused, there's so much going on.'

Nipper gave his most disarming smile.

'We had a rowdy bunch of Liverpool supporters in custody, apparently they don't like it when their team loses.'

Rodney Nopes couldn't hold Nipper's stare and looked down at the table.

What will be the bail arrangements, I assume my client will be released on his own recognizance.

'We intend to keep your client in custody for twenty-four hours, after that we can discuss bail arrangements,' said Nipper, smoothly.

The following day, after pressure had been exerted to hurry along the DNA results, Nipper once again sat before Peter in company with his lawyer, Rodney Nopes.

The night locked in a cell had done nothing for Peter's demeanour. He had spent the entire night awake, contemplating a lifetime in a similar cell along with other criminal types. How would he survive?

Nipper calmly read out the time, day and date of the murder of Rita Hemsworth.

'Where were you?'

'Can't remember,' said Peter, realising he now fought for his life. No death penalty existed in England, but the prospect of spending thirty years in prison is not a great deal better.

'The dead woman had been liberally sprinkled with your DNA, can you explain that?'

'No, it's not mine.'

Nipper stared into Peter's eyes for what seemed like minutes.

Peter crumbled, he couldn't bluff it out in the light of the incontrovertible evidence of DNA.

'Alright, I'll tell you exactly what happened, but I didn't kill her. She was alive when I left.'

Nopes began making notes as Peter tried to explain how he had run into the house and collided with the victim, temporarily knocking her out.

'Why did you run into the house in the first place?'

Peter blushed.

'I had been spying on my ex-wife, Maggie Trowbridge, she lives in the next street.'

'Why would you do that?'

'I wanted to see the bloke who's having her now,' he said, anger coming to the surface.

'And then?' said Nipper.

'This is very embarrassing,' said Peter.

'So is a murder charge,' replied Nipper savagely.

Peter's voice descended to a whisper.

'Louder for the tape,' urged Nipper.

'I pulled down her underwear and ejaculated over her,' said Peter, flushing red, and looking down at the table top.

'What made you do that?' asked Nipper.

'I don't know. It's a kind of uncontrollable urge, I suppose.'

'Do you often get these uncontrollable urges?'

'No.'

'Ever done it before?'

'Sometimes, when I was younger and my date had drank too much. But I never harmed them.'

'But this time it all went pear-shaped, didn't it?'

'No, that's all I did, I swear.'

Nipper paused just long enough for Peter to think he might be off the hook.

'But she woke up, didn't she? Looked up and saw you standing over her with your plonker hanging out? She tried to cry out and you couldn't have that, could you? So, you panicked and killed her.'

'No, I swear to you, I left before she woke up. It must have been someone else that killed her after I left.'

'Is that why you made the anonymous call to the police about Stephen Pendle? Do you think he did it?' said Nipper.

'It might have been,' said Peter uncertainly.

'Nonsense!' exclaimed Nipper, slapping the table and shocking Peter into sitting up straight.

'You wanted to finger him because he's the one seeing your ex-wife. Too hard to take, is it? That your ex-wife is seeing another man?'

Peter's rage built at the mention of Maggie with another man, a man who had taken his place in her bed.

'She's an unfaithful bitch!' he exclaimed, spittle escaping his mouth and spraying the table top.

Nipper leaned back in his chair, adopting a calm attitude.

'That's quite some temper you have there, Peter. You must have felt so bad when Rita woke to find you looming over her. That's what happened, isn't it, you lost your rag and killed her to cover your embarrassment?'

Peter began to sob.

'I didn't kill her.'

Nipper ended the taped session and told lawyer Nopes his client would be charged with the murder of Rita Hemsworth.

Nopes contributed by urging his client to say nothing more.

Nipper smiled at him.

'Bit late for that, don't you think?'

Peter, duly charged and remanded in custody pending a trial date, looked to his lawyer to apply for bail. However, owing to the seriousness of the charge, bail had been refused.

Later, in his office, Nipper called in the team.

'We got lucky with this one, but there are still the others. There is nothing linking chummy to any of them, so we still have another killer on the loose.'

As he sat in a cell awaiting trial for a vicious murder he didn't commit, Peter became even more depressed. Other inmates were not helpful. As a remand prisoner, he had been kept separate from those already convicted of various crimes, but it didn't stop them making verbal threats. Those making the threats looked as if they were more than capable of carrying them out, and Peter knew he would be in for a rough time if convicted.

His lawyer didn't help. Peter thought Nopes agreed with the police. He had no confidence that his defence would save him from a lengthy prison sentence.

He had no cellmate and left his own personal little prison twice a day to visit the exercise yard in company with others on remand.

Lawyer Nopes informed Peter the trial had been set down to be heard at The Old Bailey in eight weeks. Two months to stew in his own juices, to contemplate life in this place for the many years to come. But not alone. He would have the other inmates to contend with, and they would know what he had been convicted of. There would be no sympathy there.

Peter descended into a dark place. He lived with fits of temper at the injustice of it all and, in his eyes, Maggie's infidelity. At other times, he would lie on his bunk curled up like a child, sobbing.

He had not been listed as a suicide risk. Most inmates experienced a similar mind set over the period of their remand. Therefore, he had been afforded the minor luxury of sheets for his bunk.

They found him one morning hanging in his cell from a rough noose fashioned from a bedsheet. Peter had ended his life knowing it would happen at some time, so he might as well get it over with and avoid the pain of the trial. A foregone conclusion he would be convicted because no one would take his side.

'Fuck it!' exclaimed Nipper on hearing the news. He had been robbed of the glory of convicting a savage murderer. Peter had cheated him in the end.

Maggie appeared to take the tragic news in her stride. Stephen worried she might suffer some psychological trauma. However, she showed no signs of anything out of the ordinary.

Penny, on the other hand, withdrew into herself at the news of her former lover's death. Secretly, she had never believed him capable of such a gruesome murder. The sexual part she could accept. Peter had been capable of some minor perversions, but cutting someone up? Never.

Chapter 35

Maggie stamped her foot in anger.

'How could you? Penny is the last person you should be helping. You two were lovers, for Christ's sake.'

Stephen drew back at the strength of the tirade.

'She needs help from a professional perspective, that's all.'

'You are talking to another woman here. I'm well aware of her little game. Are you so blind?'

'I think you are being very uncharitable. Peter and Penny were very close for a while, and his sudden death has come as a shock.'

'They were very close until I came onto the scene, that's what you really mean, isn't it?'

'No, Maggie. You're overreacting.'

'Really? You and she were close, as you put it, until we met. Then you dumped her for me, just as Peter did. Can't you see she's trying to get back with you? She's using the distressed little girl act. And of course, like all men, you're falling for it.'

Stephen's annoyance showed in his face.

'I had better go, this is getting us nowhere.'

'Go, see if I care,' spat Maggie, as he turned to leave.

Without a backward glance, Stephen walked out into the street, furious.

That did nothing to assuage her anger and she slammed the door behind him.

Standing in the hallway for a moment to collect her thoughts, she wondered herself at the recent loss of her normal aplomb. She seemed more on edge lately.

The scream began from nowhere. Very quiet at first, the volume increased as Maggie looked down the hallway. The scream increased in pitch, forcing her to cover her ears.

It became so loud it affected her vision, blurring her eyes. At the end of the hallway, an outline appeared. She couldn't tell if the form was male or female. The scream didn't appear to be emanating from the figure, but now filled the entire house.

Reaching back for the doorhandle meant uncovering one ear, but she had no choice, she had to get out. As the door behind her pulled open, the figure rushed forward at speed.

Terrified, Maggie stepped over the threshold onto the pavement. The door slammed itself shut violently, the scream ending abruptly, leaving her with ringing ears.

'Are you okay?' said a voice beside her.

Maggie hadn't noticed anyone as she left the house, but standing beside her stood her neighbour, Jane.

As Maggie pulled herself together, she laughed nervously.

'The door slammed itself shut. Must have been a draught from the back door. Good job I didn't have my fingers in there.'

Jane reached for the doorknob and opened the door into the hallway.

'There, the draught must have been a gust of wind. It's fine now.'

Maggie tentatively poked her head inside.

'Quiet as the grave,' she said.

Jane thought that an odd thing to say but kept quiet. The house had been playing tricks again.

'I thought we could have a wine and I can bring you up to date on the local events,' suggested Jane.

'Good idea,' replied Maggie. A few glasses of wine would make things better, especially in Jane's company. Things always seemed to get better when she arrived.

Stephen had disappeared around the corner. Annoyed at her attitude, he made for home, looking forward to a quiet evening without the cloying attentions of women.

It wasn't to be. Standing outside his door with eyes puffed from crying stood the dejected form of Penny. Thinking her as not at her attractive best, he nevertheless invited her in. The caring psychologist element of his personality kicking in.

He knew it had been a mistake the moment she wrapped her

arms around him, crying and talking volubly about the sadness in her life.

'Nobody wants me,' she cried, 'perhaps I should end it all like Peter. At least he had the guts to leave this horrible life.'

Stephen sighed, here we go again, he thought. No wonder he spent one day a month in the company of another psychologist, unloading the burden of other people's grief. They all did that for each other, taking it in turns. Without this, they would soon succumb to their clients' woes, taking on their problems as their own. Once a month they flushed their minds clear, it had always been a necessity.

Settling Penny onto the settee, he sat opposite and began the routine of gently delving into her mind to free her from her troubles.

Stephen knew he shouldn't. It would have been sensible to refer her to a colleague. He being far too close to her.

The recent argument with Maggie didn't help. He felt he needed to talk that problem out with a professional, but here he sat, attempting to console someone else.

Penny came to the end of a bout of sobbing.

'Do you have anything to drink?' she asked pitiably.

Of course the answer should have been, no.

'Maybe one glass of wine might help you relax,' said Stephen.

'Please join me, I hate to drink alone,' said Penny.

Pouring two glasses of wine, he held out one for Penny, choosing to sit opposite, out of harm's way.

Penny sat herself further back in the chair and sipped the wine, emptying half the glass in seconds.

Stephen drank his wine as more of an escape, wondering how he could persuade her to leave him in peace.

Penny held her glass out.

'Perhaps one more?' she asked, measurably calmer than before.

Stephen topped up her glass and his own, still sitting opposite.

The wine settled on his empty stomach, making the world

a rosier place. He smiled at Penny. She smiled back, stretching languorously, and in doing so, managed to give him a glimpse of her thighs.

Stephen reached over to top up her glass and emptied the remainder of the bottle into his own.

He found himself warming to the situation and, draining his glass, got up to fetch another bottle.

Penny made no comment, merely sipping her wine as he opened the new bottle.

Still sitting opposite, he had refilled her glass, this time to the brim. She laughed as wine spilled onto her dress.

'Oops, I should soak this or the stain will never come out,' she said, draining the glass in one gulp.

Stephen drained his glass, feeling considerably the worse for wear, and merely nodded in agreement.

Penny, knowing she now stood on safe ground, swiftly slipped off the dress to stand in front of Stephen revealing her bra and panties.

Stephen groaned. Why, oh why, did he invite her in? It was bound to happen and he was unable to resist the temptation.

He reached out, gently brushing the back of his hand over her exposed stomach.

Penny sensually pulled her panties down to fully reveal herself.

All too much for Stephen, he put his arm around her waist and led her into the bedroom.

Penny woke up beside the man Maggie had usurped from her. Now she had him back. That would teach the bitch.

She compounded last night's tryst by attacking Stephen before he woke. She threw herself on top of him, using every trick in the book to get him aroused.

Penny couldn't resist phoning Maggie later that morning.
'Care for drinkies this evening?' she asked.
Maggie, at first, baulked at the suggestion but decided to find

out what had caused Penny's sudden euphoric change of mood.

'Sure, why not,' she said, attempting to match Penny's mood but falling short.

All day, Maggie wondered what lay behind her old friend's cheerfulness. Whatever it turned out to be wouldn't be good for Maggie, of that she felt certain. People like Penny held grudges, similar to Maggie herself and most women, if truth be known, she admitted.

True to her phone call, Penny arrived clutching the mandatory bottle of wine in one hand and an expensive greeting card in the other.

'Pour vous,' she said in a barely discernible french accent, handing Maggie the card.

Moving through to the kitchen, Maggie opened the card, a friendship card printed with gold lettering in Fairweather Script. The writing smacked of romance, and Maggie held back, waiting for Penny's little act to play out.

Filling two glasses, Maggie sat opposite.

'So, do tell, why so jolly?'

'Well, you won't believe it. I have no idea what happened between you and Stephen, but we spent the night together and it was wonderful. I'm sorry you two didn't work out, but all's well that ends well, as they say.'

Maggie sipped her drink, studying her erstwhile friend over the rim. Inside, she seethed.

'That's nice for you,' she said through pursed lips, sensing that Penny enjoyed her little victory.

Inside, she cursed both Penny and Stephen. Her for being spiteful and enjoying her revenge and Stephen for being stupid like most men in allowing his cock to rule his brain.

The evening proved to be the longest in living memory for Maggie. At last the wine had been finished and she didn't offer to open a second.

'Well, we should call it a night, I have things to do at work in the morning, and I want to be at my best.'

'Of course,' said Penny cheerily, I'll be off. 'I'm half expecting a call from Stephen later.'

The pair parted at the door. Maggie had to force herself not to slam it, her temper had been building silently all evening. As she climbed the stairs to her bedroom, still seething, she didn't notice the sudden drop in temperature.

Chapter 36

Nipper chewed the end of a new pencil like a hungry dog savaging a fresh bone.

'Caught one, lost one, and now some other sick bastard is at it.'

'Might be the same one who did the first two, same method except the new one isn't a prossie,' said Sergeant Jones.

'Well, in any event, we are back where we started. What's the location of the latest one?'

'Whitechapel, gutted from top to bottom. This time, whoever killed her cut her from her vagina to her throat. It isn't pretty. Her guts spilled out onto the pavement.'

'Jesus, who found her?'

'An early morning commuter, he's in hospital suffering from shock, and I don't blame him.'

'Did you see her?'

Jones paled.

'Yes, the uniforms called me first, I'm on call.'

'Did they establish an identity yet?'

'Yes, her handbag hadn't been interfered with. Her name is, or rather used to be, Penny Pickering.'

'Married?'

'Not sure, she wasn't wearing a ring, but these days that means nothing. Lots of married women choose not to wear a ring. Something about not wanting to be seen as being owned by a man.'

'Modern bullshit,' growled Nipper.

'My missus makes me wear a ring, maybe it works the other way around too,' said Jones, thoughtfully.

'I'm not looking forward to it, but we better get down to the autopsy,' said Nipper, heaving himself out of his chair and spitting the remnants of yet another HB pencil into the waste bin.

The text message read:

'You just couldn't wait, could you? No doubt we would have made up our little row, but you had to go and fuck Penny! Consider us finished!'

Stephen re read the message.

He wasn't happy. He really liked Maggie and thought they might have made it all the way, marriage even. His one slip had cost him dear. Knowing Penny, he guessed she would have been quick to spill the beans about their brief encounter. Not so brief, he acknowledged. They had spent the night in bed together.

After Penny left, he had spent an hour berating himself and his weakness. He should never have invited her in, despite her apparent distress at Peter's suicide.

Thinking about it in the cold light of day, he admitted she hadn't been that upset, successfully luring him into the bedroom. Her cries of ecstasy, real or acted for his benefit, didn't fit in with the recent loss of a loved one.

Too late, he realised Penny had deliberately set out to ruin his relationship with Maggie.

Well, she wouldn't be getting him back. He would phone her today and tell her under no circumstances would she ever darken his doorway again. The thought gave him no satisfaction. His relationship with Maggie appeared to be dead in the water, there would be no reconciliation.

The four men gathered around the body on the stainless-steel autopsy table, showed different reactions to the gory sight that lay before them.

The pathologist displayed his usual professionalism. The assistant, always slightly different in Nipper's view, wore a perpetual smile. Nipper's face remained impassive while Sergeant Jones looked very uncomfortable.

The body that used to be the vibrant Penny Pickering lay stretched out on the table with an ugly open gash from throat to pudenda. Her entrails lay outside her body, heaped in a pile beside her, still connected to her main organs inside.

As the procedure began, the pathologist cast a quick glance in Sergeant Jones' direction.

'Are you okay, sergeant? You've turned white as a sheet. Might be best if you wait outside.'

Jones moved away from the table. He had attended many autopsies in his career, but this one might get the better of him. He took the hint and moved towards the door.

However, he didn't quite make it and fell flat on his face, connecting with the unforgiving tiled floor.

The mortuary assistant helped him to his feet and led him outside, parking him on a bench. He left Jones with a box of tissues to wipe the blood off his face, giving him a cheery wave.

'I'd better get back in there, the doc is lost without me.'

Jones doubted that very much but didn't comment, he had met a few mortuary assistants in the course of his career and they all seemed a little odd. He guessed that it takes a certain disposition to attend to dead bodies on a daily basis. Jones thought the pathologist must have a similar outlook on life and death.

Meanwhile, the pathologist carried on with Nipper in attendance.

He spoke into an overhead microphone as he worked in an expressionless clinical voice.

'From the marks around her neck, I would say she has been strangled first before the killer used a very sharp knife or scalpel to inflict the injuries. The victim has been cut from her vulva to her throat, as if a sharp instrument has been inserted into her vaginal opening, then drawn upwards in a single deep cut.

On closer examination of the wound, I would suggest the instrument might be a scalpel. The entrails were roughly drawn from the body but all major organs appear to be intact. I would suggest that whoever did this might have acted in a fit of rage, and over in seconds. There is no evidence to suggest the victim had been killed to harvest her organs.'

Nipper raised his eyebrows at this, and the pathologist

switched off the microphone to elucidate further.

'In a few countries, especially Africa, people are killed for their organs to be sold to hospitals for organ transplants. These people are well organised and know how to remove the organs and store them in ice. Tragically, they work on an order basis, knowing exactly which organs to take.'

'Unfortunately, the other side of the trade is for parts used by witch doctors to make up their medicines or Muti. This practice has been commonplace for hundreds of years.'

He turned the microphone back on and continued the autopsy, removing the major organs to examine them in detail.

At the end of the procedure, everything removed, including the brain, together with the displaced entrails, were stuffed back inside the body cavity after which he sutured. It wasn't pretty, but it didn't have to be. The body would either be interred or cremated within days.

Chapter 37

Penny waved cheerily over her shoulder as she left Maggie standing in her doorway. She knew the hurt she had caused, but to her, it seemed justified. Maggie stole Stephen away, just as she had Peter. Now Peter lay dead and in a way she blamed Maggie for that, too. She strode down Petrie Street, and turning the corner, Penny almost broke out into song. She enjoyed the sweetness of revenge, how good it felt to pay Maggie back.

The tube station wasn't far and although the streets were deserted, she remained unafraid. That time when she thought she might be about to be attacked long since faded from memory. After all, the poor man copped a face full of pepper spray and, more than likely, probably innocent of any evil intention.

However, Penny's heart skipped a beat when she noticed a mist beginning to rise like before. The air definitely cooled considerably, and she shivered. She picked up the pace and walked as fast as possible. The tube station wouldn't be far away now, but the bloody mist had risen, so that vision became severely limited.

Penny glanced up, she wondered where the bright streetlamps were. Once again, the only feeble light she could see emanated from old-fashioned street lamps, the type that used gas.

Fearfully now, Penny began to trot, merely walking, much too slow to get her to the tube. It surely couldn't be much further.

She passed an unseen alleyway as a hand shot out, grabbing her around the throat. Another hand joined the first and she turned in horror to see a man's face staring at her. Even in her desperate state, she couldn't help noting that he wore a top hat and appeared to be clothed with a cape. The face snarled as the hands gripped even tighter.

Penny wanted desperately to scream, but nothing escaped the

stranger's grip. She slipped into blessed unconsciousness as the stranger lowered her to the ground. He maintained pressure on her throat until her open eyes glazed over in death.

Unclipping an old-fashioned black leather doctor's bag, the stranger reached inside for his long scalpel.

'Whore,' he yelled as he ripped at her clothes until she was fully exposed to the cold, misty night air.

In one movement, he inserted the scalpel into her vagina and pulled it all the way up to her throat, opening her body for its entire length. No eruption of blood ensued, as Penny had already succumbed to death. The stranger reached inside her abdomen and tore out coils of colon, dropping them beside the body.

'Serves you right, you whore. So may you all die.'

Walking swiftly away, the stranger pushed through the mist and disappeared.

Penny now lay sprawled grotesquely on the pavement in a bright circle of white light provided by the modern overhead LED streetlamps.

She lay there until the first early morning commuter, heading for the tube station, came upon the horrendous sight that used to be Penny Pickering.

Chapter 38

Maggie paled when she heard about the death so close to her home.

'The news reported the victim was a woman,' she said to her workmates at the office.

'Yes,' replied a young assistant, 'it's getting scary after the other two found in our projects.'

As she sat in front of the television, watching the evening news, Maggie dropped the plate of food she had been ferrying to the table.

'The victim has been named as Penny Pickering. Police have so far not revealed any details of the crime except that it is confirmed as murder,' said the newsreader.

Maggie stared at the mess on the floor, too shocked to clear it away. Instead, she poured herself a stiff drink and sat down to watch the rest of the news, although nothing registered. She could only think of poor Penny. The woman she had only last evening slammed the door on. Penny, she realised, must have been attacked shortly after leaving. Who, and furthermore, why, had she been attacked? The East End still held dangers for the unwary, but surely in this day and age such crimes were rare.

She thought back to the murdered woman found in her own projects. Maggie realised there could possibly be some connection. There were at present no details of the attack, but she would ask Jane at the earliest opportunity. The gruesome murder in the next street still played on her mind. The police maintained they had found the killer in that case, but had they? Whatever Peter's faults and they were many, she had been unable to view him as a killer. Especially as the protagonist in such a vicious murder.

Her thoughts recalled the time when Peter had accidentally cut his finger. It had been a deep cut, with blood spurting from the wound in an arc, spraying the surrounding floor. Maggie had only just managed to catch him as he fell in a dead faint. She didn't believe he would be capable of the bloody crime that Jane had described to her in the strictest of confidence. Peter would have been far too squeamish.

'Just as bad as the others,' said Jane.

Maggie sipped her wine.

'We think it may be the same killer,' Jane added.

Maggie replied thoughtfully.

'So, poor Peter, bumbling idiot that he may have been, probably didn't commit the murder on Elton Street.'

Jane looked down at her glass in embarrassment.

'Perhaps. Although the evidence leaned heavily towards him. Especially with the victim having his DNA all over her.'

'That makes him a pervert, not a killer,' replied Maggie, forcefully.

Jane acknowledged that with a nod.

'It's a shame he killed himself.'

Maggie drained her glass.

'More than a shame, it's a bloody disaster. The police got it wrong once again!'

Jane squirmed in her chair. She hated it when the force came under criticism but could hardly defend it in this case. Peter had decided to end his life because the police had left no doubt in his mind that he would be convicted and sent to prison for a very long time. He had known he would never survive in a prison environment.

'Explain Penny's death, what exactly did the killer do to her?' asked Maggie, 'did he rape her?'

Jane gratefully accepted the proffered top up to her glass.

'No, there wasn't any sexual contact. She had been strangled before being cut.'

'Cut?' said Maggie, wanting more of an explanation.

'I can't really tell you all the details, it's more than my job is worth. The media mustn't get hold of the details, far too gory for the general public,'

'Only between us, then. You know you can trust me to be discreet.'

Jane hesitated before continuing.

'She has been cut all the way down her body and her intestines pulled out.'

Maggie blanched.

'That must have been terrifying for Penny.'

'Horrific to look at, but at least the poor woman had been killed before that happened.'

'The killer must be completely insensitive. A psychopath,' said Maggie, 'Jack the Ripper must have been like that.'

Jane's eyebrows lifted in surprise.

'Why would you bring that up? Whoever he may have been, he would have been dead for years now.'

'But evil perpetuates throughout time,' said Maggie.

'On that rather disturbing note, I'll say goodnight,' said Jane, forcing a smile.

'Before you go, did you hear any more about next door? The empty house that I didn't find so empty.'

'No,' said Jane, 'but it's odd that you are apparently the only person to see the old couple. I've asked around, but everybody seems to believe the place has been empty for years.'

Maggie looked at Jane quizzically, but she looked away quickly. How could she tell Maggie about the figure at the top of the stairs next door? Even worse, how would she explain the girl in Maggie's back bedroom? Jane had the 'gift' from childhood, but never discussed it. People would think her crazy.

Days passed until the following week a large bunch of flowers arrived by messenger. The arrangement so big it barely fitted through the door of Number 15.

Maggie carried the flowers through to the kitchen, where she spotted the note lodged in between a collection of stems. They were from Stephen. The note had been carefully written in old English characters.

I'm sorry, how can I make it okay between us? S.

Maggie put the flowers in water. They were far too nice to throw in the bin. She dialled his mobile.

He must have been sitting on it because it only rang twice.

'Hello, you got the flowers. Can we at least be friends?'

Maggie paused before replying.

'Stephen, believe it or not, I understand the way a man's mind works. I accept that Penny would be hard to resist, but like most men, you have very little control.'

'Ouch,' said Stephen.

'However, what's done is done and we can't go back to how it used to be between us,' said Maggie, 'besides the poor woman is lying in a fridge somewhere and you are trying to come back to me. Don't you think that is a little odd, psychologically speaking?'

Stephen stayed silent, wincing at the rebuke and secretly acknowledging the truth in what Maggie said. It smacked of complete insensitivity on his part.

'To try merely to be friends might be difficult. Let's leave it the way it is, no hard feelings, but we both need to move on,' said Maggie.

Stephen, reluctant to admit defeat, nevertheless understood Maggie's logic.

'Okay. But I live in hope,' he said.

'Bye,' said Maggie, ending the call, worried that he might not be so easy to lose.

The next morning, she came out of a deep sleep to a thunderous noise coming from the apparently empty house next door.

As she peered out her bedroom window, Maggie saw a group of workmen standing outside.

Dressing rapidly, she opened her front door to investigate.

'We're fixing up the house,' one workman offered.

'Has it been purchased?' Maggie asked.

'Buggered if I know,' replied the man, 'we've been sent in to get rid of the junk and redecorate.'

Maggie wondered if any of the workmen would come up against Ada and Ernie. She would, no doubt, hear the yells if they did.

However, the work proceeded with gusto, and soon the skip stationed in the street began to fill with the old couple's belongings destined no doubt for the rubbish tip.

Over the following few days, the workmen transformed the house. Maggie, unable to resist the temptation, asked if she might take a quick look inside.

She couldn't believe her eyes. The house has been completely revamped. Every wall and ceiling had been painted white. Polished timber flooring featured in every ground floor room. Upstairs, Maggie went into each of the two bedrooms to find the same whiteness. The floors, though, were carpeted in the finest weave, and she couldn't help but be impressed. The new owners were certainly not poor, she guessed, but why, if that were the case, would they choose Petrie Street in the East End?

Her inquisitive mind had its answer the following week. Again, awakened by loud noises from next door, she saw a large removalist van parked outside.

A hurried breakfast found Maggie hanging out of her door, watching the removalists carry in what looked to be new and expensive furniture. She realised with an inward laugh that she had become a nosy neighbour. This is how it must have been years ago when the street had been entirely tenanted with workers and their families.

An older man appeared to be supervising, and Maggie smiled at him.

'Are you, by any chance, my new neighbour?'

'Sure am, love,' replied the man in a strong Cockney accent.

'Well,' said Maggie, 'if we are to be neighbours let me introduce myself, I'm Maggie Trowbridge.'

'William Dennis, but friends call me Billy,' said the man.

'Hopefully, I will be able to call you Billy,' laughed Maggie.

Billy looked approvingly at her.

'Sure, Maggie, and I must say I couldn't wish for a better welcome.'

Maggie flushed at the brazen compliment from a stranger and retreated inside.

That evening, Jane arrived, wine bottle in hand as usual, becoming quite a habit.

'I suppose you want to know about the new neighbour?' laughed Maggie.

'Yes, is he good looking?'

'In a mature way, but I don't know if he's available. Probably married with grown up kids,' smiled Maggie.

The couple demolished two bottles of wine while fantasising about their handsome new neighbour before calling it a night. Jane said she would see herself out while Maggie washed the glasses. At the foot of the stairs, Jane glanced up. Standing at the top of the stairs were Daisy, Ada, and Ernie. Jane smiled up at them and they smiled back.

It's becoming a little crowded up there, she decided as she closed Maggie's door behind her.

Jane's chequered past had taught her to trust no one, compounded by her role as a detective constable. She had developed the famous 'Copper's nose,' that built-in instinct that never left, even after retirement. 'Once a copper, always a copper,' held true for all those past and present that referred to the police force as 'The Job.'

'Ever come across a Billy Dennis in your travels?' she asked Detective Sergeant Nelson.

'Have I ever,' he replied. He's a nasty piece of work, that one. Fancies himself as a latter-day Kray. You know, the Kray twins. They were gangsters here in the East End in the fifties and sixties until they were both banged up in 1969 for murder. Reggie Kray, a right handful and his twin brother Ronnie, mad as a hatter.

Jane told Nelson that Billy had moved in next door and looked like being her new neighbour.

'He's not short of money. I wonder why he's bought local?' he remarked.

'Maybe he's homesick,' laughed Jane.

'He's sick all right; be careful. If he gets wind that you're police, things might get a bit sticky for you. He's not shy of giving the girls a bit of a touch up, in the violent sense, I mean.'

Jane couldn't wait to tell Maggie that Mr Wonderful wasn't as he seemed, and it would be better if she avoided him.

Chapter 39

Billy Dennis sat in his newly decorated living room, looking around with a satisfied grin. He could afford to buy the whole street, but this was the old house where he grew up. He recalled how, as a young kid, how he sat in the same room amongst the filth and battered furniture, knowing no different.

His hands curled into fists as he remembered the first slap given to him by his irate father. Billy had been punched by a neighbourhood boy a year or two older than himself and sported the beginnings of a black eye. He approached his father in tears, hoping in vain for sympathy. Instead, his father slapped the side of his head.

'Learn to fight for yourself, you'll get no sympathy from me!' his father exclaimed, 'it's a tough world out there. Never take a backward step, it's kill or be killed and the sooner you understand that the better.'

Billy lived with his mother, father, and older sister, Kate. But they shared the rented house with his mum's father and mother, Ernie and Ada. The house never seemed to be quiet and neither woman appeared keen on housework, so the extended family lived in what could only be described as squalor.

Raised voices were usually a prelude to an argument that ultimately ended in blows. He couldn't recall seeing his mother without a bruise or abrasions on her face and grew to accept it as part of family life. Billy copped a few hidings from other boys but never again sought out his father for solace. He remembered his words, 'Never take a backward step,' and did exactly that. He would either win the fight or end up badly beaten. As time moved on, he began to win more than he lost, building himself a reputation for tenacity, and violence.

As he entered his teenage years, Billy Dennis began to wish

for a better life. He and his mates once ventured up west to the posher parts of London. There they witnessed how the other half lived, and Billy decided he would never be an ordinary run-of-the-mill worker living in perpetual hardship like his family.

His father worked as a stevedore in the docks, drank heavily and lived the life of his own father before him.

Friday nights, Billy avoided his father like the plague. Pay day, and his father went straight from work to the pub. After time had been called, his father would turn out of the pub with all his mates and stagger home, where he would throw the remainder of his wages on the kitchen table. That would have to pay the rent and provide the family with food for the coming week. Quite often there wouldn't be enough, and his mum would collect the coins and the odd note with a sullen look.

'What's wrong with you?' his dad would shout, 'miserable cow!'

His mum would remain quiet, knowing that anything she said would only increase her chances of receiving a beating. Nine times out of ten, his dad would belt her, anyway.

'Get upstairs and earn your bed and board,' he would yell loudly.

His mum would obey rather than be belted again, and Billy would have to wait patiently downstairs.

The East End had always been rough and tough, but in the fifties, gangs began to appear. Many battle-hardened returned soldiers didn't adapt to peacetime life. For most of their adult life, they only knew war. Although the danger of imminent death had never far away, they didn't have to work as such. On de-mob, the government gave them a few shillings and a suit. Not much to show for years of risking their lives so the fat cats at home could prosper.

There were those that never went off to war. Many were fit and able to serve but chose to seek deferment owing to some made-up health problem. The black market thrived with food and just about anything else that became harder to obtain as the war dragged on.

Many of those young men that avoided fighting slipped into gangs specialising in supplying goods this way.

After the war ended, the gangs became more organised. As goods became more readily available, they were forced to seek other means of making easy money. Prostitution and protection became their forte. The girls were run like a smooth business and any that stepped out of line were dealt with harshly. Protection worked by offering to provide the service to any business and worked on the premise that the business proprietor could count on them for protection against pilfering and robbery. Naturally, if they refused to pay for the offered service, bad things would happen to them personally and to their business premises. Most agreed to pay after a few shops suffered mishaps with fire and burnt to the ground.

Through natural selection, leaders rose through the rank to be crime bosses. Two of the more infamous were twin brothers, Ronnie and Reggie Kray. For some twenty years they reigned supreme, gradually moving from the East End to the upmarket areas of the West End. They rubbed shoulders with entertainment celebrities and lawyers, even the odd judge who frequented their casino and the various clubs they controlled.

Eventually, the pair were both convicted of separate murders and spent the rest of their lives in prison. However, in the East End, the Kray twins were still revered as latter-day Robin Hoods; always good for a handout to those ordinary working classes who might be doing it tough, and never asked for repayment.

Many would-be gangsters modelled themselves on the Krays, and Billy Dennis proved to be one of the more successful imitators. He absorbed many small gangs into his own operation after their leaders mysteriously disappeared, and now reigned supreme in the East End. He never bothered to make the move up West, preferring to stay where he fitted in. The owner of several prestige riverside apartments in the newly remodelled Docklands area, he nevertheless craved the smallness of his boyhood home.

When in his early twenties, Billy witnessed the final time his father bashed his long-suffering mother. It happened one Friday evening after his father, true to form, walked noisily into the house in Petrie Street. Billy had been upstairs and heard the shrieks of anguish from his mother. Rushing downstairs, he saw his mother laying on the floor with his father standing over her, fists bunched.

Billy didn't hesitate. A much smaller version of his father, he would be no match for him in a fistfight, but instead drew the long thin-bladed knife he always carried and stabbed his father in the back. The blade, angled upwards, entered his heart, killing him instantly.

His mother remained on the floor lying beside her dead husband, her mouth in a rictus of a scream but not emitting any sound.

Old Ernie and Ada sat in their usual chairs in front of the one-bar electric fire, nodding their heads sagely.

'He had that coming,' said Ernie.

'Serves the bastard right,' agreed Ada.

'Everybody stay calm,' said Billy, 'I'll take care of this.'

A few phone calls later, and his father had been removed from the house. His body never to be found.

Billy arranged and paid for a long holiday in Spain for his mother. His sister, Kate, would accompany her. Their every need would be met for the rest of their lives, with the strict proviso that his mother never return home or mention her husband to anyone.

That left the old couple. Billy knew he could count on their silence, they were old-school. They hated the way Eddy treated both them and their daughter. They would stay in the house, all expenses paid. Billy arranged to buy the house from the landlord. He bought it for a good price because the landlord knew better than to argue with the top gangster in the area.

'All sorted,' said Billy as he swaggered out of his old house for the final time. Ada and Ernie waved goodbye. They would miss their grandson.

Billy continued on his journey to become the top dog in the East End while the old couple stayed on in the house. They were rarely seen outside, preferring their own company.

Years later, Ada became gravely ill. She refused to go into hospital, saying she would die in the house where she spent the best part of her life. Ernie did his best to look after her, climbing the stairs hundreds of times to care for his wife.

One night, standing beside the bed, holding a bowl of Ada's favourite tomato soup, Ernie looked down at his wife with a feeling of dread. He lived with the expectation of her demise for months, but now that her time had come, he became distraught.

He placed the soup gently on the bedside table, and lay down beside her, embracing her still form for the last time. He cried as he kissed her already cooling face and pulled the covers over the two of them. He had nothing left to live for. Ernie suffered what is commonly called broken heart syndrome.

The clinical name is Takotsubo Cardiomyopathy, generally not fatal. However, Ernie's age and his deep pain at having lost the love of his life saw him drift off into a sleep from which he would never wake.

A neighbour alerted police because the old couple hadn't been seen for weeks. When officers broke in, they found the couple dead in bed.

The owner of the house had been contacted, and when the police learned it was Billy Dennis, they suspected foul play.

Billy, genuinely saddened at the old couple's passing, had been exonerated of any wrong doing but never returned to the house, leaving it locked up and ostensibly abandoned for years.

Now, here he sat. Back to where it all began. As he made his way upstairs for the first night in his old home, the old couple smiled to each other.

'Nice to have Billy back home,' said Ada.

'Back where he belongs,' agreed Ernie.

Chapter 40

Maggie's face fell when Jane cautioned her about the handsome new neighbour.

'That's a shame, he's easy on the eye,' she said.

'Don't be taken in by the good looks, our Billy has quite a reputation with us,' said Jane.

'Is he married?' asked Maggie.

'No, but that makes no difference. He's a free agent with plenty to pick from in the circles he chooses to move in.'

Maggie couldn't help showing her disappointment.

'I'm not having much luck with men,' she lamented.

Jane laughed.

'You and me both. My choices of men have never lifted above bad, actually, downright rotten would be a better description.'

The two women toasted each other,

'Here's to, mister perfect.'

'We need two of them, now, one each,' laughed Maggie.

Days passed without any interruption to Maggie's nights. She began sleeping without the fear of being woken by strange noises and those frightening screams.

Arriving home after dusk, she turned the key in her lock as Billy opened his door.

'Hello, lovely,' he joked.

'Hi, neighbour,' said Maggie.

'Eating alone, or would you care to join me? I'm going up West to a lovely little Italian restaurant?' Billy asked, boldly.

Taken aback, Maggie wasn't sure how to answer, but the idea of a meal being cooked for her appealed, she hadn't eaten all day.

Making a quick decision, she nodded.

'Give me a minute to make myself decent.'

Billy smiled, his face showing the beatific smile that his friends loved and enemies feared. The smile hid Billy's true feelings, giving nothing away.

Maggie, like most women, experienced an inner glow at the smile. Her insides twisted with the now rare experience of sexual excitement.

It had been some time since her relationship with Stephen had soured, and since then, she had met nobody that came close. Until now, and despite Jane's well-meaning warnings, Maggie's heart and needs betrayed her.

By the time she freshened up, a cab stood at the door, engine idling as Billy stood holding the door open for her.

The cab drew away from the kerb as Jane walked past. Maggie didn't see her, engrossed in idle chatter with Billy, but Jane stopped in her tracks, shaking her head from side to side in silent admonishment.

'This will end in tears,' she said aloud.

The evening proved to be a total success. Jane hadn't enjoyed herself so much for ages. Billy appeared not to have a serious bone in his body. The night passed with Billy cracking jokes and ordering the best the restaurant could supply. French Champagne, served by a snooty waiter who Billy assured had been no closer to Italy than Marble Arch.

However, the food had been truly delicious, complemented by premium Italian wine. At the end of dessert, Maggie felt a little squiffy. Try as she might, everything appeared to have a double until she closed one eye.

Billy held open the cab door.

'Your carriage awaits, my lady,' he joked.

Billy's ability to hold his liquor had been developed over many years. Still feeling sober, he lightly touched Maggie's hand.

'Bed for you,' he quipped.

Maggie raised an eyebrow.

'Alone,' said Billy meaningfully.

True to his word, Billy helped her inside Number 15 and propelled her upstairs. He sat her on the bed and turned to leave.

Maggie's snores made him laugh,

'Another time, Princess,' he said quietly.

'How did the date go?' asked Jane the following evening.

'Perfect,' replied Maggie, 'I got a little drunk, but he remained the perfect gentleman.'

'You mean.......'

'I mean, he is the perfect gentleman. Billy helped me up to my bedroom and left me to sleep it off.'

'Well, I never,' said Jane, 'perhaps the boys in the squad have it all wrong.'

She doubted that, but for now felt it better to let Maggie have her moment.

Next door had been quiet for a week, and Maggie wondered if Billy might have moved on. Maybe he intended to sell the place after renovating.

She began to prepare an early dinner when a knock at the door interrupted.

Billy stood there, all smiles.

'Hello, Princess. Fancy another night out?'

Maggie explained that she had almost finished preparing a meal, but more than enough for two if he would care to join her.

An hour later, they sat in front of their plates together with an empty wine bottle. Maggie turned the lights down to set a more convivial mood and Billy relaxed in his chair, jacket draped over the back.

The age difference had certainly not escaped Maggie, she guessed Billy would be at least twenty years older if not more than herself. That part didn't worry her, but she wondered if Billy had been married or perhaps was still married. Jane said he wasn't, but perhaps she had been wrong, and did he have children?

He caught her looking at him.

'That's a very thoughtful look.'

'Sorry, I didn't mean to stare,' said Maggie, blushing.

'I think I can guess what you're thinking. I'm not married,

never have been and I don't have any kids. My life has been busy enough without that.'

'Sorry, I didn't mean to pry,' said Maggie, flushing red with embarrassment.

Billy laughed.

'That's okay, and in case you're wondering, I'm considerably older than you.'

'That doesn't bother me in the least,' said Maggie, with a touch of eagerness that she instantly regretted.

'How about I slip next door and get us a nice bottle of red?' suggested Billy.

Maggie guessed he normally drank better quality wine than she could offer and laughed.

'Okay, that sounds good.'

While Billy went next door, Maggie opened up the living room and lit the gas fire. It would be more comfortable than sitting in the kitchen cum dining room.

Billy walked into the warm room carrying two bottles of wine.

'In case we develop a thirst,' he laughed.

Inevitably, they ended up sitting together on the sofa. As the wine flowed, they laughed and joked until Billy made his move. Maggie felt perfectly safe since their first evening out when he looked after her. He never attempted to take advantage of her inebriated state, which impressed her no end.

However, Billy Dennis made a lifetime career of seducing women. He knew that patience offered the key to success. He bedded so many women that the sexual thrill had long since ebbed. He craved the pursuit now, far more satisfying. If a woman refused his advances, so much the better; he loved a challenge.

'I love your perfume,' he said, moving his face into Maggie's neck.

'I'm not wearing any,' said Maggie.

'So much the better, you could bottle your own and make a fortune,' said Billy smoothly.

For a reason that Maggie couldn't understand, she now began

to feel uncomfortable. The man sitting close to her changed from being the perfect gentleman to something a little creepy. She tried to move away, but his hand around her waist became insistent.

'We really should call it a night, I have to get into the office early tomorrow,' said Maggie, knowing how lame that sounded.

'Nonsense, we have another bottle of red to polish off first,' said Billy.

Maggie tried to placate him.

'Well, maybe just finish this one and save the other for next time,' she said.

Billy reached over for the bottle and poured her another glass, emptying the bottle.

'That's a good idea,' he said.

Maggie turned her head away as he nuzzled her neck, so didn't notice the small pill Billy covertly dropped into her glass. The pill dissolved immediately and as she sipped, had no idea her drink had been spiked.

The remainder of the evening remained a mystery to Maggie. It became like a bad dream. She vaguely remembered the room spinning slowly and strange sounds that she couldn't make out.

However, she awoke upstairs in her bed. Raising the covers, she saw she still had all her clothes on. Her head thumped rhythmically to the beat of her heart, and her mouth felt parched.

She got out of bed and looked at the clock, dimly aware it registered almost noon. Fortunately, the story about her early office appointment had been a white lie.

Struggling out from under the covers, she examined her clothes for any signs of interference. There were none.

She undressed and went into the bathroom to wash. At that point, she noticed bruising around her upper thighs.

Maggie sank down onto the closed toilet seat, trying to remember what happened the previous night.

Downstairs, the living room appeared tidy and a bottle of

red wine adorned the glass-topped coffee table, together with a single long-stemmed red rose.

Maggie felt far from being thrilled at the gesture. It had been obvious during her shower that Billy had used her sexually at some point in the evening, and the rose merely compounded his deceit.

Billy disappeared yet again and a week passed before Maggie confronted him with the events of their last meeting. She knocked on his door and when he opened it, wreathed in smiles, she stormed inside.

'Exactly who the hell do you think you are? You took advantage of me last week and don't try to deny it.'

Billy's smile broadened.

'Don't get the hump, Princess, you enjoyed it as much as me.'

Maggie's fury bubbled to the surface.

'I can have you arrested for rape!' she exclaimed loudly.

'What rape, you started it by groping me,' said Billy cheerfully.

His attitude compounded her anger.

'No, I most certainly did not,' she said.

'Remember it well, do you?' he said with a sly wink.

The penny dropped, and Maggie saw red.

'You bastard, you drugged me!'

'Prove it,' he laughed, 'be a bit difficult after a week, Princess.'

Maggie, left speechless, realised it would be impossible to prove. Any test for drugs would be pointless after a week. That's why he absented himself, to cover his tracks.

'How about we start that nice bottle of red I left at your place last week?' said Billy, he enjoyed a challenge and knew with this one he couldn't lose. After a week, there would be absolutely no evidence. He hadn't even bothered to use protection, taking care of that many years before, paying handsomely for a vasectomy at a private clinic.

Maggie slapped him hard before storming out of his house. Billy put a hand to his reddening cheek.

'Another notch on the bedpost,' he said, the trademark smile disappearing, 'the stupid bitches never learn.'

Chapter 41

Billy stayed away for the following month. It would give his neighbour time to calm down. He considered doing the same thing with the other neighbour, Jane, but when he found out about her job, he changed his mind. It would, of course, have been the ultimate challenge, shagging one of the filth, as the police were known in the local vernacular.

The residents on the other side represented no interest to him. A middle-aged couple who were both highly unattractive. Billy possessed some standards, arguably not very high, but just the same, he had to draw the line somewhere.

He stayed instead in one of the plush new apartments reconstructed from old dockside warehouses. West India Docks Road used to be a hive of activity when a working dock. Warehouses lined the dockside and had been standing for almost a hundred years. Now, though, they represented the newest status symbol and didn't come cheap.

Billy, one of the first buyers, selected an apartment in a prime position overlooking the River Thames. Paradoxically, the flats were designed by Maggie's firm.

After one month, he decided it should be calm enough in Petrie Street for him to return, and as dusk fell began the journey back to his old home. He decided the walk would do him good, too much of the high life beginning to slow him down. No longer a young man, he concentrated on his fitness, determined to reach old age in better shape than most. After a lifetime of shady dealings, he had amassed a fortune with no one to leave it to. The irony didn't escape him. In some respects, his life turned out to be a total waste.

Billy carried his small Louis Vuitton overnight case and left the apartment. He wore clothes to complement his bag, knowing that without quality matching gear, everyone would assume the expensive bag a cheap copy from China. Unfortunately, as soon as Billy opened his mouth, that assumption would be made, anyway.

All in all, he was happy with his life. His enemies were tucked away where nobody would ever find them and he ruled the East End, comfortable in the knowledge he had become unassailable.

Making his way towards Petrie Street, Billy walked slowly. Nobody dared touch Billy Dennis. The local villains knew him both by sight and reputation. Small bands of petty criminals were controlled by larger groups, that were controlled in turn by larger gangs, but all ultimately led to Billy. He represented the kingpin behind all organised crime in the area. In the old days, he always employed minders. Tough men who would accompany him everywhere, forming a protective ring. Now, though, he rarely bothered. There were no competitors, all having been dealt with long ago.

He knew every street in the area and soon found himself close to his new home. Night fell unexpectedly fast, must mean more bloody rain, he supposed. He picked up the pace, not wanting to be caught in the rain with his expensive get-up.

A chill sprung up, but without a breeze to accompany it. Looking down, Billy wondered at the mist around his feet. It appeared to be increasing, moving up from the ground gradually encompassing him completely.

His sight, now limited, obliged him to peer through the gloom. What happened to the street lights he wondered? They used to be as bright as daylight. Now, he passed ancient looking green cast-iron lamps that hissed with the gas powering them. The dim yellow light battling unsuccessfully to light his way.

For the first time in many years, Billy felt the first tingling of fear. He sensed danger and turned his head constantly, searching for any threat.

A refined, educated male voice came from the mist.

'Can you please direct me to Buck's Row?'

Billy stared into the mist, trying to make out the man, but the mist seemed to cover him from head to toe.

'I'm sorry, I've never heard of it, and I know every street around these parts,' said Billy.

Out of the mist emerged a pale hand. He saw the glint of steel as something incredibly sharp stabbed into his throat. The blade passed through his throat to exit from the back of his neck. Standing stock still, Billy stayed on his feet as the shock of what happened made its way into his senses. The blade, swiftly withdrawn, struck Billy once again in the throat, but this time at an upward angle, piercing the roof of his mouth before stabbing into his brain. Billy sank to his knees, instantly dead from the blow.

The stranger walked away, still shrouded in mist as Billy lay dead on the pavement. In seconds, Billy became illuminated in the harsh, white glow of the overhead street lights. The mist completely gone, leaving Billy lying in full view like an actor at centre stage.

Screams rent the air as commuters returning home came across the bloodied corpse. Police arrived and set up a crime scene. The untouchable Billy Dennis had been murdered.

Jane knocked on Maggie's door.

'I don't suppose you've seen your handsome neighbour lately?' she asked.

'No, actually, I haven't even heard from him in a month,' replied Maggie truthfully.

She never mentioned Billy's attack. Something she now wanted to forget. If she told Jane, no doubt the rest of the police force would soon know that Maggie Trowbridge had been forced to have sex with the East End's most notorious gangster. A few would offer sympathy, while most would wonder if Maggie brought it on herself.

Jane raised an eyebrow.

'Are you sure nothing happened between you two?' she asked suspiciously.

'Nothing,' replied Maggie, 'he is the perfect gentleman. Why all the questions?'

'Billy Dennis was murdered this evening, not far from here.'

Maggie paled.

'That's terrible.'

Jane left without the customary glass of wine. She needed to remain alert. The murderer could well still be in the area.

Maggie didn't have any such reservations, and quickly uncorked a bottle of white. Sitting in the kitchen, she drank quickly, recalling that night with Billy, the night that remained only a hazy memory.

Wine spilled from her glass as the piercing scream broke the silence. It had been absent for quite a while and its re-emergence stunned Maggie. It built to a crescendo, the noise became unbearable and Maggie rushed along the hallway onto the street outside. As usual, the scream ended abruptly as soon as her feet hit the pavement outside her front door.

Two days later, a knock at her door revealed a large bunch of fresh flowers carried by a smiling Stephen.

'I thought you might need a little cheering up.'

Chapter 42

The flowers stood between them on the kitchen table.

'What made you choose now?' asked Maggie.

'I don't give up easily,' said Stephen, 'I really like you, Maggie, and I'm sorry for what happened.'

Maggie felt weary. The events of the past two days left her rather fragile, and Stephen's arrival at the door seemed propitious. A shoulder to cry on would be most welcome.

'I heard what happened to your neighbour, rumour has it that it may have been some kind of gangland killing.'

'That's what the police think,' said Maggie.

'What was he like?' asked Stephen.

'He seemed nice at first, but I think underneath the façade, Billy might have been all bad. He probably got what he deserved.'

Maggie couldn't help emphasising the final phrase, still smarting from Billy's assault.

Stephen reached across the table for Maggie's hand, but as his fingers touched hers, she drew away quickly.

'Perhaps we can at least be friends,' said Stephen.

'Maybe friends,' replied Maggie, 'but nothing else.'

Stephen sat back in the chair as if he had been slapped. Rejection is always hard to suffer, but in Stephen's case, it brought back suppressed memories.

Coming from an underprivileged background made it difficult for any bright student to rise above their station in life. Stephen Stoppard had been a prime example.

Stephen's life, always tough in the East End, had been exacerbated by his father, Frederick, who always carried a chip on his shoulder which had passed down through generations of Stoppard's. Frederick Stoppard had to live with the shame of his own grandfather's execution.

Percy Stoppard had been convicted of a policeman's murder in 1924 and hanged. But the Stoppard family never believed in his guilt. Percy wrote to his wife on the day of his execution pleading his innocence and naming one of the Pickering kids, Keith, as the likely killer. That scrap of paper, handed down from generation to generation, now belonged to Stephen.

It meant nothing now, of course. Time moved on and most people forgot about that old crime. Except for the Stoppard family, they were forced to wear the stain of having a murderer in the family.

Stephen excelled at school, winning a scholarship to university. After earning an honours degree, he set up practice and became a successful psychologist.

Enamoured with Penny from their first meeting, it took some time before her surname clicked in his memory. It didn't take too many questions to elicit from her that one of her antecedents proved to be Keith Pickering. The same man who apparently framed his great grandfather, Percy, leading to his execution.

From that moment, Stephen's relationship with Penny began to cool. He couldn't get Percy's hand-written note out of his mind and spent many evenings poring over it.

For most of his life, he lived under the dark cloud of his great grandfather's untimely end at the end of a rope. To him, it became the ultimate rejection. Studying psychology did not help. He self-analysed far too much and made himself a victim.

Any rejection towards him became a trigger for his own victimisation, and Maggie's metaphorical slap in the face did exactly that.

Glowering across the table, Stephen's face darkened. Maggie noticed his anger, making her feel nervous.

'Thank you for the flowers,' she said, getting up from the table.

Stephen followed her obvious move and stood up.

'Please give me a call sometime,' he said, hating the almost begging nature of his words.

Maggie closed the door behind him, thinking that she wouldn't be calling her former lover anytime soon. The look he displayed in the kitchen sent a chill down her spine. Something about Stephen didn't add up.

'I can't help worrying about what has been going on since I moved in,' said Maggie.

Across the table, Jane nodded her head in agreement.

'You have had a rough trot. First, your ex-husband, then your friend, Penny, and now the next-door neighbour, Billy Dennis.'

'Not forgetting those other poor women, they were all killed not far from here, and in the buildings I had worked on,' said Maggie.

Jane omitted to tell her about the ghostly apparitions both upstairs and next door. She had yet to receive a visit in her own place but lived in expectation. If Maggie knew, she would be off like a shot. But so far she appeared not to have seen anything, only the odd scream, as if that wasn't enough.

Jane admitted to herself her reluctance to lose Maggie as a neighbour if she chose to move away because of the recent events. She experienced some kind of bond between them. Nothing she could put a finger on, more of a sense of déjà vu.

'I wonder what will happen next door. Billy said he wasn't married and had no children,' said Maggie.

'Perhaps it will revert to what it has been for years, an abandoned house,' laughed Jane.

'What is it about this place,' said Maggie, quietly, 'the entire street gives me the creeps now. Have you noticed that nobody appears to know their neighbours, where is that old East End camaraderie everyone talked about?'

'Buried in the past, I daresay,' said Jane, 'folks don't have that sameness anymore. It used to be that everybody shared the same poverty, but these days they want to be better than their neighbours. One-upmanship, they call it. People are so consumed by their own lives they become insular and forget they have others living close by.'

The two sat in silence for a while as the bottle of wine edged ever closer to being empty.

'What happened to that other guy you were seeing, he seemed nice?' asked Jane.

'Stephen, yes, we enjoyed each other's company for a while until he slept with his old girlfriend.'

'Oh, yes, I recall him seeing the murdered woman, Penny Pickering, what is the story there?'

Maggie found herself recounting the saga of herself, Penny, and Stephen.

'Sounds like the proverbial love triangle,' said Jane, 'they always end in tears.'

From Maggie's countenance, Jane realised she crossed an invisible line; time to go, she thought.

Their parting became a little frosty, and Maggie closed the door behind Jane gratefully.

The scream began as Maggie entered her bedroom, and this time she reacted differently.

'Shut up!' she yelled at the top of her voice.

The scream ended abruptly.

'That's better, now fuck off and don't come back.'

Maggie enjoyed a peaceful night, not one sound disturbed her slumber.

Chapter 43

Nipper sat at his desk chewing an already destroyed pencil.

'This bloke — could he have been murdered by the same killer?'

The team had gathered in his office. Jane, sandwiched between Bob Wilson and the doorjamb, spoke, her voice muffled by the sergeant's back.

'They were all killed with a sharp instrument, the only difference, the lack of mutilation. But here's the thing, the victim was a man. The other victims were all women.'

'So the pattern has either been broken or we are looking for another killer. Billy Dennis had few enemies, he eliminated most of them. Lot of villains would like to see him dead, but few would have the bottle to do it,' said Nipper.

'I think it must be a rival gang,' said Detective Sergeant Wilson. After a pause, he continued.

'However, the media sees it differently. It's much better for their ratings to suggest a connection with Jack the Ripper. They are suggesting that whoever it is has taken on the same modus operandi as the original Ripper and operates in the same areas of the East End.'

Nipper spat out the remains of the pencil.

'No, the bloody media isn't helping. People have stopped going out at night and even the local prossies are operating in-house only.'

'Perhaps he will stop as suddenly as the original Jack the Ripper? Nobody knows what caused him to stop his rampage against East End prostitutes, maybe this one will do the same,' ventured Detective Sergeant Wilks.

'Very bloody helpful,' said Nipper, 'in which case we will be labelled as useless as our lot were in the 1880s.'

An uncomfortable silence reigned as detectives shuffled their feet and looked down in an attempt to avoid the penetrating stare of Chief Inspector Nipper.

Nipper ran his eyes around the room.

'I suggest you get out onto the streets and find this bugger. Never mind about Billy bloody Dennis, he no doubt deserved his comeuppance. Let's concentrate on the woman-killer, none of his victims deserved their untimely end.'

Nipper's office emptied as the team moved out into the general office, collected their coats, and made for the door. Sadly, not one of them had any idea what to do next, but it would be better to sit in a local café than face the accusatory stares of their boss.

The newly promoted Detective Sergeant Wilks cornered Jane.

'How about we pay the local girls a visit? One of them might have seen someone out of the ordinary lurking about.'

Jane hesitated, there would be danger in case any of her old associates recognised her. However, she now looked completely different to the old Avril Graystroke. Chestnut coloured short hair replaced the long, bleached, blonde look, and the gaudy clothes with mismatched mini skirt were replaced with a smart suit.

'Okay, why not,' she said, 'it can't hurt.'

Jane hoped that would be the way it turned out, and they might get lucky.

The back streets of Stepney housed a few brothels. Prostitution flourished, no longer illegal in Britain as long as business is conducted in-house and not on the streets.

However, the brothels demanded a quick turnover and charged handsomely for use of their premises. Many prostitutes, both female and male, still illegally used the streets as their place of business. The punters' cars or a rented flat shared amongst the girls used for conducting business instead of a room.

It would be a long shot, but the pair of detectives decided to visit a few of the legal brothels during the morning when most participants would be either sleeping or resting.

House after house they visited drew the same result. A big

fat nothing. The girls gave nothing away, most too frightened to talk openly in fear of retribution by the brothel owners. The police were never welcome on premises, scaring away any potential early customers. Prostitution had become a 24-hour service since legalisation.

'Perhaps evening would be better,' suggested Wilks, 'the street girls might be easier to talk to seeing as they are still operating illegally.'

Jane reluctantly agreed to join him after dusk in the streets frequented by kerb-crawlers looking for a cheap thrill.

It had just turned 9 p.m. and Jane, in company with Sergeant Wilks, set out on their quest for information. The night air turned cold with a dampness that suggested impending rain. Jane recalled the nights she walked these same streets in search of clients. She wondered now, as she did back then, how anyone could feel the need for sex in such dismal weather surrounded by equally dismal surroundings.

A few girls stood nonchalantly beside the kerb, most sucking hungrily on a cigarette, looking for likely punters while keeping a lookout for plain-clothes police.

Twice, Jane turned abruptly, thinking that someone appeared to be following them, but the street behind appeared to be empty.

The damp coldness increased as a white mist began to swirl around their ankles. She looked back again with the same sensation of being watched but found it hard to see more than a few yards. The mist seemed to be denser behind them than in front.

They approached a tall girl dressed in a cheap imitation leopard-skin coat.

'I don't know anything,' said the girl before they had even asked a question, 'I'm waiting for my uncle, he should be along any minute now,' she said, unconvincingly.

Wilks flashed his warrant card and the girl didn't flinch, she knew exactly who they were. Jane smiled inwardly, she had developed the same instinct about police early on in her old profession.

'Seen anyone a bit out of the ordinary lately?'

'What, apart from you,' said the girl acerbically.

Jane said nothing while Wilks persisted.

'We're trying to help you lot,' he retorted in the same vein.

'Well, you can help by fucking off and not queering my pitch,' said the girl, turning her back.

Jane pulled Wilks gently by the sleeve.

'Come on, we'll try elsewhere.'

'Cheeky bitch,' said Wilks.

Jane couldn't help laughing gently.

'It's not a bitch, sarge, it's a him. He's transgender, popular with the punters these days.'

Sergeant Wilks looked over his shoulder in wonder through the encompassing mist.

'Bloody hell, it takes all types.'

'Indeed it does, sarge, indeed it does,' murmured Jane.

Moving further along the street to the next girl, Wilks looked at Jane enquiringly.

'This one's a girl,' she assured him with a grin.

They asked the same questions to a few more girls, but they all seemed reluctant to answer.

Admitting they weren't getting anywhere, Wilks said they might as well call it a night. Besides, they couldn't see much in the mist and they both shivered as the cold seeped through their clothes.

'Wait a minute,' came a cry from behind.

Jane turned to see the caller and saw the last girl they had spoken to.

She walked up to them, stopping in front of Jane.

'Fuck me, is that you, Avril? Fancy seeing you here and with the Old Bill, too.'

Jane paled, but her change of colouring passed unnoticed, her face already drained from the cold.

'Sorry, my name's Jane, Detective Constable, Jane Wilmot.'

'Who do you think she is?' asked Wilks before Jane could say any more.

'She looks a lot like one of my old pals, Avril, never knew her surname. We shared a flat not far from here.'

'Well, you are patently mistaken,' said Jane acidly.

'Sorry, I'm sure,' said the girl, adding under her breath, 'fucking coppers.'

'Funny, we all have a double, so they say. Hilarious that yours is a prossie though,' laughed Wilks.

They headed back, each to their own home. By the time Jane reached Petrie Street, the mist had cleared, and the surrounding air felt distinctly warmer.

She Looked at her watch, deciding it a little too late to call on Maggie. Instead, she popped a frozen meal into the microwave and settled in front of the television.

Jane felt drained and tired, so stretched out on the sofa. The soporific drone of the television lulled her to sleep, and when she woke with a start, morning had already broken. Showered and dressed, she made her way to the police station, where yet another meeting appeared to be in full swing.

'Nice of you to honour us with your presence, Constable Wilmot,' said Nipper.

The room quietened and Jane felt herself colouring with embarrassment.

'Sorry, Guv.'

Nipper paused before going on.

'As I already said. There has been another killing, and it looks like the same as the rest of the women victims.'

'Whereabouts?' asked Sergeant Wilks.

Wilks and Jane glanced at each other as Nipper revealed the name of the street where the unfortunate girl had been killed. The same place they were the night before.

'Bloody hell,' said Wilks, 'Constable Wilmot and I were in that same street last night talking to some of the street girls.'

'Well, in that case, you two can get down to the morgue and see if you recognise her,' ordered Nipper.

With great trepidation, Jane walked into the morgue where the autopsy would be carried out. She feared the worst and as she looked down on the face of the body lying on the stainless-steel examination table, her fears were confirmed. It proved to be the last girl they talked to, the girl who had recognised her, an old friend from the past.

'Have you identified her yet?' asked Wilks.

'No, she had nothing on her,' replied the pathologist.

Jane bit her tongue, she almost blurted out the dead girl's name. It was Mandy.

Jane and Mandy shared a flat around the corner from the street where Mandy had been found. They used the flat for clients, alternating in one-hour shifts, the maximum time they allowed for their pickups. Sometimes they only needed a half hour, they were the easy ones. Quick and to the point, rushing to get back to their wives at home.

She recalled Mandy's quick wit and kindness. Jane had been all business. Never feeling anything remotely like affection for any of her pickups, regular or casual. To her, it simply became a mechanical task performed for money, and nothing else.

Mandy, on the other hand, quickly formed relationships and often talked to Jane as they lay in their shared double bed after business had concluded for the night. It seemed to Jane that Mandy lived in a Walter Mitty world where she would someday meet the love of her life and be whisked away to some distant land and live happily ever after.

Now, here she lay on a cold steel table, dead and mutilated.

Jane turned away, unable to bear it anymore.

'You look very pale. Better go outside. I'll stay for the gorier bits,' offered Wilks.

Jane nodded and left the room, making for the outside fresh air.

After a few enquiries, the dead girl had been identified as Mandy Blackwell. Strange, thought Jane. I never knew her surname, everyone used first names only and most of those were false.

Again, no clues could be found and the search for the killer once again hit a brick wall.

Jane, though, couldn't rid herself of the memory about the strange sensation that she was being followed that same night. She mentioned it to sergeant Wilks but he said that apart from the cold mist, he saw nothing.

'Strange that she thought you were someone else. What name did she call you?'

Jane, about to say she didn't recall, thought better of it. Sergeant Wilks might be on a fishing expedition.

'Avril, I think she said.'

'That's right, Avril. I wonder if she might know something. I'll ask around the manor.'

Sergeant Wilks spent the following two days shlepping around the streets favoured by working girls. He desperately wanted to find Mandy's old friend, Avril. Perhaps she might hold a clue to the killer?

Time after time, he had been stone-walled by the girls. The unwritten rule to never help the police held strong.

He got lucky only once when an older woman, herself now a retired prostitute owing to the fact that no one in their right mind would pay to have sex with her, agreed to talk for a price.

'Lovely girl, Avril. All business mind, no mucking about with the Johns. In, out, and pay up were her saying.'

Wilks stifled a laugh.

'Where is she now?'

'Don't know love. Some geezer got himself killed and they fingered Avril for it. We never saw her again. If she had any sense, she would have run for cover. Gone anyplace where they couldn't find her.'

'You mean the police?' asked Wilks.

'Police, gangs, the only difference is that one lot is legal,' laughed the woman.

'Now give me the money and piss off before anyone sees me talking to the filth. I got me pride, you know.'

The following day, Wilks filled Jane in on his enquiries.

'Strange, I've searched records and there's no trace of any crime associated with this Avril girl. There are plenty of unsolved killings, but not one mentions a prostitute by that name.'

He looked oddly at Jane, who bridled at the stare.

'Don't look at me like that, just because I've got a lookalike. I'd hate to see what yours looks like!'

Wilks laughed.

'Come on, I'll buy you a coffee and you can recount your story of when you were on the game.'

Jane suppressed the desire to floor him with one blow and laughed.

'I don't know where to begin, sarge, how about the one about the detective with the tiny dick?'

Both chuckling, they left the station, heading for the closest coffee bar.

Underneath her laughter, Jane breathed a sigh of relief. In any event, she had escaped detection over Eddie's killing, and could rest easy for the rest of her life as Jane Wilmot.

Chapter 44

Maggie at last enjoyed a few nights of sound sleep. No uninvited screams came to terrify her. Maybe her angry outburst quelled whatever or whoever was behind the ear crunching outbursts.

Jane had been quiet lately and Maggie began to wonder if she should check on her. However, she found she enjoyed her own company more and more. She didn't need anybody else to lean on and decided to resist the temptation.

The back bedroom remained a mystery in that things appeared to move themselves. Twice now, she opened the curtains to let in some daylight, but when she re-entered, the curtains were closed. It seemed cooler in there than the rest of the house and she wondered how anybody could sleep in the constant chill.

Maggie dismissed the thought, leaving the door closed. She didn't bother to go into the room at all, her own bedroom all that she needed.

Her happy solitude came to an end the night Stephen knocked on the front door. Maggie opened it and sighed out loud.

'What do you want?'

Stephen looked at her with his puppy dog eyes and began to speak.

'I miss you. I wish we could be friends.'

Maggie felt a mixture of anger and compassion, although the level of anger surpassed the compassion.

'How many times do I have to tell you? It's over.'

'Not for me, it isn't. I can't get you out of my mind.'

Stephen genuinely cared for Maggie. Her rejection only served to make her more attractive.

His professional training should have told him it was the reaction of a disturbed mind, but he had passed beyond reason. His desire for Maggie eliminated any other thoughts. He cancelled all his appointments on the pretence of sickness and didn't bother to go into his office anymore. Maggie became a fixation.

The walls of his apartment were festooned with photographs of her. Taken through a telephoto lens, he had caught her in all sorts of postures. A couple of his most treasured shots showed her semi-dressed at the bedroom window.

On one occasion, he had been aiming his camera at her bedroom window and captured her almost naked. His insides churned as he watched through the net curtains. What he saw and photographed next shook him to the core. A man standing beside her in the room.

That particular photo, now displayed in the middle of his bedroom wall, showed the couple standing close together. The man's face couldn't be identified through the net curtains, but he had definitely been there and every time Stephen studied the picture, his anger increased. The mystery man had become the target of Stephen's venom. How could she be with another?

His obsession, together with the effects of sleep deprivation, drove him to the same spot every evening, staying until Maggie's bedroom light switched off. However, the mysterious man never made another appearance, which made Stephen even more psychotic.

His need for her surpassed that of mere friendship, but if that remained the only way to gain admittance to her good graces, so be it.

Once again in the late evening, he stood at her door begging her to be friends. His furtive glances around Maggie made her nervous, but Stephen wanted to see the other man, wanted to know the competition. He at last noticed a chink in her reserve, a sudden softening of her eyes, he repeated his entreaties, to the point of desperation.

Maggie knew he would never give up. She recognised the light of mania in his eyes and decided that perhaps allowing him into her home for one more time, might make him more reasonable.

'You can come in if you promise to behave,' she said, reluctantly standing to one side.

Stephen eased past her into the hallway.

As she closed the door, he slid his arms around her, pulling tightly so she could feel his arousal pressing against her.

'Friends, I said!' said Maggie, forcefully.

She forced his arms away from her with a strength that surprised him.

'Come on, Maggie, you know you want me as much as I want you,' said Stephen, his breathing becoming heavier with increased desire.

Maggie continued to hold him at bay until he spun her around, clamping one hand around her throat.

'Upstairs, Maggie. I know what you like.'

She went as cold as ice, this is what she feared. Allowing him in had been a mistake. Stephen had lost control.

Frog-marching her upstairs, he appeared to have superhuman strength. Maggie, through her panic, wondered if he had taken medication he normally prescribed for his patients.

At the top of the stairs, Stephen forced her into her bedroom, pushing her face down onto the bed.

As quick as a flash, Maggie sprung up and bolted for the door. Not to be thwarted so easily, he caught her by the back of her blouse, gripping it tightly.

Stephen pushed her violently against the opposite bedroom door, it opened and he followed her in.

The atmosphere changed dramatically as the coldness of the room became instantly apparent. Stephen hesitated, why did the room feel so cold?

Maggie lay sprawled on the unmade bed where he had unceremoniously pushed her.

Stephen eyed her licentiously, the coldness of the room forgotten in his urgent need.

Maggie rolled over onto her back, her skirt rode up and she lay with only underwear shielding her nakedness.

Stephen smiled, but it wasn't the smile of her old lover. Instead, Maggie looked up into the leering, twisted face of a madman.

'Got you, now,' he shouted loudly.

Maggie stared up at him, her face darkening with rage.

The scream began softly and they both paused, looking for the source. It appeared to be coming from a corner of the room. They looked in the same direction but could see nothing. The scream grew louder.

Stephen dismissed the scream in his madness, grabbing at Maggie and tearing at her clothes even as the scream increased.

Maggie fought him with both hands, but he seemed to grow stronger as the scream intensified to the point where she felt the desperate need to cover her ears.

The savage vignette appeared to freeze in time as Stephen stood bolt upright, his hands leaving Maggie. He turned slowly to face away from her and she could see a long-handled knife protruding from the centre of his back.

Beyond Stephen stood another figure, Jane.

'It's okay, Daisy,' Jane whispered, 'the nasty man will be gone soon.'

Maggie looked from Jane to the corner of the room where the scream appeared to originate and now began to fade away to a whimper.

'Who is there?' asked Maggie, curiosity overcoming her fear.

Jane calmly answered.

'It's a young girl, named Daisy. She was killed here, in this room, many years ago.'

Stephen slowly sank to the ground, a look of shock on his face. The knife still embedded in his back.

'I heard the scream,' said Jane unemotionally, 'and grabbed the first thing that came to hand. Luckily, the door wasn't locked.'

Maggie looked down at Stephen.

'Is he dead?'

Jane put her hand to the side of his neck, testing for a pulse.

'Dead as a doornail,' she said lightly.

'This will be hard for you to explain,' said Maggie.

Jane shrugged her shoulders.

'You could call it déjà vu.'

'What do you mean?' asked Maggie.

'The same thing happened some time ago, in this same room. I killed another worthless man. I suppose this will be the end for me.'

Maggie got to her feet.

'Not if I can help it,' she said, ushering Jane from the room.

'Go back next door and stay there. Go to bed as if nothing happened. Say nothing to anyone about this, trust me, everything will be alright.'

Jane did as Maggie instructed. Still numb due to the enormity of what she had done.

Maggie looked down at her erstwhile lover's body. She bent down and pulled the knife from his back, it slid out effortlessly covered in a slick film of blood.

Carefully, she wiped the handle to eliminate any fingerprints that Jane may have left behind.

The room had become even colder than before, and as she breathed, a fine mist of expelled breath hung in the air.

Maggie looked down at the knife in her hand as, inside, she fought someone for control.

Her physical shape began to change. A man's body briefly occupied her space before it flicked back to her own. It happened again as the figure attempted to wrest control from Maggie, but she fought hard against him to prevent the change completing. He had succeeded so many times before, using her as a vehicle to carry out the vengeance he harboured against all women. Especially those who sold their bodies.

Maggie didn't want to die, but she knew that no other way would end this nightmare. Doctor Ralph Jessop, alias Jack the Ripper, would carry on through time as he had since 1888 if she did not act now. He would use others to carry on his work, retribution against the prostitute, Mary Smith, and all those like her. They carried the curse of syphilis, the disease of madness, his own madness.

This house, Maggie realised, carried his spirit. How she regretted her decision to buy this place of death. But it had proved all too late. He had used her to carry out his foul deeds, and it must end now!

Kneeling beside Stephen, Maggie undid her blouse to expose soft white skin. She held the knife in both hands, the point touching her delicate midriff, and pulled it towards her savagely. The lack of any instant pain surprised her. Without hesitating, she drew the knife upwards in a sawing motion until the blade reached her ribcage.

The agony commenced in that moment, a searing pain that seemed to pierce her very soul. Uncontrollably, her lips parted as the torment travelled through her vocal cords. The shriek grew louder, its pitch shifting from her own high-pitched cry to a deeper, more masculine scream, until she collapsed on the floor, coming to rest beside Stephen.

The room was shrouded in an eerie silence as the shadowy figure slowly emerged from Maggie's motionless body. His long black coat billowed around him like a cloak of darkness, and the top hat perched atop his head cast a sinister shadow over his face. In his gloved hand, he clutched a black leather bag tightly, as if it held the key to his otherworldly existence.

As he fully materialized, his face contorted with venomous hatred, and his eyes gleamed with malevolence. It was clear that his days of exacting vengeance had come to an end.

Maggie lay still on the floor, her body now free from the sinister presence that had possessed her. She was pale and weak, but her eyes held a glimmer of relief as she watched the figure recede into the shadows, knowing that whatever dark vendetta had driven him was finally over...

www.raymondmhall.com

CASSEY
THE DARKNESS IS COMING
Raymond M Hall

"Circumstances are beyond human control, but our conduct is in our own power" – Benjamin Disraeli

"BEWARE, THE DARKNESS IS COMING!"

The old priest nodded sagely at the poster. They were everywhere, and he idly wondered who or what group was responsible. He knew of the dire warnings for mankind predicted in the Old Testament and supposed that one day they would come true, but surely, not yet............

Chapter 1
Whitechapel, London, 1962

Father Clough nodded his head sagely as Mr and Mrs Dennis left his office. They had arrived earlier, Mr Dennis, cap in hand, to ask for his help.

'Honestly, Father, I don't know what to do with our little Rose. She is a sweet girl, but she worships an old doll she found. She calls it Cassey; it's a disgusting thing to look at, most of the hair pulled out, one eye permanently closed, and the open eye seems to stare constantly at you,' said Arthur Dennis.

'Rose's personality has completely changed,' said his wife.

Father Clough smiled at the vision this conjured up.

'Most young children become attached to an object or toy. Sometimes it's a Teddy Bear or fluffy dog; your daughter has found a doll, probably thrown out by a family with no further use for it. But to Rose, it has become her friend, her confidant if you like. I bet she talks to it all the time.'

Sally Dennis nodded her head in agreement. 'She does, Father;

but it's worse than just idle chatter. I get the impression that the doll is talking back to her.'

Father Clough raised an eyebrow quizzically,

'I hope you haven't heard the doll speaking to your daughter?'

Arthur Dennis smiled grimly.

'No, we have not, but I wouldn't be surprised; there's something not right about that darned doll.'

'Not, right?' asked the priest.

'Bloody thing is evil, pardon my language!' Arthur exclaimed.

'Well, maybe I had better call around and see for myself,' said the priest, making a note in his diary, 'will the day after tomorrow suit?'

The couple left his office and Father Clough settled back into his chair. Odd folks around here, he thought. A mixture of cultures. The Jewish fraternity had their own beliefs stretching back to the beginning of time. There were a few Catholics like Arthur and Sally, but most people in the East End were Church of England. All had one thing in common: an undying belief in the *old ways.* Superstition ran rife in the entire community; all religions appeared to have a common thread, that of the occult and witchcraft. The ability of some to cast spells to the detriment of others.

He would speak to the girl but had no doubt it would be, as he suspected, merely a child's preoccupation with a toy. However, deep down, the priest suspected the supernatural was very real. If one could believe that the Father, Son, and Holy Ghost were one unseen entity, then surely one must allow for other supernatural forces.

It would be interesting to talk to young Rose Dennis; she was only nine years old, but sometimes the young were wise beyond their years.

Rose sat on the front doorstep of her house. It was scrupulously clean, as were all the doorsteps in the street, a matter of pride for the women occupants. The condition of the doorstep said a lot about the inhabitants.

Cassey was in her arms as usual. Rose talking to her endlessly, as if they were in mutual conversation.

The boy from three doors down approached, a mischievous

look in his eye.

'You should throw that old thing in the bin, it's probably full of germs,' he said, casually cuffing the nearly bald head with his hand.

'Go away, Michael. You are not to hurt her!' Rose exclaimed.

This drew a laugh from Michael. He was older than Rose by a year and at the ripe old age of ten thought himself vastly superior to the soppy girl sitting on the doorstep nursing a dirty old doll.

'Go on, throw it away. It's ugly,' he insisted.

Rose bridled at the insult.

'She is not ugly, you are, with your twisted legs.'

Michael saw red. He was very conscious of the condition of his legs, twisted from rickets, a common symptom of poor nourishment.

'Give me the doll, and I'll get rid of it for you,' he said, grabbing the doll from Rose's clutches.

Rose exploded to her feet.

'Give her back or I'll tell!' she yelled.

'Telltale, telltale,' jibed Michael, turning on his heel and running for the alley leading to the rear of their terraced houses.

Rose followed as fast as she could, pursuing Michael running on his thin misshapen limbs.

In the back lane, Rose caught up with him, grabbing Cassey by the legs and dislodging the doll from his grasp.

'Don't you dare touch her again,' yelled Rose, swinging Cassey by the legs, aiming at Michael's head.

There was a sickening thud as the doll's head made contact.

Rose stepped back, still holding the doll, amazed at the amount of blood pouring from Michael's shattered skull. She didn't know what to do, so simply walked away, without looking back.

Cassey lay in the kitchen sink surrounded by dishwashing bubbles, languishing in warm water, as Rose gently washed away Michael's blood.

'There, there,' cooed Rose softly, 'that nasty boy won't bother us again.'

Cassey's face looked up at her from the serenity of the warm water, both eyes open. She was smiling.

Chapter 2

Father Clough had been informed of Michael's accident and made his way to his parent's house to offer comfort.

'What happened?' he asked gently.

The bereaved couple sat on a small settee opposite.

'We don't know; the police said that on the face of it, Michael was the victim of a violent attack,' said Michael's father angrily, 'possibly gang-related they said.'

Michael's mother cried out.

'Gang-related! What the hell are you talking about? He was ten years old. How could it be gang-related?'

'It's what the police told me,' her husband said, crushed by the force of her outburst.

Father Clough took her hand.

'Now, now, Mrs Blacksmith, try to calm down. Your husband is doing his best.'

'They said he must have been struck with a hammer,' she said, tears spilling down her face.

'One blow was all it took. According to the Inspector, his skull was smashed,' said the father, impervious to the effect his words were having on his wife.

Bill Blacksmith, Billy to his mates, turned to the priest,

'Father, we need help, not just prayers, but real help. We must find out who killed our boy.'

'I will do my utmost to assist the police to find the killer or killers,' he said, adding, 'I'm so very sorry for your loss. We can talk later about the arrangements for Michael's funeral.'

At the mention of the funeral, Mrs Blacksmith dissolved into tears, becoming incoherent. The priest left the pair in peace. There was nothing he could say or do for them at present.

The Dennis family was only three doors down, so he brought his visit forward. No doubt they would be aware of the murder and may need some words of comfort themselves.

Arthur and Sally sat in the kitchen. He knocked, then made his way through the house. Doors were seldom locked in the street during daylight hours, and neighbours were at liberty to come and go as they pleased.

Father Clough explained why he was calling a day early and they merely nodded, indicating that he should take a seat at the table.

Rose was busy at the sink.

'Hello Rose,' said the priest, 'you look very busy.'

'I'm giving my baby a bath,' replied Rose, letting the water out with a gurgle. 'She's nice and clean now, aren't you Cassey?'

The old priest smiled.

'May I see your doll please?' he asked, putting out his hands.

Rose gently placed Cassey in the priest's arms, standing close by.

He saw an old doll with sparse strands of hair and one closed eye. Rose had put her clothes on and smoothed the creases from the still damp dress.

'There, you take her. She might be more comfortable in your arms,' he said. 'Are you her mummy?'

'No, I'm not,' said Rose indignantly, 'Cassey is my friend.'

'Sorry,' said the priest, taken aback by the girl's vehemence.

'Perhaps this is not a good time for a visit,' he said to Mr and Mrs Dennis. 'The entire street is in shock over the boy's death.'

Rose walked off with the doll, but Father Clough caught the disconcerting glimmer of a smile on the young girl's face.

'Terrible business,' said Arthur Dennis, 'I don't know what the world is coming to; there's a rumour that a gang may have been responsible.'

The priest shrugged his shoulders.

'Hard to believe that any gang would target a ten-year-old child.'

Sally Dennis looked past Father Clough to her daughter carrying the doll.

'Who knows these days, it seems that nobody is safe.'

He spent only a short time with the parents, more interested in speaking with little Rose. Making his excuses, he walked down the hallway to the front door.

Rose was sitting on the doorstep nursing her doll, and the priest gently lowered himself down to sit beside her.

'You're very fond of that doll, aren't you?' he ventured.

Rose flashed her eyes at him, 'She's not *that doll*, her name is Cassey.'

'Sorry,' said the priest, realising the little girl was deadly serious, 'where did you find her?'

'I didn't just find her. She was a gift,' said Rose.

Father Clough knew he was conversing with an intelligent child, but it seemed like she was a great deal older and wiser than the average nine-year-old.

'A gift from a neighbour?' he asked.

'No,' said Rose.

The priest paused for a moment, not wanting to rush the child with too many questions.

'Then, where did she come from?' he asked.

Rose narrowed her eyes and looked at him suspiciously.

'Why do you want to know?' she insisted.

Again, the priest was bemused. Was he really talking to a child?

'Oh, no reason, I'm just curious,' he answered. 'It's my job to get to know everyone in the area in case they need help.'

Rose stared at Father Clough with her dark eyes, but he could not hold her look, instead, turning away with the distinct feeling that he was no match for the girl. The pretty little nine-year-old possessed an inner power that challenged his idea of an adult-child relationship.

Deciding he wouldn't get any more information from her, he got to his feet.

'Bye Rose, we'll talk again,' he said.

As he walked away, he could feel her eyes on his back. Pivoting quickly, he caught Rose staring at him. But not only the little girl. The doll appeared to be standing up in her arms, both eyes open and staring. Father Clough gave an involuntary shudder as he walked away.

Rose sat down on the step once again, encircling Cassey with her arms.

'Don't worry, he won't bother us. Nobody will,' she said, laying the doll on the step next to her. The doll's eyes closed, assisted by the internal mechanism. When Rose lifted her again, one eye opened but the other remained shut.

'You're playing tricks again, Cassey,' laughed Rose.

She loved Cassey and had done so since the day they first met. A special bond existed between them........

Is Cassey Rose's doll OR is Rose Cassey's little girl? The doll has history, and it's all bad!

www.raymondmhall.com

Printed in Great Britain
by Amazon